EL DAVINCI:

A Young Adult Novel

El Incognito

This novel is dedicated to my children, Nick, Bri, and Z. No matter what, just keep your feet moving forward. And this is also dedicated to all you young knuckleheads out there, the ones with mad potential, the ones who give their teachers a hard time, who gave me a hard time. May this novel serve the purpose for which it was intended. Trust me when I say, follow your dreams, because real talk, nothing is impossible!

Preface

What's happening, *mi gente*? I have to say, *muchas gracias* for reading this preface. I mean, who reads the preface anyways, I usually don't. But because you're taking the time, I'll try to make it short and sweet, and somewhat entertaining.

So, here we go! Back in the day, I remember my high school counselor threw out his most famous spiel at me. The only ace up his sleeve he pulled out whenever one of his students seemed to be going astray. And let me tell you, back then, I was becoming a real teenage-dirtbag. To my counselor's credit though, his speech was fairly poignant, having to do something with the tragedy of wasted potential. What really stuck to me, and probably because of its comical nature, was this one phrase, and I'll quote it for you, he said, "Life's an adventure, one that'll take you through rough seas and smooth sailing. So don't give up on yourself, don't give up on your potential."

Seriously? Life's an adventure? I mean, going through life in an Indiana Jones theme-park ride sure sounded good, though a bit farfetched. I can't be too hard on my counselor, because I have to admit, like so many youngsters out there, I too, was a casualty of Walt Disney's mission to create a protective bubble around my innocence, or rather, around my ignorance. How could any child exposed to such wonderful fairy tales ever be prepared for when the bubble bursts and life turns out to be more like the stories from the Brothers' Grimm. And I'm talking as grim as the grim reaper.

So, after years of witnessing the harsh realities and unexpected tragedies a lifetime can offer, I view life more as a ten-round boxing match. Each round serves as a decade, and if you're lucky enough to live through all ten rounds, you're a bonafide legend. Truth be told, most of us won't live long enough to attain that specific title. But then again, life offers us many opportunities to obtain titles, even though it may not seem like it sometimes.

This is where I do agree with my high school counselor. Don't give up on yourself, and by God (because straight up, there is one), don't give up on your potential. What really shows our true grit, is not how long we last, but in how we react when we get knocked down, and trust me on this, life will knock you straight on your ass from time to time.

So, when that moment comes, and you find yourself looking up from the flat of your back, what will you do? Will you throw in the towel? Or, will you get back up every time, and keep your feet moving forward.

That's what my high school counselor should have conveyed to me, the pearls I'm passing on to you—that life is a straight-up fight, and somehow, someway, you must dig deep within and find that special thing you were born with, and use it to achieve victory.

And that, *mi gente*, is what this novel is all about. What I want you to ask yourself at the end of this story is, what will you do, when you're laid out looking up from life's canvas?

-With Love and Respect,

El Incognito

I. Guilt

idnight. "Are they chasing us!?!" With panic kicked into high gear, Sterling jerks the steering wheel to the left, branding the asphalt with a crescent moon as the midnight-black Buick Regal screeches around the corner of Logan Avenue and 28th street.

"I don't freakin' know! You keep turning too damn fast, homes! I can barely hold on!" Lenny's brown hands turn pale as he gouges his fingertips deep into the dash. "Ughhh! Damn, Sterl! Slow the hell down or we gonna' crash!" he says, like he's about to get tossed like a rag doll in a hurricane.

Hold on tight, little vato! Cuz' you about to get tossed! Hold on tight! A chorus to an original rap song forms in his thoughts.

Another 95-mph tail-whip around a corner easily loosens Lenny's grip on the dash pressing him hard against the passenger side door. The Regal narrowly escapes plowing into a life-sized mural shared by Roberto's taco shop and Maggie's *Dulceria.*

"Damn it, Sterl, I said watch out! We almost hit Cesar Chavez and Rosa Parks, man!" Lenny's rap remixes, *Survive the night, little gangsta! Or you won't live to see eighteen! Survive the night!* He recites it in his thoughts like a prophecy coming to pass.

Though he's never driven on his own before, Sterling steadies the steering wheel like a professional Nascar car driver. Aside from a few wanderers willing to brave the notorious *barrio* after dark, the streets of Logan Heights can be as treacherous as an ex-girlfriend ravenous for revenge.

"Don't be a scary-ass Mexican! Check if they're chasing us, Lenny!" Sterling shouts, his eyes engorging with panic.

"Forget you, Sterl! You're the one driving all crazy! You look back for the *jura!*" Lenny yells back, clinging onto the dash as if his life depends on it.

Time seems to slow as another obscure thought flashes in Lenny's mind, *will I get to see my dad, if I don't make it through the night?* He grinds his teeth, building up the determination to take a look, "Fine! I'll look back for the *jura,* alright, Sterl!" Lenny takes a deep breath, releases hold of the dash, and twists his body back to peer out the rear window. "I think we're good!" he says, exhaling with relief. "I don't see no one chasing...!"

At that moment, Sterling yanks the steering wheel to the left, making another hard turn. The lowrider reacts, tail-whipping out of control towards the opposite side of the street. "Shit, Len! I lost control!"

Lenny doesn't finish what he was about to say, tensing instead as the sidewalk invades his peripherals in a flash, "We're gonna' hit!"

Sparks ignite as the rear Dayton rim warps like a busted lip against the curb. Lenny's tossed again, this time twice as hard. The passenger side window shatters against his skull with a deafening burst. "Ahhh! My head!" The rush of cold, night air instantly numbs his senses.

Sterling stomps down on the gas pedal and tightens his grip on the steering wheel, somehow regaining control of the bucking Buick. The Regal screeches away in a trail of smoke. He makes another quick turn into a quiet residential street crisscrossed with hidden alleyways—good for giving someone the slip. "Damn, that was crazy, we almost died back there, Len! Says Sterling with excitement and disbelief. "Are the po-po chasing us!?!" Sterling's query goes unanswered. "Lenny! Can you hear me!?! Are the po-po's chasing us!?!"

All Lenny can do is rock back and forth, corralling his head in incapacitating pain.

"Damn it, Lenny, what's wrong with you? Snap out of it!" Sterling tries to shake an answer out of him, "Come on, boy, are you alright? Can you hear me!?!

Lenny remains stuck in agony.

"Damn it, Len, I'll just look back, then!" With the rearview mirror gone and both side views busted, Sterling has to twist his body back to peer out through the rear window. He looks out into the darkness for a good five seconds. "Pshew! I don't see any po-po back there!"

As soon as a sigh of relief escapes from his breath, an object of considerable weight and size smashes against the windshield, tumbles over the roof of the car, and rolls awkwardly onto the middle of the street.

"What the hell was that!" Sterling shouts, slamming his foot down on the brake pedal. The stolen lowrider zigzags to a screeching halt.

The sweet aroma of night-blooming Jasmine—so common in a clear San Diego night—is marred by the bitter odor of charred rubber. The sudden stop whips Sterling's head against the steering wheel and Lenny's cheek against the dash.

"Ahhh! What the hell, Sterl!" Pain sent Lenny into a daze, and pain snaps him back into the present.

"Damn! What was that, Len? Man, I think I cracked my dome!" Sterling taps on a small gash beginning to leak from his forehead.

Then, as if suddenly induced into a mechanical seizure, the stolen Buick convulses, and then flatlines. "What the hell!" Sterling quickly tries to turn the ignition over, but the car remains unresponsive. Anxiety swoops in like a sandstorm in the Sahara as the teenager's stare at each other speechless. Only their eyes communicate, *What the hell is happening?*

They exit the car cautiously. White steam begins seeping out from the hood, followed by a snake-like hiss.

"Damn, the car's smoking! What the hell did we hit? It must've been a big-ass dog or something! It straight-up messed up our g-ride!" Sterling glares at the indentation on the hood as he slams the door shut.

"I...I think it was," Lenny tries to speak, "It was a.." but his words skip as he fixates on the blood and skull fragments encased in a web of broken glass on the windshield. *It wasn't a damn dog! It was a person! We straight-up hit a person!* His thoughts yell out loud and clear, but he can't verbalize it.

"What is it, Lenny? What are you tripping off of?" Sterling notices the look of shock on Lenny's face and tracks his gaze. When his eyes hit the skull fragments attached to human hair, the fear knocks the air from his lungs, like an uppercut to the gut. "What the hell is that?" he says, without breath.

It takes two seconds for it to register—one for Sterling's eyes to meet Lenny's, and another for both of them to turn around and look past the rear of the car.

As they peer into the stillness of the night, the young boys become trapped, as if suddenly caught by Spider Man's web. Their mouths gape at a figure lying motionless in the middle of the street.

"Shit, Lenny, it wasn't a damn dog! It was a person! We straight hit a person! Let's get the hell outta here!" Panic snaps Sterling into action, vanishing down a darkened alleyway as fast as a phantom out of the corner of your eye.

A single lament entombs Lenny as he remains motionless. *Perdóname, ma, I broke my promise.* Suddenly, A hauntingly familiar scream pierces his eardrum, like an omen of bad things still yet to be had. Lenny drops to his knees and peers around, expecting to find his mother petrified by the notion that she's about to lose her only son to the juvenile justice system. He realizes quickly enough that the shriek didn't come from her or from anyone at all, but from deep within his soul.

Lenny was about to surrender to the grief and sob when self-preservation shoves him into action."Sterl, where are you!?!" He yells out. "Sterling!?! Where the hell are you!?!" He calls out again, now realizing he's a lone prisoner in a cell of regret. His heart speeds as the fight or flight response kicks into overdrive. Not understanding why, Lenny darts towards the figure lying motionless on the asphalt. The only thing he's sure of is that a terrible sensation stabs deep into his chest. A sensation that feels more like guilt than fear.

II. Supernatural

Thirty-years later. Picture frames fly off the walls in Lisa's ridiculously overpriced town-house as the front door slams shut with a resounding *thud*.

The chic, forty-year-old television hostess would've paid any amount for a place overlooking the bluffs of Los Angeles, especially for one that inflates her ego.

"Why!?! Why is this happening to me!?! I can't believe it! I mean, I'm Lisa Deveroe, damn it!?! She sighs in a frustrated-emotional kind of way.

"Seriously, after all I've been through, how could it all go so wrong!?!" She tosses her keys on the entry table. "I get courtside seats to all the Laker games, backstage passes to any concert I want, VIP service in any club! I've even dated a celebrity or two, damn it! How can it all suddenly go so wrong!?! How!?! It can't. It just can't, damn it!" She peers into her Venetian entryway mirror, falling helplessly into the windows of her soul.

"I need a drink fast!" Lisa smirks as if what she had just said was a punchline to a bad joke. "What am I saying? I need a few, maybe even a few more after that!"

Hoping the bottom of a bottle will reveal what she so desperately needs, Lisa flings her briefcase onto the couch. She storms straight into the kitchen with one goal in mind. "Where's the damn tequila!?!" She rifles through her liquor cabinet, "No Patrón, no Don Julio, no Henney!?! How can there be no Henny!?! What the hell happened to all the hard stuff!?!" Three seconds later, she smacks herself on the forehead with the palm of her hand. "The dinner party!" A long, sigh escapes from her belly. "I should've stocked up!" She goes through her cabinet once more. "Wine?" Lisa reaches for the only thing she has left worth drinking—a $1,000 bottle of Pinot Noir. "It'll have to do."

Sweet, scented plumes escape from the wine bottle as droplets of luxurious crimson spill onto her marble countertops. Lisa's decor exposes her luxurious tastes, but does nothing to reveal what's really locked up inside.

"Why is this happening? I've worked so damn hard, sacrificed so damn much!" An unsettling haze darkens her thoughts. "After all I've been through, to get my show, my house, my Benz, my celebrity status for Goodness sake! Well, semi-celebrity status, I mean. And to let it all just slip away! Really!?! I mean, really!?!"

She downs the glass in two gulps and pours another. She takes it down just as fast. Two more drinks later, Lisa turns and bangs her head against the French balcony doors and gazes out into the darkness. The glare from the Hollywood sign grabs her attention. She steps out into the night, drawn by its irresistible power.

You're destined for big things, Lilyboo, a familiar voice says in her mind.

"Yeah, really big things, alright!" Lisa tears up.

A gentle Santa Ana breeze sweeps through the hills, caressing her face as if attempting to console her.

"Why did you put that stupid idea in my head." She quickly stops herself. "I didn't mean that. It's just, look at your precious little

Lilyboo, now, all alone and soon to be standing in the unemployment line."

Lisa takes heavy steps back into her house. She turns, taking one last look at the larger than life sign. *Hollywood, where dreams come true.*

"I've worked so hard for my show," she says. "And now, I'm just a breath away from getting canceled, and there isn't anything out there in entertainment for a forty-year-old hostess like me." Melancholy bares its menacing jaws, like a Great White before a strike.

"What the hell! I had a good run, fifteen years," she shrugs her shoulders. "Oh well. It's just my time I guess." She tries to convince herself of the inevitable. "Oh hell no! Forget that!" Lisa looks around, desperate. "I'm about to lose it." She reaches for the bottle and pours the last of it. She downs it in a flash. "Thousand dollar bottle my ass! This isn't working. I need something else." The stress begins to suffocate.

For some reason, Lisa fixates on the coat closet door. She finds herself moving towards it, as if on autopilot. Her hand suddenly stops on the doorknob.

"Really? This might not be the best time." Apprehension squeezes, but not hard enough. She twists the doorknob open. "What the hell, it'll take my mind off all of this, I hope.

Finally hit with a lack of inhibition, Lisa struggles to maintain her balance. "Damn, the wine is finally kicking in." She reaches clumsily for a plastic container buried on the top shelf. Written on a strip of duct tape securing the box are the words, *Don't open.* Lisa runs her hand through her hair, once again second-guessing herself. "I've kept this locked up for so long. Do I really want to open it now? Pandora's box."

Lisa's lives a high-society type lifestyle, but she has always carried the fear that she will one day be exposed for growing up in one of the most poverty-stricken neighborhoods in Los Angeles—known more for its criminal element than high society debutants.

She heads to her quaint little living room with her box in hand. "The hell with it, I might as well put these damn couches to good use." Lisa sinks into her imported couches. She places the container at her side and caresses the exotic material, mesmerized by its luxurious feel.

"Dayum! I won't be able to afford anything as nice as this anymore, not if the road doesn't change for me soon."

A small dust cloud billows as she blows the cover of the container clean. She rips off the tape, unsnaps the handles, and pulls off the top. Lisa hesitates, and then reaches in. She pulls out an old football cap—the black and silver logo is unmistakable. "L.A. Raiders, baby! I haven't seen this thing in forever." She secures it on her head with a twist and reaches back into the container.

"What? No way! My papa's fave! He used to sip on this all the time." Lisa pulls out a clear, pint sized-bottle with an old Gin label on it. She brings it up to her ear and shakes it. "And there's still a shot left." Lisa twists off the cap and downs the last remnants.

"Oh, geez, papa," she says in between gasps, "That's harsh. I can't believe you used to down it like water!" Lisa lays the little bottle on the couch and reaches back in the container. This time she pulls out a large photo album. "Yep," she says, with a melancholic laugh. "If this can't help me, nothing will."

Just as on the day of her middle school promotion, Lisa traces over the gold-trim lettering imprinted on the cover, *Memories Are Who You Are*. She closes her eyes, transporting herself back. A rush of anxiety grabs hold of her as it did back then.

"Congratulations, Lilyboo." Mia Deveroe says, handing her twelve-year-old daughter a brand-new photo album decorated with a large purple bow. "It's for to keep your memories safe."

"*Nanay,* you shouldn't have spent money on this," Lisa says with concern. "There are more important things you need to spend money on."

Mia kisses her daughter on the cheek and whispers in her ear. "I'm so proud of you. You're always putting others first, but your papa wanted you to have it." Her eyes gloss over with emotion. "It's so you can look back and remember where you came from. He would've been so proud of his little Lilyboo." Mother and daughter embrace, trapping the sadness of losing the man they loved to themselves.

The nostalgia brings a warm smile to Lisa's face, but then anger yanks her back to reality. "Memories are who you are, huh? More like, memories can come back to hurt you!"

Lisa flips over the album. Messages from high school friends long forgotten adorn the back cover in permanent ink. One, in particular, grabs her attention.

Don't forget us when you're rich and famous, Lilyboo, and don't forget you grew up in the hood, girl. Your homegirl, Lil' Sasha.

In a peculiar state of grief mixed in with a shot euphoria, Lisa flips the album back to the front and tries to open it. "What the...?" She tries again, but the album remains shut. She places it on its side and notices the problem, a tiny, hourglass keyhole with a latch. "Damn it! I forgot it was locked, but where's the key?"

Lisa scans the living room, trying to recall the last time she's held the tiny skeleton key bracelet in her hand. "Has it been that long, or am I just faded?"

She sighs. Then, her recollection and reaction move simultaneously. Lisa reaches back into the container and corrals a small wooden keep-safe in her hand. The tiny box serves to hold the little silver key bracelet captive. "No turning back now." Lisa takes a deep breath and inserts the key into the lock. She winces as the latch flings open with a subtle twist of her wrist. "Maybe you'll bring me luck, little key," Lisa says, fastening the bracelet around her wrist.

"*Nanay!*" Self-loathing instantly stabs at her side as she flips to the first page and gazes at the highlight of her teenage life frozen in a photograph—a mother and daughter caught in a loving embrace. The caption reads, *Compton High's class of 95' graduation.*

"Oh, *nanay*, I'm so sorry. I never forgave you for marrying Jon." She caresses the image of her mother. "I couldn't see past my anger. I shouldn't have pushed you away. I guess I felt you were betraying papa's memory. Only now, do I understand, it's hard not having someone to share your life with."

Lisa flips to the next page. A smile creeps out from the side of her mouth as she gazes at another picture—a row of teenage girls with her at its center. They all sport different color prom dresses, but the same blue Chuck Taylor tennis shoes. The shot was snapped as the girls were contorting their fingers in the most peculiar ways. The captions reads, *Compton's most wanted bad-ass-bitches. Prom night.* She chuckles as she throws up the sign of her crew—something she hasn't done in ages, and it felt extraordinarily good.

"My homegirls," Lisa says, shaking her head. "I left and never looked back. I guess I must've thought I was too good or something. I'm such an idiot." She exhales with deep-rooted regret. "Only around you girls, could I be myself, my real self."

Lisa flips to the next page. A jolt of emotion steals her breath away. "Papa!" Her most cherished childhood memory captured on an old Polaroid photograph—a robust African-American man leaning against a custom-built 1964 Chevy Impala lowrider, propped on three wheels. The man's proud, 9-year-old daughter straddles his shoulders, raising a trophy in triumph—best lowrider in show.

Lisa examines the caption written in her father's handwriting. *My two prized possessions, my Lilyboo and my six-fo.*

Lisa sighs again. "I remember that day. I can still hear your voice." She closes her eyes as her father speaks softly in her mind. "You see, Lilyboo, that's why you never give up, no matter how rough the road gets. Just keep your feet moving forward, baby girl, through all the nonsense, through all the drama, through all of it. If you can do that, baby girl, you'll get through anything." He motions towards his lowrider, "Remember when this was an old rust bucket, and how pissed your mamma got when I bought it? Now look at it, shining bright like a diamond." He places Lisa in the driver's seat of his car. "You're destined for big things, Lilyboo. I can see it every time I look into your eyes. Just remember, baby girl, the road's gonna' get rough, but as long as you keep your feet moving forward, it'll smoothen out sooner or later. I promise."

Onlookers snap photos of the prize-winning lowrider. Lisa waves. "It's the paparazzi! Look at me, daddy!" She says, raising her little arms, "I'm famous, like Janet Jackson!"

Lisa's emotions manifest on the corners of her eyes as the memory fades. She reaches for her briefcase and pulls out a handwritten note with a phone number written on it—a substantial offer to buy the lowrider. She fought so hard with her mother not to sell it, even though they needed the money. She can still recall how happy she felt when her mother finally gave in.

"Yeah, well, I'll need the money if I'm out of a job," she tries to convince herself. "It's time to get rid of it. I mean I haven't driven it in years, and I'm just throwing away money keeping it in storage."

Lisa begins dialing the number on the note but stops short of punching in the last digit. "No way! I can't! I won't! I'm sorry, papa. I know how much you loved that car. I love that car, too, even more now." She crumples up the note and tosses it over her shoulder. "I gave up my friends, my self-respect, even my mother, and for what, to let everything I worked so hard for slip through my fingers." Lisa glances at her expensive fingernails. "Hell, no! Hell-to-the-no!" Lisa tries to shake the thought away, but the negativity seems impenetrable. "Just keep your feet moving forward," she recites like a mantra.

"I need a shower, help me reset, get some clarity." After a long hot shower, Lisa dries off with a towel made of fine Egyptian cotton. She applies the best skin moisturizer money can buy. "I feel better, now.

Time to figure out how to bring back the ratings." Lisa programs her Bose stereo to a soft jazz station. The Saxophone's hypnotic melody induces an immediate state of relaxation.

"That's what I'm talking about," she says, swaying her hips side-to-side. "Thank you, Kenny G! Work that sax, baby."

A myriad of ideas run through her head—the Kardashian's, Kanye West, Charlie Sheen— but they've been done already. "We need something different, something fresh. A new angle for a show, but what? What's out there nobody's done yet? Something life-changing." She kisses St. Anthony, the oval-shaped charm around her neck. The one she never takes off. It was a gift from her father on her eighth birthday. "Papa, I could use your help. Talk to St. Anthony for me. Ask him to help me find what I need." Lisa closes her eyes and whispers a prayer. As she utters the last phrase, a thought strikes her unexpectedly.

"The intern?!?" Lisa recalls the rather ordinary event with extraordinary clarity. "The hottie with the little white blouse showing off her boobs. What did she say again?"

It occurred two days ago. Lisa was waiting in an unusually long line at the Starbuck's kiosk right outside her building. Two interns were engaged in a casual conversation about the network's crisis. She overheard the conversation but paid no mind to it. It was just a simple suggestion, but one she now realizes merits some serious consideration.

"Why don't they look through the commentaries from the network's website. They should just listen to what the fans have to say," the long-legged intern had said.

Lisa was engaged in a critical decision at the time—it was either a cappuccino or an espresso, which is why the comment passed unnoticed. "Look through the viewer commentary. Why the hell hadn't I thought of that!?!" With renewed vigor, Lisa jumps to her feet and rushes to her laptop.

"This is crazy," she says with excitement. "My heart is racing. I have a strange feeling about this. I've always believed in the supernatural, but if I end up finding something worthwhile, I'll never doubt again."

Lisa accesses the network's website and scrolls through the comments from the past several month. "Let's see what our viewers have to say. I mean, they generate the ratings after all."

Lisa scans through the headings, searching for a metaphorical needle in a haystack. The network receives hundreds comments. The board doesn't take them very seriously though, allotting only a lone employee to manage them, in addition to other more important duties.

"Maybe a good idea slipped through the cracks. If I get lucky, I'll make sure to thank her."

Lisa skims through the posts. "I should go through these more often," she says. "They're freakin' hilarious." She forgot how a simple compliment from a fan, though comical as it may be, can refill her with a sense of self-worth.

Lisa scrolls on. "What's this?" On the seventieth post, something strikes her unusual. The title of the post reads, Tattoos by El DaVinci.

"I don't remember doing a segment on someone named El Davinci, or did I?" The post reads-

By username: *BRYAN619*

I loved your segment on rockers-n-tats. I'm a total tattoo freak myself, and I love to see new ink on my favorite rockers. I've followed some of the best tattoo artists in the world, and I have to say that Anthony Kiedis from The Red-Hot Chili Peppers has some of sickest ink I've ever seen. I'm totally interested in the tattooist he called El DaVinci. His work is completely bananas. You should devote a whole segment to his tattoos.

"Oh, yeah," Lisa recalls, "I remember Anthony talking about his tattoos, but I need something more solid than tattoos."

Lisa reads on. Then again, on the eightieth post, a familiar theme. "There he is again, this El DaVinci person." The post reads-

By username: *RapMonster*,

Damn son, that Lil Wayne segment was off the chain. He's a straight-up lyrical genius. His new tattoos are stupid sick, boy! Who the hell is this El DaVinci guy? Where can I get a tat from him? Please do another segment on Lil Wayne and his tats quick! I'm Out!

Lisa runs her fingers through her hair. "I do remember Lil Wayne mentioning his tattoo artist, but he didn't go into much detail about him." She muses over it and then moves on.

Another fifteen posts later, he's mentioned again—El DaVinci. Then again, a few posts after, and again after that. Lisa counts all the references made about this unknown tattoo artist.

"Damn, this guy's mentioned a good twenty-five times. The only other person mentioned more is Justin Bieber, and he's been interviewed to death. Who is this mysterious tattoo artist?" A strong sense of curiosity begins forming. "How come nobody talked about who he is? I mean, this guy tattooed some high-profile celebrities."

She pauses, then a thought quickly sprouts in her mind. She walks over towards the balcony doors and peers out at the Hollywood sign.

"Can this be it? What I've been looking for? An undiscovered talent, a secret among celebrities." A smile crosses her face as she rushes back to her laptop. She what any person would do. She googles him. "Damn! Damn! Damn!" she says, banging her fist on the table. The only matches that appear reference the Renaissance painter, Leonardo da Vinci.

"Let me try Yahoo." Lisa narrows her search with keywords—El Davinci, tattoos, artist, celebrities. "Damn it! Nothing on a tattoo artist named El DaVinci!" She tries Bing, Ask Jeeves, and several other search engines. "Shoot! Not a damn thing on this guy! There has to be a way to find out who he is!"

Again, Lisa runs her hand through her hair. "Wait a minute, duh!" For the second time that night, Lisa smacks herself hard on the forehead with the palm of her hand. She quickly reaches for her cell phone.

"It's real late, but the hell with it. I hope she answers. If there's anybody who can find out who this guy is, it's Maria from research. That little latina has crazy talent for getting the low-down on anyone."

Lisa stares at the computer screen while dialing Maria's number. The tiny hairs on the nape of her neck electrify." This just might be supernatural after all!"

III. The Proposal

wo-days later. "Just what exactly are you proposing, Ms. Deveroe?" Joseph Theodore Blunt III—also known as Mouthpiece, is the spokesperson for the executive board. He and two other members make all the decisions for Entertainment Weekly, a broadcasting affiliate for the popular World News Network.

Entertainment Weekly has held the top spot in the Nielsen ratings several years go, but now they're just trying to stay in production.

"I'm proposing we sponsor a live interview with this guy." Lisa has pitched a promising idea before, like that bit on a day in the life of the paparazzi, where she intended to stake out high-profile celebrities with one of the most controversial photographers out there. The board voted against it.

"Please tell us you're joking, Ms. Deveroe. Let's just get straight to the pudding shall we, no one in our target audience is going to be interested in a convicted felon, especially one with absolutely no celebrity status and," he pauses to give the other board members a *this-is-a-complete-waste-of-time* look. "And Who's serving life for murder no less?" Mouthpiece turns and stares Lisa straight into her honey-glazed eyes expecting her to buckle.

"Yeah," Lisa says, nodding her head. "You mean vehicular manslaughter, and that's what makes his story even more compelling." Lisa reciprocates with a stare-down of her own. "This guy has been behind bars since he was fourteen years old! Fourteen! How is it that he's tattooed some of the biggest names in the celebrity world?"

"Ms. Deveroe," Mouthpiece clears his throat. "We may be in need of ratings, but what you're asking is completely out-of-character for this network. We do entertainment news, not exposés on criminals, and to even suggest going live with it," he pauses for a breath. "Is absurd. We cannot portray that we're desperate for any story that may be out there," Mouthpiece says, adjusting the tie on what used to be trendy business attire, but now only compliments his outdated notion for entertainment.

"Ms. Deveroe, I have to agree with Mr. Blunt. There are thousands of these Latinos incarcerated all over the country. And the political atmosphere being what it is, I'm afraid the ratings won't favor an interview with someone like him, Pitbull maybe, but a criminal serving life? Such a proposal only portrays desperation, Ms. Deveroe." The only female board member cuts in with her stinging skepticism.

"Desperation? " Lisa has to turn away. She knew the men on the board would be difficult to convince, but she was banking on the only women member to have her back. Lisa stands there, taking long, controlled breaths, fighting hard not to lose it.

The board members give each other skeptical glances. Lisa finally turns around to face them, "Are you all serious right now? You are all aware where we stand with the ratings, right?" Lisa asks with sarcasm of her own. "With all due respect, ladies and gentlemen of the board, we are ridiculously, no wait, let me get straight to the pudding," she stares at Mouthpiece. "We are hilariously desperate! I've been part of this network for a long time, and I don't want to see it go down in flames either!"

Though she's been keeping her cool, Lisa loses her composure for only a second, but it's long enough for her to pull out a stack of enlarged photographs from her bag and fling them in their direction. They slide across the high-polished conference table. "This guy isn't just any Latino," Lisa says, "He's a Chicano, which makes his story an American story, and seriously, his ethnicity shouldn't matter because his story has the potential to touch the entire world, not just us our little corner of the planet. It's that big! I mean, look at how incredibly talented he is. Words like prodigy, savant, even genius have been tossed around when asked about him. The inmates, the guards, even the warden of the prison call him a prodigy."

Mouthpiece smirks. "Prodigy, really? How come none of us have heard of him, and we've been in this industry for quite a long time as well, Miss Deveroe."

"Exactly! Lisa motions angrily towards the photographs spread out across the table. "And with all due respect, I've been in this industry for a long time, too. Trust me, I know a scoop when I see one. Just look at the photographs. All the celebrities on those pictures rave about how amazing this guy is." Lisa exhales hard. "Look, I know they're only tattoos, and not some grand pieces of contemporary art, or something." She picks up a photograph from the table. "But look! I mean, really look!" She points the images. "Look at the tattoos on Drake's back. They're not ordinary tattoos. Check out the detail, you can't deny his ability speaks for itself!" How did he get so good? I mean, he's been locked up since he was fourteen. How are high-profile celebrities getting his tattoos for goodness sake? We have to get this scoop before some other network does, like TMZ. Don't you see, this will be something completely different from what we've ever done, a live interview with a convict, and not just any convict, but a lifer with a secret reputation among celebrities. This guy reached the stars all the way from Prison. From Prison! Come on! You can appreciate that, right? We are a news and entertainment network after all, aren't we? And this is entertainment news at its best!"

The members of the board pass around the photographs, showcasing the inmate's artistry. Even still, they give each other skeptical looks.

"Look, let's be realistic here," Lisa continues. "Our numbers need to improve, yes? On that, I'm sure we can all agree. I believe, deep in my core, our viewers are sending us a message. They're getting bored with the Kardashians of the world. They need a fresh dose of reality, and I mean one they can make a genuine emotional connection with. I'm talking about a gritty, true to life drama, here! One that everyone can relate to, or at least be compassionate about!"

The other male board member, who is quite a bit older than the others, and who happens to be the president of the network, is an extremely reserved fellow but with a willingness to gamble on innovative ideas. He shifts through Lisa's proposal, singling out a close-up mug shot of the inmate. He analyzes it for a moment. Something in the inmates' eyes resonates with him, as if the inmate is withholding some deep-rooted regret desperate for redemption.

"And besides," Lisa interrupts. "Look at all the comments from our website about this guy." She walks over to the large windows overlooking downtown Los Angeles and pulls up the blinds, letting in the light. She peers down at hundreds of people going about their daily business—from so far up, they look like ants. "I mean, he already has a following, and he isn't even famous, well, mainstream famous, I mean." Lisa turns and faces the board. "Look, with all due respect to this board and to this network, we need this. We need to captivate our audience again!" She says, pointing out the window. "I mean, how is it that this guy's reputation spread from prison to the celebrity world? Seriously, think about it! It's amazing story, I'm telling you!" Her eyes meet Mr. Blunts. He glances at the other members.

"This is the kind of story that will bring back our viewership! I know it!" Lisa's concludes her pitch.

"Ms. Deveroe, we've heard what you had to say, now would you please give us a moment to consider your proposal in private." Mouthpiece points towards the exit.

Trying her best to keep her frustration in check, Lisa calmly steps out of the conference room. The moment the doors shut behind her, she lets loose. After a few Muay Thai kicks in the air, she comes back to her senses. She presses her ear up against the doors, hoping to pick up a hint to their decision. "Damn it! Thick mahogany doors! I can't hear a thing!" Again, Lisa runs a frustrated hand through her silky hair, a thing she's been doing a lot lately. "They're going to vote." She sighs with frustration. "They have to go for it. Things are different this time. Our rating are the lowest they've ever been! They'll be complete idiots if they don't go for it."

Lisa paces the hallway, twisting her hand back and forth, feeling the little key bracelet swing against her wrist. "Come on, little key, bring me luck!"

Twenty minutes later, the handles to the conference room crank open. A member of security personnel signals Lisa in. "Mrs. Deveroe," he announces, "They're ready for you."

"Here we go, Lisa, girl," she says. "You can do this."

The security guard steps aside and ushers Lisa into the conference room. She sits calmly, trying to read the board member's facial expressions, but like professionals in the World Series of Poker, they reveal nothing. Lisa endures a brief, uncomfortable moment of silence, then the president of the board cues Mouthpiece.

"Ms. Deveroe, after a good, hard look at your proposal, and with some serious debate, I might add," he pauses.

Lisa's mind goes for a loop. *These idiots are going to deny me again!* Right when she's about to jump to her feet and yell, *This such BS!* Mouthpiece announces, "You got your show."

Lisa's eyes widen, "Wait, what!?! Did you say, I got my show?" she asks, wondering if her mind is playing tricks on her.

"Yes, Ms. Deveroe, you got your show." This time the president of the board answers.

"I got my fucking show!" Lisa's enthusiasm echoes throughout the room. She covers her mouth.

Mouthpiece stands and walks over to her. He hands Lisa back her proposal. "Congratulations, Ms. Deveroe," he says, nodding his head in a show of respect. "That was quite a proposal."

The female member of the board can't help but to put a damper on Lisa's moment. "Ms. Deveroe, I want you to know, I voted against it, and I feel it's my responsibility to inform you that your neck is way out on this one. We've always strived to keep the reputation of our network second-to-none. With that said, if you fail to produce the ratings projected in your proposal, we will have no choice but to terminate your contract, do you understand?"

Lisa stares the woman down. The contempt in her glare makes the woman shift uncomfortably.

"And if I may offer some advice," continues the board member, not wanting to back off. "It wouldn't hurt to watch your figure a little more carefully. Data shows slenderness tends to attract a higher viewership."

"Those are some harsh words, Ms. Haterly, especially after all my years of loyalty to this network. Don't forget, I brought this show to the top spot in the ratings not too long ago. But you know what? I'll do that," Lisa says sarcastically. "I'll watch my figure, and I'll accept the consequences, and the recognition for getting this network back on top." Lisa turns and struts out of the conference room, her long, black hair dances in triumph.

The director of broadcasting, a crafty, eighty-year-old gentleman, and a bit-of-an-acquired taste catches Lisa as she's exiting the conference room. "Well, doll, did ya' manage to pull it off, or did they eighty-six ya', again?"

"Oh yeah, old man, we're off and running!" Lisa pumps her fist and dances around like she just scored the winning goal in the world cup.

"Lisa, honey," says the old man, "For your sake, I sure hope this Mexican fella' is everything you made him out to be."

Lisa unzips her leather-bound proposal and examines the inmate's mugshot. "You mean this Chicano fella', you old geez. And me too, because everything I know about him is right here on this lil' ol' sheet of paypa'." She says, impersonating him.

"Great! We still goin' live?" he asks, hoping she changed her mind at the last minute.

"You know it." Lisa nods, "Ain't nothin' wrong with some good ol' fashion risk takin'. Sound familiar?"

"Yeah, yeah, put this on me why don't ya'. I guess I'll be on my way den'." The director strolls down the hallway, whistling a somber tune.

"Where you going?" Lisa asks.

"To start preppin' the team," he shouts back. "Someone's gotta' warn em' about the risk ya' takin', specially since we along for tha' ride."

"I guess there's no turning back now." The butterflies in Lisa's gut begin to flutter.

Lisa strolls down the hallway when the intern happens to pass by with a platter of bagels in her hands. "Wait! Excuse me, Carla, isn't it?"

The intern stops and turns. "Yes, Ms. Deveroe."

"I just want to thank you." She walks up to her and gives a strong hug.

The intern accidentally drops the platter on the floor. "Ok, thank you for that, but what did I do?" she asks, bending down and placing the bagels back on the plate.

"You were right. It was a great idea. I'll make sure to put in a good word for you with the higher-ups." Lisa turns and walks away.

"Huh? Wait! What was a great idea!?!" Carla shouts, reaching for the last bagel.

"All we had to do was listen!" Lisa shouts back.

The intern shakes her head as Lisa strolls away. "What is she talking about, listen to who?"

IV. Showtime

Three-months later. 11:00 a.m. "Let's get a mo...?"
Bewildered from not hearing his voice, the wily, old show director bangs on the megaphone and rolls the volume all the way up, as inmate 1-9-0-4 (also referred to as inmate Santiago, and by a more exclusive moniker) squeezes black tattoo ink into a circular container just big enough to contain a sweet pea.

"OK, folks, this time it's fer' real." The director raises the megaphone and squeezes the trigger. "Let's get a move on it, boys and girls, twenty-minutes till showtime!"

11:01 a.m. Upon hearing the call, the crew step it up, surrounding the inmate with a perimeter of video cameras, television monitors, and lighting equipment.

Under his direction, the seven-member team has earned the reputation as the top broadcasting team in the business. For over ten years, they've gotten to know each other's subtle innuendos, especially the nuances in their director's tone. They know when they're meeting his rather unrealistic expectation, or when they need to hit the gas. This particular moment falls in the latter, and this particular crew has never disappointed.

11:02 a.m. Inmate Santiago tucks in his white, tanktop undershirt and glances to his left. He smirks at two correctional deputies standing overly rigid. Their stiff facial expressions exude arrogance, resting their forearms on the mace canisters fastened to their Batman-like utility belts. Like a pair of action figures in pose, they stand watch over the commotion behind matching mirrored sunglasses scanning each member of the crew.

Deputy Jones and Deputy Smith are both fresh out of the academy and follow protocol down to the letter. Inmate Santiago was the first to learn this the hard way as he tried to barter with one of them. A friendly exchange—a realistic charcoal portrait for a Snicker's bar—should have been viewed as just a slight bend in the rules. Instead, inmate Santiago received a two-week stay in solitary for attempting to coerce an officer of the law.

11:03 a.m. Catching a strange-looking figure mimicking his every movement from the corner of his eye, inmate Santiago quickly averts his gaze to the right. He smiles and nods at his reflection, coming from the one-way security mirror. The observation room concealed behind the glass now serves as the arena where Warden Weisel and several high paid executives from the network will engage in a battle of verbal wit. Unbeknownst to the execs, the warden brings his uncanny ability for negotiation to the match.

11:04 a.m. The warden strikes first "Gentlemen, gentlemen," he says in a calm, non-threatening tone. "I understand you have significant capital invested in this endeavor, but what you must understand is that I do as well, possibly more. I had to pull some very large strings to make this event possible, and that's not mentioning additional overtime hours I had to approve for added security measures. I don't need to reveal how much this is costing our taxpayers, do I?"

He turns and glances at El Davinci through the glass. "Please don't misunderstand my intentions. I agreed to do this show because Inmate Santiago's ability is truly something extraordinary. You should see his work with oils. I have one hanging in my office right now. I swear you'd confuse it for a Monet. It's not a stretch to say he rivals any of the great painters of the Renaissance. He's that good."

11:05 a.m. The Warden approaches the glass. His mongoose-like figure makes it easy for him to cross his hands behind his back. He stares at Santiago with an ambitious glimmer in his eye. "I'm sure we can come to a financial agreement for all parties involved, of course." A slow, devilish grin crosses his face.

11:06 a.m. Angling his ear upward, inmate Santiago catches a faint echo coming from the hallway where Lisa's high-heel red bottoms tap on the tile floor, sending word that a lamb is lurking in the wolves' den. And not just any lamb, but one dressed to kill—with a cream-colored Armani fitted dress, a diamond necklace and matching chandelier earrings that sparkle like stardust.

She glances up at a deputy pacing the gun-rail with his AR-15 assault rifle hanging off his shoulder. "My personal guard dog," Lisa says, trying to shake off the jitters. "How the hell did I get myself into this?" She rehearses a series of questions on a script, occasionally glancing down at her bracelet. *You've brought me luck so far. Don't stop now, my little key to success.*

Lisa Deveroe, hostess of Entertainment Weekly, makes a lucrative living delving into the glitz and gossip of the celebrity world. She's hosted many interviews within the confines of multi-million-dollar mansions. Never had she thought that one day she would host a show that delves into the dark and underground world of prison, and conduct it from within the cold, hard confines of a maximum-security detention facility no less.

But Lisa made a strong case for the inmate and his ability, even without knowing much about him. Strangely, she can relate, being once unknown herself, but in the high-profile world of entertainment. In fourteen-minutes and counting, Lisa will try to prove to the network that she still has what it takes to be relevant in show business.

11:07 a.m. Inmate Santiago tears open a package containing a long, thin single-point needle. He examines it for any bends. Then, he inserts it into a handheld device, like a sniper inserting a bullet into his trusty rifle.

11:08 a.m. Inmate Santiago runs his tattooed fingers down the length of a long rubber tube attached to a small electric generator. The red needle in the pressure gauge dances as he taps on it with his fingertip. With the flip of a switch, the generator comes to life, sending a crisp buzzing ricocheting throughout the room. The sensation of vibrating metal massages his right hand as he gently steps on a small, circular footswitch.

11:09 a.m. With his left hand, Inmate Santiago rotates a circular knob, adjusting the velocity of his tattoo gun. With this top-of-the-line piece of equipment, he can easily control depth, speed, and force of application with pinpoint accuracy, resulting in the works of art that elevated him to legendary incognito status.

11:10 a.m. The inmate looks up at the speaker fixed to the upper right-hand corner of the ceiling as a haze of static morphs into a muffled voice.

"Inmate 0-3-0-1 entering observation A." Inmate Diego Martinez awaits just outside in full-body restraints. He orchestrates a melody of rattling chains as he takes short, awkward steps into the room.

11:11 a.m. Inmate Martinez is watched carefully through what's referred to as the eye in the sky, as he makes his way into the bubble of tech equipment. The escorting deputy reaches for the shackles and inserts an oddly shaped key into the locking mechanism, releasing Martinez from his captive state. The inmate scans the unusual surroundings through his peripherals, like an undercover agent deep in foreign territory. His gaze stops dead on several packets of brand new tattoo needles.

"Inmate Martinez!" Sensing his intentions, the deputy shakes his head side to side, "Don't even think about it. We'll be watching." He nods up towards the camera.

"*Chalé*, punk-ass *jura*!" responds the lanky yet muscular inmate as the deputy walks away. Then, He glances up at the camera and flashes the bird.

11:12 a.m. Inmate Martinez unzips his prison-issued jumpsuit and slips off his undershirt, exposing his illustrated chest. He sits on a plush chair placed in the center. Similar to what you would expect to find in your basic tattoo parlor, beautifully sketched images—religious symbols, indigenous figures, tribal designs, stylized letters—adorn the walls of the room.

11:13 a.m. "*Qué onda, loco*, how the guards treating you, homes," asks inmate Santiago.

"*Chalé*, they gave me the rundown, homes, sit, and don't make trouble." Sarcasm accompanies Diego's smirk, "Like I can do that, homes. You know me, I'm all about trouble, ey'. But don't trip, homes, for you, I'll be cool."

"*Órale*, no need to trip, chocolate chip. It's about time to get this show on the road, *qué no*?" says inmate Santiago, also known as El DaVinci, the tattoo prodigy.

11:14 a.m. "We're live in six, people!" The director shouts through his megaphone as he begins his final pre-show routine, involving scrutinizing every cable from every piece of equipment. A true stickler for details, he motions angrily to the youngest member of the crew— the newly hired sound technician's assistant—to double-check the amplifier connections.

"This is *firme*, people on the outs gonna' see this, homes. You're finally gonna' be famous on the outs, homes," Inmate Martinez says, nodding his head to the hype.

"*Chalé*, Big D, we're gonna' be famous, homes. You're part of this too, *qué no*?" El DaVinci reaches out and gives Diego a Chicano-style handshake.

"*Órale, simón!*"

11:15 a.m. "Alright, Lilyboo, it's time." Lisa shakes her wrist once again, feeling her tiny key bracelet swing back and forth. "Eat your heart out, Oprah, here I come!" She gathers as much confidence as she can muster and approaches the convicts.

"Hello, gentlemen. I'm Lisa Deveroe. I'm the host of the show." Her confidence wanes, swallowing nervously at the sight of the two intimidating-looking figures. Still, she reaches out her hand for a formal introduction. El Davinci stands and stares at Lisa, dumbfounded by her magnetic energy. His heart races as his mind searches for something to say. Strangely enough, David's voice (his childhood friend) pops into his head. *It ain't no big deal, foo'. You ain't gotta be scared to talk to girls. They won't bite. Just make them laugh, foo'. That's what I do.*

El Davinci takes a breath and takes her hand gently. "My bad, *mija*. You can relax, ey', we're not all animals, even though we do live in cages. I won't bite, I promise." He winks at her and releases her hand.

Lisa smiles.

11:16 a.m. "I'd like to introduce you to my homeboy, Diego, a young, down-ass *vato loco*."

Diego responds with a head nod, "*Órale*, what's up, homegirl?"

"Well, it's very nice to meet the both of you," Lisa replies. "So," Lisa says, facing the star of the show. "You're the famous Leonardo Santiago, is that right?" Lisa's intoxicating scent—accentuated by Clive Christian perfume—invades his senses. It makes his heart palpitate.

"*Simón!* That's what my *jefitos* named me, but in here, I'm called El DaVinci."

11:17 a.m. The director peers into all six monitors assembled to look like one big screen. Each monitor displays a different angle of the room. "Wait a minute," he says, glancing at his watch and then eyeing the monitor facing the entryway. "You know what? I just got me one heck of an idea." He bolts towards the door. "Scottie boy, grab that there portable and meet me outside, stat! We only got a couple minutes! Let's see if we can't rouse up some good ol' fashion anticipation."

Scott pauses for a beat and then nods with a smile. "Oh, you're good boss, you're very good." He snatches up the portable and heads outside. "That's why you get paid the big bucks, ey', boss!"

11:18 a.m. "Excuse us, fellas." The director takes Lisa by the hand and whisks her out into the hallway. "Listen doll, in a minute, you're gonna get the chance to sell this for all it's worth. This is your moment!"

"Ok, thank you for that, but what are we doing out here?"

"Don't worry, boss. I know what you have in mind," Scott says. "We got this."

11:19 a.m. The director nods and rushes back into the room.

"Scott, what the hell's going on? Why are we out here?" Lisa asks with anxiety, watching the director head back into the room.

"Don't worry, Leese. The old man wants you to spice it up a bit before the big reveal. You know what I'm saying, build up the wow factor." Scott says as he snaps in an extra power source into the video camera.

"Damn," Lisa says, nodding her head with approval. "He really is a genius." Lisa reaches for the tiny microphone attached in her collar. "You hear that old man, you're a genius. I'm selling this for all its worth!" she says with conviction.

"You finally caught my drift, huh?" The director eyes Lisa through the monitor.

"Did you bring the picture of your *jefita*?" asks El DaVinci.

"*Simón*," Diego reaches into his waistband and pulls out an old creased-up photograph. El DaVinci graces over it, examining every detail of the woman's face—the shape of her eyes, the sharpness of her nose, the outline of her lips. "She's beautiful, ey'."

"*Simón*, that's where I got my good looks from, homes." A sliver of sentimentality escapes from Diego's voice.

El DaVinci places the picture on a stand so he can refer to it as he tattoos freehand.

11:20 a.m. "Positions, everybody!" The director lassos his finger in the air. The mechanical door shuts.

"Here we go, boys and girls, it's showtime!" The director places the megaphone to his mouth, and commences with the final portion of the countdown. "We're live in 10-9-8-7-6-5-4-3-2-," he concludes by motioning with his index finger.

"*Órale*, let's do this." El DaVinci blesses himself with the sign of the cross.

Outside the prison, somewhere on the mean, urban streets of Los Angeles, a fourteen-year-old, freshly-initiated gang member sits laid back in a shabby two-room apartment smoking a joint in his room. Juan Gonzalez, or now known in his hood as Lil' Playboy, changes the channel on his small, old fashion television. He searches for something to watch before starting a new drawing on a brand new sketch pad.

"Man, this TV sucks! I have to get a new one when I get some more *feria*." Lil' Playboy happens to be a talented artist. It came to light early in his childhood. Once he hit seventh grade, he realized he could make some money off of his ability when one of his classmates contracted him to draw an image of Mickey Mouse holding a heart for his girlfriend. He made $20. His newest venture will bring him $100, an Aztec calendar which his homeboy will use as a template for a tattoo.

"What's this?" he says, eyeballing Lisa on TV. "Damn, she's pretty fine. Entertainment Weekly, huh?" He leaves it on the channel and begins drawing.

34

Back at the prison, the show begins. "Whoa, whoa! Hold on a sec. I'm not done framing my shot. It has to be perfect." Scott maneuvers the lens, focuses on Lisa's curvy figure, trying to hide where they're broadcasting.

Lisa's eyes widen, noticing the camera isn't live yet. "We're supposed to be on!" She mouths the words knowing Scott is watching her through the lens.

"Ok, ok." Scott taps on a switch, converting the ambiance to black and white for a more dramatic effect. The director maintains his patience for as much as he can before unleashing some good old southern-style profanity right into Scott's earpiece.

As cool as the other side of the pillow, Scott gently taps the live-feed button, and the red LED light flashes on portable. The camera goes live.

Lisa jumps right in. "Good evening, everyone, I'm Lisa Deveroe, and welcome to a special edition of, Entertainment Weekly, the show that gives you an intimate glimpse into the secretive and high-profile world of entertainment."

The sound technician spots his cue and keys a switch, activating the show's theme music.

Scott Leon Jr., lead cameraman for the network, has an uncanny ability for getting the perfect shots. His talent for filming from unique and dramatic vantage points, along with an unnatural willingness to enter dangerous situations, landed him his dream job right out of college. He became an action cameraman for a news network committed to exposing human atrocities. He's traveled war-torn parts of the world in a bulletproof vest alongside armed battalions to cover events like The First Gulf War and the ethnic cleansing in Rwanda. And yet, even those emotion-hardening experiences can't stop his temperature from rising. The notion that a disgruntled prisoner can approach him from behind and use his neck as leverage for unreasonable demands, punctures holes in the psychological barrier that took him years to build. And it's all due to the safety and security meeting held earlier by the Captain of the guard.

"Listen, folks," said Captain Briggs at the meeting. "It's my responsibility as head of security to inform you, we never negotiate with prisoners." He selects a bulky, shotgun-like weapon from a weapons cache and loads in a canister of tear gas. "Look, people, I'm not going to sugarcoat this, tell you everything will be fine, or there's nothing to worry about. I'm not programmed that way. The truth is, you should worry. Each one of you is a potential hostage in here, and there are always casualties in hostage situations, especially in a place like this." The intensity in the Captain's eyes is matched only by his no-games demeanor. "Listen folks, If you find yourself in a crisis in here, do whatever you need to do to take cover when you see the gas." He lifts the launcher and aims it in the air, "Because that'll mean only one thing, we're coming in fast and we're coming in hard."

Scott takes a deep breath as the captain's words still echo in his ears. He winces as a bead of sweat runs into his eye, causing him to shake the camera slightly. It attracts the director's attention.

"Steady, Scottie ol' boy. We can't afford any mistakes." The director covers his microphone, making sure to conceal his concern. As their leader, he carries a general-like obligation to bear the pressure for his team. When the board approached him and expressed their expectation for a flawless broadcast, he assured them that his team always delivers.

The show's theme music concludes, and Lisa commences with her intro.

"As some of you may already know, our station has received numerous inquiries about a mysterious tattoo artist mentioned only briefly by many celebrities we've interviewed at Entertainment Weekly," Lisa says. "All we knew about him was that he goes by El DaVinci, and that he left his mark on the likes of Flea, bassist from the Red Hot Chili Peppers, and multi-platinum rapping sensation Drake, just to mention a few on an expanding list of high-profile celebrities."

Lisa displays several photographs scaled up for the audience to see. She cycles through them like cue cards. Scott zooms in on the images.

"It has always been our mission to keep you, our loyal viewers, informed and entertained," she continues. "So, our network launched an investigation into the identity of this mysterious tattoo artist. It took some serious digging, but I'm happy to report, we solved the mystery." Lisa winks, hinting that she's about to reveal something extraordinary.

"What we found was so compelling, our network agreed to put on a special two-part segment, where I will interview this underground tattoo artist as he showcases his remarkable talent right before your very eyes. Ladies and gentlemen, we are broadcasting live from California's notorious Donovan State Penitentiary."

Scott pans the camera around.

"Stay tuned, folks, you don't want to change your dial, we'll see you right after these short messages from our sponsors." Lisa winks flirtatiously into the camera, attempting to arouse interest for the upcoming segment.

"Cut!" The director shouts in his calm, just another day at the office way. "We're back on in three minutes and forty-five seconds, folks," he announces over the megaphone. "Lisa honey, that was smokin', my temp just spiked." He says, teasing hrough his microphone. The crew members laugh, partaking in the joke.

"Hey, I'm just trying to entice our viewers, that's all." Lisa snaps back.

"Oh, I'm enticed, alright."

Lisa shakes her head. "Geez, you're too much, old man."

Jenny, the make-up artist, hops out of her chair and waits by the entryway. "Come on, come on, my girl Lisa needs me. I only got two minutes!" She stomps her foot on the floor. "Hurry up! Ok, what do I need to do? Tighten up her lip-liner, powder her nose, soften her cheeks, dust off her collar off." She sighs in frustration as she wiggles her way through a small crack emerging as the door opens at its mechanical pace. The director shakes his head, waiting calmly for the door to open fully before making his way towards Scott.

"You alright there, Scottie ol' boy? I've never known ya' to falter the portable, specially' durin' a live feed."

"Yeah, yeah," Scott chuckles. "I should've known your old eagle eyes would've caught that." He removes his Dodgers cap and wipes his brow with a handkerchief. "I'm cool, boss. This place just got in my head a little. It was that damn security meeting. Thank Captain Briggs for that."

"Yeah, he is a rather intense fellow. Alrighty' then, I'll leave you to it. By the way, genius switching the color scheme to black and white." The director nods. He eyes his timer and turns towards Lisa.

"Lisa, honey, I forgot to give ya' this." He pulls out a perfect short-stem rose from his shirt pocket and clips it to her lapel."

"Where were you hiding that?" Lisa asks.

"Never mind that, you just keep showin' em' what yer' made of, doll." He turns without saying another word and makes his way back into the room. "Close these doors! Jenny, that's enough of that, get your butt back in here, we got 30 seconds!"

El DaVinci preens his goatee as he studies the rough, porous, canvas of Diego's back. "How big do you want your tat, ey'?"

"I want her to cover my back, homes. She gave me life. I wanna' honor her with the skin off my back, *qué no*?"

El DaVinci nods. "*Simón*, that's the love of a son, ey'," he says with shame hiding in his voice. He closes his eyes, shutting out the surrounding chaos like a Tibetan monk in deep meditation. Within a few seconds, the tattoo begins materializing in his mind's eye. "*Órale*, I can see it now. That's gonna' be a big piece, homes." He rotates his hands at various angles like a photographer setting up for the perfect shot.

"That's right homes." Diego glances up at the photograph. "She's beautiful, *qué no*? My jefita." He clenches his jaw, forcing his emotions deep inside.

"*Qué si*, homes, she' s beautiful." El Davinci places his hand on Diego's shoulder, "Don't trip. I know the feeling, homes."

"You still got your *jefita*, *qué no*?" asks Diego.

El Davinci turns away, hiding the pain escaping from his eyes.

"*Simón*, I'm sure she's still around. I haven't seen her in years, though."

"*Chalé, disculpas*," Diego says as melancholy begins to stir.

"Don't trip, ey'. It's all my fault. Anyways, young *vato*, I'm gonna' get down on this tat for you, homes. Your *jefita* will be my Mona Lisa."

"Mona-what, homes?" Diego turns and looks up a him, not quite knowing whether to take the comment as disrespect.

El DaVinci quickly notices his confusion. "My Mona Lisa, homes. You know, that famous painting of that one *heina*."

"Nah', homes. I don't know what *heina* you talking about?" Diego says, shrugging his shoulders.

"Don't trip, ey'. It just means your *jefita* is gonna' be my masterpiece." El Davinci slips on a pair of black, latex gloves and wiggles his fingers in place, like a surgeon preparing for surgery.

"*Órale*, I already know, homes. Everything you do is a masterpiece."

The director swoops in suddenly. "Excuse me, fellas, I just wanna' let y'all know, when Lisa enters through that door, the cameras will be rollin', and it'll be yer' time ta' shine."

"*Órale*, we got this." El DaVinci studies the contours of Diego's back one more time, assuring the best possible place for the tattoo.

"Positions everybody, we're back on in ten seconds!" The director peers into the monitors. He glances off to the side, "Are you ready for your big debut, son?"

"As ready as a virgin on prom night, ey'!"

Scott cracks his neck and rolls his shoulders and with one smooth motion, he hurls the sixty-five-pound portable onto his shoulder. "Are you ready, Leese?

"I was born ready. Are you ready this time, Scott?

"Yeah, yeah. Here we go! We're live in 5,4,3,2." Scott and the director motion with their index finger at the same time.

"Hello out there, welcome back to an Entertainment Weekly exclusive."

Scott zooms the camera out, exposing Lisa standing in a hallway. She paces forward as Scott follows in close, giving the cinematography a gritty feel. He switches to full-color mode, focusing on Lisa's red bottom high heels as they tap on the tile floor. Lisa suddenly pauses. Scott switches back to black and white and slowly moves the camera upward, exposing a large, steel door with the words, OBSERVATION ONE stenciled above the door frame. Lisa turns and faces the camera.

"Ladies and gentlemen, we are broadcasting live from a place that houses the most dangerous criminal's society has to offer." She alters her voice to just above a whisper. "We're in a place so dark and dangerous that armed guards are posted throughout various locations." She points to her right, Scott pans the camera up and to his left, where a pair of black, military-style boots pace the gun rail. He zooms in on the deputy in full tactical gear with his assault rifle hanging off of his shoulder.

Scott pans the camera back towards Lisa and zooms out, revealing two Sheriff's deputies standing next to an entryway. One of them nearly succumbs to the excitement of being on TV. He cracks a smile, fighting back the urge to yell out, "Hi, mom, I told you I'd be on TV one day!"

Lisa quickly peers around as if something grabbed her attention. "As we speak, professional marksmen scan the facility from elevated positions, ready to subdue any situation." She glances up at the officer in tactical gear. Scott follows her every movement.

"These concrete walls protect us from murderers, rapists, and other hardcore criminals." Scott pans the camera along the concrete wall of the hallway. "What place I am referring? Well, California's own, Donovan State Penitentiary." Lisa raises her arms. Scott rotates the camera 360 degrees, giving the audience a panoramic view.

"Behind these concrete walls and razor-sharp fences," she says, pouring on the drama. "Lies a beautiful little secret. A rose has emerged, spreading beauty to such an unlikely place." Lisa unclips the rose attached to her lapel and twirls it slowly. She is a master at incorporating impromptu dramatization on the fly.

"Oh, you're good, Leese, I got this." Scott switches back to full-color mode and zooms in on the flower.

"Ata' girl," the director say. "That's how you give it a touch a' flair." He shoves the young sound technician's assistant standing beside him. "You see that, that there was my idea."

"What beauty can I possibly speak of in a place as dark and as menacing as this?" Lisa says and then pauses, staring directly into the camera. "Well, tattoos."

Scott zooms in on one of the deputies as he reaches for a small walkie-talkie attached to his vest. "Open up observation one."

The steel door hisses to life and slithers open. With the camera following close, Lisa enters and makes for the center of the room. Scott signals the sound technician and camera number two and three activate. He places the portable in its case and heads to camera three just as Lisa is leading into El DaVinci's debut.

"I'm standing in front of an inmate with the reputation for creating the most amazing tattoos anyone has ever seen. Some have even gone as far as to say that Inmate Leonardo Santiago, also known as El DaVinci, is a tattoo prodigy and might very well be the best tattoo artist to have ever lived."

Scott swivels camera three to the right and zooms in on the walls of the room. He pans by beautifully sketched smile now cry later faces,

Aztec figures, religious symbols, tribal designs, and many other sketches he's tattooed over the years.

"Folks, this is our mystery man, and with his permission, and with the support of Warden Wiesel and the deputies here at Donovan, we will take an intimate glimpse into his life as an inmate in a maximum-security prison and as a secret, highly sought-after celebrity tattoo artist. And so, without further ado, I'd like to introduce, El DaVinci, the tattoo prodigy."

All six cameras turn towards El DaVinci. He glances at the lens of one of the cameras and eyes his reflection staring back at him. It makes the butterflies to stir in his stomach. In that moment, he's whisked back into his childhood as the anxiety triggers a memory.

"*Hijo*," his father says. "We all get a chance to do something great in life. Many are scared of it. Others don't realize it came and went. *Pero hijo*, there are some who grab the chance with both hands and never let go!"

Little Lenny looks up at his father, and right when he was about to ask, his father answers. "Don't worry, *hijo*, *lo sabrás*," he says. "You'll know when it's your time. You'll feel it in your gut."

El DaVinci freezes, caught between panic and excitement.

The young sound technician's assistant leans over. "Is he going to say something?"

"Shhh! Give him a minute," responds the director.

Scott zooms in on El DaVinci's face, exposing the facial features forged by a violent merging of cultures. A man in his forties but with the distinction of one eighty-years wiser, his eyes are large, but his constant squint conceals their true size. Deep crevices contort on his forehead with each expression, complimenting the wrinkles beginning to spread from the outer edges of his eye sockets. His jet-black hair shimmers against the artificial lighting along with his finely trimmed goatee with several greys residing within. His shoes are spit-shined to a high-polish, and his tank top is tucked neatly under his meticulously creased khakis behind a full-body artist's apron.

This is it. This is my time. El DaVinci's heart races, and yet he calmly nods at the camera. "*Qué pasa,* out there in the real world. Welcome to our little corner of hell, or what we cons refer to as home."

With clipboard in hand, Lisa sits and crosses her legs. "OK then, let's begin."

El DaVinci reaches for a spray bottle and squirts a misty solution onto Diego's back. The mixture of alcohol and bactine creates kind of lubricant over the skin, making it easier to tattoo while reducing the possibility of infection.

El DaVinci turns and peers at the photograph of Diego's mother, focusing on the shape of the woman's face. Then, he commences with his pre-tattooing routine, cracking his neck from left to right and snapping every knuckle in his hands. He dips the point of the needle into the ink and begins outlining. He tattoos for a short time, then stops to wipe, and then continues again—stopping at about thirty-second intervals to wipe again. Such is the tedious process of tattooing, and El DaVinci is second to none.

"*Òrale,* let's get this show started, ey'."

Lisa clears her throat. "Ok, then, but before we begin, may I ask, what will you be tattooing for us today?"

"Check it out, *mija,* I'm gonna tattoo a portrait of a very special lady on my homeboy Diego," he says, adjusting the air pressure on the compressor. He hands the picture over to Lisa.

"She's resting in peace with our lord and savior, ey'," says Diego.

"Oh, I'm sorry to hear that. When did she pass?" Lisa holds up the photograph for Scott to zoom in.

Diego turns his head, "She's been gone a long time, ey'."

Lisa places the picture back on the easel. "Well, I'm so sorry to hear that, Diego. Let's begin the interview, shall we?" Lisa quickly moves on before it can get awkward. "I would like to start with your moniker,

El DaVinci. It seems very appropriate you being a tattoo artist. How did you get that name?"

El DaVinci smirks. He stops tattooing and slowly wipes Diego's back. He gazes down at a familiar face staring back at him from the inner portion of his left forearm. Scott zooms in on the tattoo on El Davinci's arm then back at his face.

"*Chalé*, that was a long time ago, ey', back when I was young and dumb. Man, the things a young, hard-headed little *vato* will do for a life of respect behind bars. And you know what, it was all because I lost a hand in a poker game." His mind flashes back.

V. Paid in Full

*F**lashback.** "Washa, locos!* The game is No-Limit Texas Hold'em." Beto eyeballs the *vatos* sitting around the aluminum recreation table, all of who could have easily been cast for the gangster flick, *American Me.* Shaved heads, prison tats, chiseled physiques, characteristics all too common in such a hardened environment.

The *carnales* enforce this section of the rec hall at the infamous Folsom State Pen. That's what they call themselves, *carnales*, which in *Caló* terms means, brothers—a term less menacing than the alternatives. Any inmate caught lingering about without their consent is subject to brutal and sometimes fatal repercussions.

"For you *vatos* that don't know," Beto says, staring deep into the eyes of a freshly turned eighteen-year-old inmate sitting awkwardly among them, and trying his best not to show it. "It's called no limit, homeboys, cuz' there's no limit to what you *vatos* can throw into the pot, ey'." Beto waves his menacing tattooed-skeleton-bone finger, "But if you *vatos* can't cover the bet, *chalé,* you still gotta' pay the piper, *qué no,* homeboys?"

"*Simón, carnales!*"

"That's right, homes."

45

"*Simón qué si*," several of the *carnales* answer out.

"Don't forget what happened to *Carlito's*," says Beto, "That *vato* got overconfident, lost a big hand, ey', and when he couldn't come up with the *feria,*" Beto shakes his head, "*Chalé*, you *vatos* know how that story turned out.*"

"That's fucked up, ey'!"

"What a disgrace!"

"No good, homes!" the *carnales* respond. Their facial expressions carry a silent warning, *don't make bets you can't afford to cover, or you'll end up six-feet under*!

"Hey, homes," calls out the young inmate with his chin held higher than it should.

Beto says nothing, baiting the young inmate into a confrontation.

"Hey, homes!" the young inmate says again with his voice raised high. Silence suddenly spreads around the table. Beto's evil grin expresses, *you took the bait, kid, hook, line, and sinker*.

The young inmate peers around with that, *Oh crap, I think I just messed up*, expression on his face. He clenches his jaw as his thoughts run wild, *no backing out now, I can't look like a chavala in front of these hardcore vatos*. The thought makes his heart nearly beat out of his chest. It should've have cued him to the danger lurking ahead, like a hazard sign before a deadly curve—but the young inmate still takes it at full speed. "I wanna' know how the story turned out, homes!" he says, aggression residing in his tone. Talking up to a *carnal* is dangerous enough, but talking loud to a made head can practically sign your death warrant.

Facial expressions turn serious as the *carnales* glance at Beto, ready to pounce on command.

"What'd you say, homeboy!?!" Beto stares the young inmate down. Then, his enlarged jaw cracks another evil smile.

It sends a cold chill running down the young inmate's spine, making his legs tingle—another warning sign—and he still won't back down.

"I said, I wanna' know how the story turned out, homes!" He says, grinding his teeth, trying to match Beto's level of intimidation.

"I heard you, fish!" Beto turns towards the *carnales*. "*Washa'*, check out the *huevos* on this youngster." He nods his head, "But I like that, little *vato*, I like that a lot!"

Hardened from the fires of prison brutality, Beto probes the young inmate for signs of fear. His penetrating gaze shocks the teenager's heart, but the young inmate holds steady.

"Alright, little vato, you wanna' know how it went? Beto says, "I'll tell you, homes. Carlitos worked off his debt," he pauses for a moment, "In other ways." he says, jerking his hand in a sexual motion.

A look of complete shock contorts on the young inmate's face, followed by a look of disgust. Beto breaks into a fit of laughter. "Check out the little *vato's* face, *ey'*, I bet he shit his pants, homes!"

The *carnales* sitting around the table join in the laughter, that is, except for the young inmate named Leonardo Santiago. He grins and nods his head, taking in the joke with as much humility as he can muster.

Lenny may have just graduated from juvenile hall to the state pen, but he's no rookie to incarceration. He's learned when a situation calls for him to be smart and not a smart ass. His celli back in juvenile hall schooled him on prison etiquette. "My big homie told me all about the *pinta*," Lil' Boxer had said. "You gotta' always be on your game, Lenny, cuz' you gonna' be a small fish in a pond full of *tiburones*."

Unfortunately for Lenny, these particular sharks are all members of one of the most violent and feared prison gangs on the West Coast. The *carnales* are known by other more nefarious names, and just a mere mention of them brings about a sense of apprehension and fear.

Lenny scans the *carnales* sitting around the table as a single thought jabs relentlessly at his side. *How did I get myself into this?*

Taking stock of his opponents, Lenny glances to his left, where *Pelón*, a seasoned prion *veterano,* sits hand-rolling a cigarette. His strong jawline and face cratered with acne scars is the typical portrait of a hardened convict. Most assume *Pelón* got his moniker from his obvious bald head, but only a hand full of *carnales* know that the true meaning of his name comes from his daily ritual of shaving his head bare to the skin with the same razor blade he uses to slice at the jugular of enemies.

Lenny turns to his right, where *El Gallo*, also known as Fighting Rooster, taunts the carnal sitting next to him. What *El Gallo* lacks in his 5-foot-5 stature, he more than makes up for it with his ability to throw down. The 50-hash marks etched into his left forearm keeps track of his victories. Whenever there's trouble on the yard, it's an easy wager that *El Gallo* is at the center of it.

Sitting on the other side of Fighting Rooster and blowing off his taunts with high-pitched laughter is the self-proclaimed George Lopez of the bunch. The meaning of Joker's name isn't too difficult to decipher. He has talent for bringing comic relief to such an emotionless environment. Again, the *carnales* who know him best know never underestimate his playfulness, because when it comes to matters of money, he wields his prison shank like a brain surgeon wields a scalpel.

Beto—the carnal taunting Lenny—sits to *Pelón's* left. Tall, lanky, and with a long Native American ponytail, Beto is the spokesperson for the gang, responsible for delegating orders to their *soldados*. If a soldier fails to carry out a mission, Beto dictates whether the punishment is as minor as an *El Gallo* beat down or as severe as *Pelón's* razor blade across your neck. On the surface, he's the leader. Under the surface, though, a deeper secret resides.

Sitting directly across from Lenny is the man referred to simply as *Villa*, named after the famed Mexican civil war General, *Pancho Villa*. Reserved and observant, aside from being a *carnal,* his involvement in the organization is unknown, but by how the other *carnales* speak to him, Lenny knows he commands enormous respect.

Beto shuffles through the deck and dishes out two cards to every player. Lenny lifts the corners just enough to reveal his hand. "I fold," he says, laying down his cards. He looks around the table thinking, *I better check out the competition before playing with these vatos*. Lenny throws away a king of diamonds and ten of hearts.

El Gallo, who's next to act, takes every opportunity to live up to his aggressive reputation, even though he's also known for something else when it comes to cards. "*Órale*, I'm in five reds, homeboys." He says, tossing five cigarettes into the pot.

"*Chalé, Gallo*, I know you bluff a lot, but what do I look like, your old lady's butt cheeks? I'm not gonna' let you spank me with these odds." Joker's comedic talent is matched only by his ability to calculate numbers in his head. He tosses his hand into the pile of dead cards known to as the muck. Villa follows suit, flicking his hand into the muck without saying a word.

"I'm in." *Pelón*, the most experienced player at the table, calls the bet. "You know you *vatos* fucked up, ey'." Beto exudes overconfidence, calling the bet with a mediocre hand. As dealer, he takes the first card and places it under the deck—this action is known as the burn—and lays three cards face up in the center of the table. In the game of Texas Hold'em, this is called the flop, and it reveals a queen of spades, jack of clubs, and ace of hearts.

"*Órale*, I just hit top pair, homes!" exclaims *El Gallo*. "I'm in a fresh pack, *carnales*. Let's see who's down for a little throwdown with the Fighting Rooster." If a single cigarette has caused many altercations in prison, you can imagine what a new pack can do.

Pelón stares *El Gallo* down, searching for a telltale sign of a bluff—a vein popping out, body shifting, eye twitching, and the like.

"*Órale, Gallo*, I'm down," *Pelón* notices something and ups the stakes with another pack of cigarettes and two packets of shrimp ramen soup, "Let's see what you're about, *carnal*."

"Too rich for my taste. You *vatos* can fight it out, but I'll catch you on the flip." Beto tosses his cards away.

"That's a legit raise, *Pelón*. Shrimp ramens are the business, *ey'*, *pero sabes qué*, Fighting Rooster never backs down." *El Gallo* matches the bet by throwing in two jars of Tres Flores hair grease.

"*Órale*, pot's right." Beto burns another card and flips over a fourth. This is called the turn, and it shows the two of hearts.

"I check to you, *Pelón*." Utilizing the strategy of the check, *El Gallo* gives his opponent the first move, hoping to lure out information about his hand. Unfortunately for *El Gallo*, *Pelon* checks back.

Beto burns one more card and flips over the fifth and final card of the hand. The river, as the final round of betting is known, reveals the seven of clubs.

"I got your *número*, *Pelón*, I know you were chasing that straight, homes, that's why you checked, but it didn't come. *El Gallo* tosses four cigarette packs into a lucrative pot. He also reaches behind his back and pulls out his favorite Playboy magazine from his waistband. "You sure you want to call, *carnal*," he says, flinging the magazine into the pot. All heads turn towards the half-naked woman on the front cover.

"*Órale*, that *guerita* is fine, *ey'*. I call," *Pelón* says, matching the bet with a carton of cigarettes he pulled out from the leg of his pants.

"What! You called me, homes? *El Gallo* asks, happily flipping over an ace and a jack of spades. "Two pair, loco, *Cheeoow*! You thought I was bluffing, *qué no*, *carnal*?" he says with victory in his tone. *El Gallo* reaches for the pot with both arms, "I thought you knew, *El Gallo* knows no defeat."

"*Dispensa*." *Pelón* flips over the red queen of hearts and the red queen of diamonds, "But today's a good day to learn. Three-of-a-kind," the *vato* says, clapping his hands, "That pot is mine."

El Gallo freezes in mid-reach. "*Chalé*! You slow-rolled me, *carnal*, and with your damn ladies." He flicks his cards in anger.

"*Simón*, my ladies are always good to me." *Pelón* stands and pulls off his shirt, exposing a tattoo covering the center of his chest—The queen of hearts and the queen of diamonds. But these particular queens don *Día de Los Muertos* motifs on their faces. He hangs his shirt over his shoulder and winks at Lenny as he rakes in the pot.

"You should've known better, Fighting Rooster," *Pelon* says, "Patience is the key."

Lenny glares at *Pelon's* hand, shaking his head. *Ace, king, queen, jack, ten! I would've won with a straight!* He makes a mental note, *don't be afraid to play your hand. You can win!*

The game plays on for another hour until Lenny finally gets involved in the most important hand of his life.

Lenny glances to his left and then to his right. He lifts the corners of his cards just enough not to expose it. Lenny peers at a pair of black aces. *Oh, snap!* He yells out in his thoughts. Again, Lenny looks around the table before looking back down at his cards. He lifts the corners again. *Yep! Pocket aces!* As slowly and secretly as he can, Lenny draws in a breath as it's now his turn to act. "I bet a pack of reds," he says as cooly as he can.

"*Órale*, looks like the little *vato* picked up a hand, *ey'*," says one of the *carnales*. Everyone folds around the table except for *Villa*. He stares at Lenny for about minute—which for Lenny feels more like ten.

"I call," the *carnal* says, matching the wager.

Beto lays out the flop. It reveals the queen of diamonds, the two of clubs, and the ace of spades.

Three-of-a-kind! At first glance of the cards, Lenny experiences a quick sense of relief. *Ok, I think I'm win gonna' win this hand*, he says in his thoughts. But then he's overcome with overconfidence. *Hell no! I am winning this hand!* He tries to put on a Oscar-worthy performance, taking deep breaths and pretending to look flustered. "Check," Lenny says, finally.

Villa leans in and rests his chin on his fist. After about two minutes, the *carnal* throws in a wager, "Two packs."

Lenny's fingers move like they're playing an invisible piano. After ten seconds, he calls, hoping to drive in the hook deeper.

Beto flips over the turn—the queen of clubs. *Full house! Aces over queens!* Lenny grinds his teeth, trying to keep his excitement from exploding out of his chest. His heart beats in his ears, but Lenny calmly motions for another pass.

Villa glances at the cards on the table, and then at his young opponent. Lenny sits upright, taking slow, deep breaths, pushing his excitement deep into his midsection. No matter how hard he tries to remain cool, a vein pulsates out from the side of his neck.

Villa notices and tosses in another wager, doubling the last. Lenny scans the *vato's* faces around the table. *I bet they think I don't know what I'm doing. I can't wait to flip over my full house and prove them wrong!* "I call," he says.

Beto flips over the fifth and final card. The river reveals a six of clubs. Lenny leads in with everything he has left—two jars of hair grease, his last pack of cigarettes, and a Sony hand-held radio bartered for some of his artwork, "I'm all in," he says pushing in the wager with his forearm and staring straight into the *carnal's* eyes.

Villa leans forward and lifts his cards to eye his hand before settling back in his chair. "That's good bet, little *vato*, but I have to raise you." Villa tosses in a sheet of twenty-four raffle-like tickets, instituted by the warden as an incentive program. Each ticket affords certain privileges—phone calls, extra hot trays, commissary items—highly valued, even to those in the highest ranks of the prison hierarchy. How he acquired them is best left unsaid.

"I can't cover that bet, homes, I'm in for everything I have," Lenny says.

Villa slips on a beanie cap and crosses his arms. "It doesn't work that way in here, little *vato*. This is prison poker, and in here, you have to match the bet or fold your hand."

"I'm not folding, not when I know I have the winning hand," Lenny says, defiant.

"Are you sure about that, little *vato*?"

"Hell yeah!" Lenny smirks, "I'm sure."

"Then you know what you gotta' do."

"And what's that?" Lenny asks.

"Pledge."

Lenny looks around the table, seeking an explanation from the other *carnales*. "Pledge? What do you mean, pledge?"

"You have to pledge your *servicio,* little *vato*," Villa says. "You give your word you'll do whatever I say, *entiendes, Mendez*? You'll be my indentured servant, homes until you make good. But you don't have to worry, since you got the winning hand," Villa says with an instigating wink. "So, I ask you again, are you sure you wanna' call, little *vato*?"

"Your servant, huh?" Lenny peers at his aces and then at the cards on the table.

"That's right, little *vato*, my servant."

No way he can beat my full house, Lenny reassures himself. You got my pledge," Lenny says. "But it don't matter because I'm not losing." He quickly flips over his cards, "Full house, homes, aces over queens. It looks like you're gonna' be my servant, homes." Lenny peers around the table, expecting to see surprised looks on the *carnales's* faces. But instead, they stare back, shaking their heads, as if saying, *ya te chingaste.*

"Damn, little *vato*, a full house, that's a *firme* hand," *Villa* says. "I see why you pledged," he calmly flips over a pair of queens. "I probably would've done the same thing in your shoes, but unfortunately, it's not good enough!"

Lenny looks down at *Villa's* cards with his eyes wide open, trying to comprehend what's happening. *Four of a kind! Are you serious!*

Villa leans in and stares up at Lenny. "You know what your problem is, little *vato*? The arrogance and impatience of youth. You should've learned from *Pelón* earlier. His lesson came back to bite you," the *carnal* says, corralling the pot and pulling it in with one arm. "Patience is the key to this game, to any game, little *vato*, even in the game of life. He pauses and then looks into Lenny's eyes, "You know what this means, right? How do you plan on making good?"

With nothing of value in his possession, Lenny's mind races for a solution.

"I know that look. That's the same look Carlitos had when he lost his hand. Now you get to find out how the story goes, ey'," *Villa* says with a smile.

Lenny glances at Beto, who's not trying very hard to contain his laughter. A horrific thought suddenly invades Lenny's mind. "Hell no! I'd rather die!" he says, balling up his fists.

All the *carnales* break into a fit of laughter. "I told you, *vatos*," Beto says in between laughs, "This youngster's got *huevos*."

In his panic, Lenny fixates on a beautiful tattoo on Villa's right forearm, and blurts out the first thing that comes to mind, "I'll do you a *firme* tattoo, homes!"

Villa breaks into an even deeper laugh, "You're right, *carnal*. This little vato does have some *huevos, ey'*." He turns towards Lenny. His expression now serious, the kind that makes your stomach bubble. "We don't let anybody tattoo on us, homes, only a true master." Villa stands and pulls up his shirt, exhibiting his chest tattoos with pride—the most stunning is Cuauhtémoc, the last Aztec king, standing on a pyramid—a true work of art on skin.

"What can a youngster like you offer me, homes?" he says, "You better watch what you say in here, little *vato*, before your mouth gets you in too deep, and I'm talking six-feet deep."

Again, emotion swoops in. It clouds Lenny's logic. "Yeah, well, I'll do the best tattoo you've ever seen in your life, homes!" he says with conviction bulging from his eyes.

For the second time in a day, silence spreads around the rec table. The *carnales* stare up at Lenny shaking their heads. This time, he knows exactly what they're thinking, *you just dug your grave kid!*

"Hey, little *vato*," *Villa* leans in and stares deep into Lenny's eyes, "You willing to put your life on that?" His ice-cold expression sends a chill shooting down to Lenny's toes—a third warning he'd be wise not to ignore.

Lenny stares back at *Villa*, again asking himself, *how the hell did I get myself into this? I can't rank out now!*

"Yeah," he answers, "I am."

"Like I said, check out the *huevos* on this youngster." Beto grabs the cards and shuffles the deck.

The space in Lenny's cell can become quite claustrophobic, but he pays it no mind as he sketches out a scene from a lasting childhood memory. His hand glides across the page, remembering the strolls he used to take on the boardwalk while swinging happily in his parent's arms.

"Hey, little *vato*," *Pelón's* voice whisks away the sound of the waves caressing Mission Beach in Lenny's mind. "*Villa* wants a word with you."

Escorted by the most feared hitman in Folsom, Lenny strolls down the bottom tier like he's walking the green mile. Inmates step aside as they make their way to the end of the hall where Joker and *El Gallo* stand in front of a cell door like a pair of secret service agents guarding the oval office.

"Good Luck, little *vato*," Joker says, laughing, "And try to smile when he's doing his thing, he likes that," he says with a disturbing wink.

Lenny hesitates for a moment as Joker's attempt at comic relief resonates in his gut. He peers inside the cell and then enters. Lenny finds Villa reading, *A Hundred Years of Solitude* by Gabriel Garcia-Marquez. *Pelón* unrolls a large blanket hung above the entryway, giving them a sense of privacy, and then steps outside. Lenny's heart races as Joker's remark lingers in his ears.

"Do you know what you got yourself into, little vato?" *Villa* says, placing an old photograph in between the pages of his book and closes it.

Lenny nods, "*Simón*. Look, homes, I know what I'm doing. I may be young, but I know what's up!"

"Oh, so you know what's up, huh? Then why do you act like you don't, with that, I ain't scared of shit attitude, when everyone in here can see you're shaking inside like a wet pussy cat." Lenny remains speechless as Villa's words sting with truth.

"I remember how it was when I first got here. There's no shame in being scared, homes." *Villa* says, easily reading the fear in Lenny's eyes. "Shit, you wouldn't be human if you weren't. But there's a big difference between acting hard and being hard." *Villa's* intimidating glare penetrates Lenny's soul. "You don't even know who I am, do you, little *vato*?"

"I do," answers Lenny, "You're a *carnal*."

Villa smirks. "Yeah, I am a *carnal*, alright, and a bit more. In fact, I'm the man, *yo soy el mero-mero*. In secret, you can call me, El *General*." He pulls up his sleeve, revealing a tattoo on the top portion of his right shoulder. "Only my *capitanes* know the mark of the boss."

Lenny stares at the tattoo in awe. He's heard rumors of a tattoo that carries the highest status for a *carnal*.

As serious and distinguished as both of his names imply, *El General* is the true boss of bosses. Observant and disciplined, he ascended the ranks of prison politics with shrewd wit and strategic use of treachery, not unlike tactics employed by some politicians in government.

He's the reason why Lenny took great risk to play in the poker game in the first place. If he could have impressed the top *carnal* with his own strategic wit to win the poker game, he would've earned membership into the gang, at least that's what he was gambling on.

"This information can get you killed, little *vato*," *El General* says.

"Hey, I didn't know, I thought Beto was the man."

"Most do, little *vato*, and that's how we're gonna' keep it. Like I said, knowing this shit can get you killed."

"So why tell me?" Lenny asks.

"That's a good question. I really don't know. Maybe it's because I know you won't make it through the week, or maybe because you remind me of myself back in the day, young and arrogant, *pero con huevos*. But don't trip, little *vato*, I know all about you, Leonardo Santiago."

"Oh yeah? Like what?" Lenny asks with a bit skepticism.

"*El Toro*, the *carnal* who vouched for you and got you in the poker game, he told me you're a *firme* artist. But I know all I need to know about you from this." He reaches for book in a small recession in the wall and pulls out a sheet of paper concealed in its pages. He scans through the formal-looking document for a moment. "Vehicular manslaughter, huh?" he says. That's serious shit, ey'. That's why the DA dropped the hammer on you, because you killed an innocent bystander, little *vato*," he says, shaking his head. "That's heavy to be carrying around for a young *vato* like yourself." *El General* stares at the young inmate. Lenny quickly averts his gaze. "I bet you were thinking, since I'm serving life, I might as well join the *carnales*, that way I can have a life of respect behind bars."

Lenny looks up at the leader, "Yeah, I do want a life of respect in here."

El General eyes Lenny up and down, "Is that right? I'm sure you already know, but you're going to hear it from me, little *vato,* so there's no misunderstanding. Once you're in, there's no getting out. Your life will belong to the brotherhood. Whatever's commanded, you do without question, without hesitation, even if it means taking your own life, *ey'*, like the samurai, *entiendes, Mendez*?"

"Yeah," Lenny nods. "I understand," he says, staring back at the leader with conviction.

"*Órale*. I can see in your eyes you mean it. Consider this your initiation, and you better take it as serious as a shank to the heart, little *vato*, because it'll probably cost you your life." He slips Lenny's paperwork back into his book and exchanges it for another. This time, he pulls out an old photograph with the image of a little girl donning two curly locks of hair—a fair likeness of Shirley Temple (beloved child actress of the 1930's). Villa gazes at the image, the expression in his eyes change for a brief moment. "When a *carnal* says he's going to do something, he does it exactly as he said it. Our reputation is everything in here." He hands Lenny the photograph.

"She's my *hijita*, daddy's little angel. She's thirty now, but back when she was a little girl and I was a hard-headed *vato* like you, I couldn't have known how the guilt would affect me to leave her all alone, *en esta vida loca* without her *jefito* to have her back." He grinds his teeth as the guilt gnaws at his insides.

"This is what she looked like the last time I saw her behind the visiting glass, and this is how I want to remember her forever," he says, glaring at Lenny. "The little girl daddy left behind. So, now you know how important this tattoo is for me, but more so for you, little *vato*," his tone now serious. "Because if it isn't the best tattoo I've ever seen in my life, you're not going to make it through the week, *entiendes*? It's gotta' be that way, especially because you said it in front of the other *carnales*."

Lenny stands there for a moment, trying to swallow a dry lump forming in his throat. "I understand," he says, swallowing hard, "All I need to know is, where do you want it." A knotting sensation twists at his guts.

"Damn, little *vato*, you do got a pair on you, homes. It's too bad you let your mouth do all the talking, instead of your head." *El General* flexes his left forearm, "I want her right here," he places his forearms together, "Next to our holy mother (the tattoo of the Virgin Mary on his right forearm), so she can protect her." *El General* looks up at the ceiling, suppressing a rush of emotion threatening to break free. "She's the only reason I'd want to leave this life behind, the only one I know how to live." The leader of the *carnales* clears his throat, "Remember, little *vato*, your word is everything in here, that's jailhouse rules."

"I understand," Lenny says, his nerves going for another loop.

"*Órale*, you'll start tomorrow. I'm done with you."

Lenny takes the cue and turns to leave.

"Hey, little *vato*."

Lenny pauses and then turns to face the leader once more.

"Don't get cocky, homes. Just because you know how to sketch, don't mean you know how to tattoo. Patience and practice, that's the key to everything in life." *El General* whistles, and *Pelón* rolls up the blanket.

"Did it hurt?" Joker asks as Lenny is walking out, "Or did you like it."

Lenny pays him no mind as he passes. As soon he steps into his cell, he begins hyperventilating. The notion of losing his life attacks him like a swarm of angry piranhas. He rubs his hands together, trying to stop them from shaking. His head begins to ache as blood rushes in too fast, and he passes out on his bunk.

Lenny is startled back to consciousness by a voice. "Lights out in five!" a deputy announces over the loudspeaker. Lenny bolts upright and then hunches over. He pulls out a photograph from his waistband and gazes at the only image he has of his father. "How would my life have turned out, *jefito*?" he asks, "If you were still here?"

Pelon suddenly materializes at his cell bars, like a ninja assassin. "Hey, little *vato*," he looks around and then hands Lenny an object wrapped in a kitchen towel through the bars. "It's from *El General*."

"What is it?"

"Call it a parting gift, if you can't back up your words." He turns and begins walking away. He takes several steps forward and then pauses. Glancing back at Lenny, he says, "Hey, little *vato*, keep your lines short, and save the shading for last. You get one shot at tattooing like you get one shot at life." *Pelón* then turns and heads down the tier as quiet as a midnight breeze.

Lenny unwraps the towel, and to his surprise, finds a small glass container filled to the top with ink, accompanied by an odd-looking contraption. "Trip out! I've always wanted to see how these worked." Lenny presses a lever attached to a small power source melted in place, and a thin-grade guitar string pulsates through the tip of a pen casing. Again, the thought of losing his life pulsates through his chest. He fights an overwhelming urge to vomit as he shuts off the contraption. Lenny lies back down on his mattress, starring at the photograph in his hand, trying control the convulsions in his stomach.

"*Papi!*" Lenny says, taking slow, deep breaths. "I don't think I can do this," he picks up the tattoo gun with the other hand and activates the lever. Again, it buzzes to life. He sits upright and looks around. His gaze stops a blank piece of sketch pad paper. "I don't need paper. I need someone's skin to practice on." He stares at the photograph, then at the tattoo gun, then back at the photograph. He does this several times until it happens. A thought hits him as hard as a titanium bat across his forehead. The hairs on the back of his neck electrify with an idea.

"Lights out!" echoes a deputy's voice as Lenny's fear turns into anticipation. One-by-one, the lights go out in the cell block. Lenny strikes a match and lights a candle. He places it on a shelf, recessed into the wall.

"*Mijo, por favor*, pray for your father's soul every night." It was his mother's last request before he pushed her away for good. Lenny places his father's picture under the gentle glow of the candle and recites the most powerful prayer he knows. "Our Father who art in heaven," even though he usually recites The Lord's Prayer in the quiet torment of his thoughts, tonight he brings to sound, though not much louder than a whisper.

"Alright, *jefito*, let's do this, you and me." Lenny closes his eyes and focuses on the details of his father's face he can still remember—his oddly-shaped hairline and how as a child he used to follow it with the tip of his finger, his crunchy mustache and how it was always finely trimmed, his diamond-shaped dimple and how it split his chin into symmetrical halves. But what he remembers most vividly of all, are his hazel chameleon-like eyes and how they seemed to change from blue to green to light brown, depending on the color of the shirt he was wearing.

With his artistic instincts fully engaged, Lenny activates the prison-made tattoo gun, dips the tip into the vial of ink, and stabs it into his left forearm. He flinches, an involuntary response from the sting, as he repeats *Pelón's* words in his mind. *Keep my lines short and save the shading for last.*

The outline proves difficult at first, especially with blood beading up through his pores. The notion that he can't simply start over taunts his confidence, but whenever he puts pen to paper, brush to canvas, and pretty much any implement to any surface, Lenny hands become as steady as a redwood in a storm.

"Patience and practice." He chants *El General's* words like a mantra as he develops a system—tattooing for short spurts then stopping to wipe away the blood. He references his father's photograph every so often and then continues tattooing. After about every fifteen minutes, he stops to analyze his progress. It only takes an hour of this for it to happen, proof of his prodigious talent—of that special thing he has inside.

"This is starting to trip me out," he says, as the endeavor now becomes effortless. Lenny could never really explain how he's able to create his masterpieces. It just kind of flows out, naturally. That's how he best describes it to people, a natural flow that just comes out without thinking, almost as if his hand knows what to do all on its own

Lenny finds that maneuvering this ingenious, prison-made contraption is becoming easier by the minute, a little too easy. Even with the burning sensation in his forearm, it no longer proves a distraction. The fear he had for losing his life dissipates like the moonlight at the crowing of a rooster as a familiar face starts to stare back at him. "Maybe I can do this! Maybe I'll be a *carnal* after all!" El DaVinci says with confidence mounting. "Patience and practice, that's the key to everything."

Lenny tattoos half the night, developing a kind of supernatural connection with his ability and the machine's capability. A little past three in the morning, Lenny wraps his left forearm with a makeshift bandage and lays on his mattress, exhausted but content.

After morning chow, Lenny enters Villa's cell as *Pelón* and *El Gallo* discuss what would be an appropriate consequence for a *carnal* who requested protective custody for the sole purpose of getting out of a debt he couldn't afford to pay.

"*Oralé*, little *vato,* I didn't think you were gonna' show," says *El General*.

"I didn't know I had a choice?"

"There's always PC, little *vato,*" *Pelón* answers, "But that wouldn't matter. There's no place in this *torcida* we can't get to."

"I see you've been practicing," El General points to Lenny's forearm. "You mind if I take a look?"

Lenny nods and removes the bandage.

"Damn, little *vato*," expresses the leader of the gang, "I didn't know you can get down like that," he slips on his reading glasses and analyzes the tattoo. "I'm seriously impressed, that's a *firme* piece. It's up there with some of the better portraits I've seen. But you're going to have to step up your game, little *vato*, because this tattoo has to be the best I've ever seen, without question, *qué no?*"

Lenny rebandages his arm. "So, where can I set up?" he asks, standing eye-to-eye with the *carnales*.

"You came to handle business, huh? You got that look in your eye, the eye of the tiger," El General nods.

"I'm just anxious to get down on this for you, that's all." El Davinci unwraps the towel and places the tattooing equipment on El General's mattress. "We should prep your arm."

"I'll take care of that, little *vato*," announces *Pelón*. He heads for the sink and pulls out a smooth, shiny object from his waistband. With a flick of his finger, out swings a razor—that infamous blade he uses at his leader's command—the one that belonged to his grandfather who raised him—an old fashioned straight razor with a large rectangular blade that folds open. How he managed to get it in prison is anybody's guess.

El General pulls off his shirt and sits cross-legged on the floor. *Pelón* applies soap on his leader's forearm, then he positions the blade at a slight angle and slides it down the length of his leader's forearm arm. He glances at Lenny with a grin and wipes off the residue with a towel. He continues in slow, precise strokes until his leader's arm is nice and smooth.

"*Listo*. As smooth as Jenifer Lopez's ass, *carnal*," he says, flicking his blade closed and placing it back in his waistband.

El DaVinci places the leader's forearm on his lap, "You ready?"

El General slips on his reading glasses and opens a book, "*Carnales*, you mind letting the little *vato* work in peace. I don't want any distractions or excuses."

The two *carnales* unroll the blanket and exit the cell. El DaVinci takes a pen and draws a faint line down the center of *El General's* forearm.

"What's that for?" asks *El General.*

"I want it perfectly centered. I mean, it's for my life, right?

El General nods. Lenny takes three slow, deep breaths and cracks every knuckle. He wiggles his fingers and peers down at them. They're as steady as they'll ever be. He activates the tattoo gun, dips it into the ink, and stabs it in El General's arm.

Three days later, Lenny carefully wipes off the last of the excess ink left on *El General's* forearm. "I'm done, homes. I hope it's a fair trade, this tat for my life," Lenny says, wiping the beads of sweat from his brow.

El General pulls off his reading glasses and places his book down at his side. He stands and twists his torso, working out the kinks from sitting in same position for hours.

"We'll see, little *vato*. I didn't want to look until you finished because I didn't want to make you more nervous than you already are."

"Don't go too far," *Pelón* says, "The reaper may be lurking." He shoots Lenny a terrifying wink.

"Look, I don't care if I live or die anymore. I just want you to know I put in one hundred on this tattoo because I know how much it means to you, because I know how much she means to you. If you need me, you know where to find me, homes." Lenny exits the cell with the uncertainty of a mustard seed, sort of like walking out of an exam you know you aced but still felt anxious for the official results.

"*Carnales*, give me a moment." *Pelon* unrolls the blanket and steps outside with *El Gallo. El General* places his forearm under lukewarm water and gently washes off the tiny droplets of blood outlining the image. He dabs it dry, slips on his reading glasses, and begins examining the tattoo. After about ten seconds, he makes his decision. Lenny's fine lines and precise shading creates the illusion that his

64

daughter is staring straight into his soul, as if expressing, *I miss you, daddy*. *El General* caresses the tattoo as tears accumulate in the corners of his eyes. He tries to fight them back, but then surrenders to them. "I know, *mija*," he says, "I've missed you too, more than this *pinche corazón* can take." For the first time since his incarceration, tears roll down unabated. He covers his face with hands and quietly sobs into them.

Several hours later, the *carnales* roll down the cellblock, like a fleet of lowriders cruising the boulevard. Inmates cut a path, showing respect for the notorious gang as they pass.

Lenny doesn't notice the group approaching as he flips through a book filled with the artwork of Leonardo da Vinci. "I see you're interested in the Renaissance," *El General* says as he enters Lenny's cell while the other *carnales* wait outside.

"You know Leonardo da Vinci?" Lenny asks, surprised.

"Come on, little *vato*, just because I'm locked up don't mean I don't know shit," responds *El General*. "I know them all, Da Vinci, Michelangelo, Raphael, Donatello. Who knows, little *vato*? Maybe you'll paint your own Sistine chapel one day."

Lenny smiles as the comment immediately triggers a memory. *That's what I told my jefe.*

El General looks around Lenny's cell and examines a drawing of the prison yard taped to the wall.

"So, did you come to take me out?" Lenny asks.

"Damn, little *vato*, you sure remind me of myself back in the day." *El General* gives his *carnales* a head nod. They turn and face away like disciplined soldiers. He glances down at his tattoo. "Look, homes, this isn't easy for a *vato* like me to say. I give orders, nothing else. I don't even know where to start. I'll just say you are a man of your word. This is the best tattoo I've ever seen in my life, just like you said," he holds out his arm. "*Mi hijita* looks," he pauses for a breath, "She looks so vivid, so real, I can hear her sweet little voice again." He closes his eyes. "I thought I lost it somewhere along the way, because of all the shit I've been through, because of all the unspeakable shit I've had to do in here to survive," he shakes his head and sighs, "But you helped me find her voice again, and I owe you big for that." He stares into Lenny's eyes. "Look, little *vato*, you're not gonna' like what I have to say. I know you want to be a *carnal*, and I render your debt paid in full, but I can't let you in."

Lenny shoots him a confused look, "What! But I…"

El General holds up his hand, "Before you say anything else, hear me out, little *vato*. I've done a lot of bad shit in here, even to our own. But now, because of you, I got a real chance to do something right, something good. You're a true *artista*, a straight-up prodigy, little *vato*, like Mozart, Einstein, shit, homes, even like Leonardo da Vinci," he says, pointing to Lenny's book. "Like all them gifted *vatos*, you got something special. You are the greatest tattoo artist I've ever seen. And let me tell you something, homes, I've seen some real *firme* artists come and go, true masters of the art, and none of them can hold a candle to you. *Serio pedo*, you have a straight-up talent, and it's your golden ticket out of this kind of life."

"Out of what kind of life?" Lenny ask, frustration growing in his voice.

"The kind that can get you killed every minute of every day in here, little *vato*. That's how your life will be in the brotherhood. You're going to have to put in work, like every *carnal* in the organization, and it'll cost you your ability sooner or later, and I can't have any part of that. You ever hear of the parable of the talents?"

"Nah', homes," Lenny says, shaking his head.

El General crosses his arms behind his back. "It's in the good book. It says you need to use the talent God gave you for good, or you'll suffer eternal damnation. I used my talent for bad, and I'll have to answer for it when my time comes. I don't want to be the reason why you have to answer for yours."

"I'm not worried about that, homes, I just want to be in the brotherhood," Lenny says.

"I don't want to hear it, homes, my decision is made. Look, little *vato*, you won't have to worry about anything while you're in here. The word's already out. You're off-limits. We'll provide you with protection and anything else you could ever need, want, or desire in here. The only condition is that you use your talent to bring pride and honor to our *Raza*, not death and destruction, like so many of us do in here to survive. Maybe, you can give our future generation hope. They need to look up to a talented young *vato* like you, instead of a ruthless old *vato* like me. That's the price you have to pay for having such a gift."

Lenny takes a deep breath. "Whoa', man, that's way too heavy. I'm nobody special."

"You are now, little *vato*." *El General* rest his hand on Lenny's shoulder, "You are now," he turns and exits without saying another word.

Lenny leans back on his squeaky mattress, watching the *carnales* stroll away. "What just happened?" He says, running his hand over his forearm, "Damn, *Jefito*, I didn't know you were gonna' do all that." He quickly lifts his head, feeling the presence of a large figure hovering at his cell door.

"*Qué onda*, El DaVinci, can you get down on a tat of a *firme ruca*, for me, homes?" asks a big Geronimo-looking inmate named *Indio*. He pulls off his shirt and points to his beefy chest, "I want her right here, homes, holding two *pistolas* and sporting a *charro* hat. What do you think? Can you get down on that for me, homes? I'll owe you a solid, ey'."

Lenny looks around, not sure if the big Indian looking fellow has gotten him confused with someone else. "What'd you call me, homes?"

"*Órale*, you didn't know, huh? *El mero-mero* gave you your *placaso*, homes. From now on, you're El DaVinci, the tattoo artist."

Present

"Amazing! So, you're saying that the leader of the most feared prison gang on the West Coast gave you your prison moniker?" Lisa asks with disbelief, "And based on Leonardo da Vinci?"

"*Simón*, and you wanna' know something funny? I'm more partial to Michelangelo," he says, laughing out loud. "Seriously, though, my prison name wasn't the only thing he gave me, ey', he straight gave me wisdom, too. Wisdom only a *vato* like that can give."

"Really? Can you be more specific? Lisa stares at him, her cat-like eyes expressing genuine curiosity.

"Well, for one thing, that *vato* taught me all about patience, ey', to stop and think, and I mean to really think, like scientifically and shit, to weigh out all the possibilities before letting your emotions get you caught up with something you'll have to live with for the rest of your life. With *El General*, I got lucky, *ey'*. I let my emotions speak for me, and I wouldn't be here, straight up, if he didn't like that tattoo, but I gambled anyway. What can I say, I was young and dumb back then."

"Yeah, but your gamble paid off, I mean look at you now, sharing your story with the rest of the world," Lisa says, glancing at the camera.

"*Simón*, but I could have easily lost my life because I let my emotions get the better of me. That was the day, El DaVinci, the prison tattoo artist, was born, *qué no*, Big D." He says, tapping Diego's shoulder.

"*Simón*," Diego responds with a head nod.

"You mean tattoo prodigy. So, what became of *El General* after all these years?" asks Lisa.

"Well, once a new *vato* stepped in and took over the brotherhood, he was sent to solitary, and never heard from again. It's said he died in there from a heart attack, but who knows, ey'."

"Wow! That's incredibly tragic, and I have to say, a little unbelievable. Did you ever get to tattoo that big fellow, the one you referred to as *Indio*?"

"*Nel, pastél*. That *vato* transferred out before I got the chance. He was a good ass boxer, too. You know, he's a big-time actor now. I guess some *vatos* are just meant for bigger things, ey'.

"Yes, I believe they are," Lisa says, winking at him. "Well, I have to say, that was an amazing story," expresses Lisa. "And you know what, it reminds me of how I got my nickname. My grandmother used to call me Lilyboo because I reminded her of her favorite flower, the lily, and the name stuck. My papa, my *nanay*, my friends, everyone called me Lilyboo." Without realizing it, Lisa's emotion begins to seep out. "She had this little garden full of Lilies, all different colors. Her favorites were the bright orange ones. "Lisa looks up, amazed at how easy it was all coming out. She sniffs the air, "I swear I can still smell them. When I was six, geez," she chuckles, "Six years old, can you believe that? I was such a runt back then. I used to sit in her garden and talk to her lilies for hours. She must have thought I was crazy or something. She used to tell my papa I had a talent for talking, and that I'd have my own talk show one day, like Oprah. It's crazy, but somehow she knew what I was going to do with my life." Lisa has never exposed so much of herself on camera, or to anyone else, but then she's never felt such a strong emotional connection with someone she was interviewing either.

"She told me before she died that she knew I was going to be on TV," Lisa pulls out a handkerchief and dabs the corners of her eyes, "And that she'd be watching me from above when the time came."

"Ata' girl, let it flow, darlin', let it all come out. The audience is gonna' eat it up like candy!" The director says, raises his thumbs.

"Ok, this is getting a little embarrassing, even my director is encouraging me to cry in front of the camera," she says with a smile. "So, shall we move on to the next question." Lisa fans her eyes as she scans through her clipboard.

"Keep it coming, *mija*. I got plenty stories to tell."

"So, was that the first tattoo you ever did?" she asks.

"For *El General*? Not really."

"Wait! What!?! It wasn't your first tattoo," Lisa says, confused, "But I thought you never tattooed anyone before *El General*."

"He was the first I ever tattooed with a prison-made tattoo gun, but I tattooed before him."

"Really? So, if you were eighteen when you tattooed *El General*, how old were you when you did your first tattoo, then?"

El DaVinci sprays Diego's back and dabs it gently with a towel. He looks up at the picture of Diego's mother, dips the needle into the ink, and continues outlining with short, methodic strokes. "Damn, I must've fourteen, ey'."

Fourteen! Wow! Are you serious?" asks Lisa, amazed. Can you tell us a little more about that?"

"*Chalé*, that was a long time ago, ey'." His mind reels back, "When I first stepped into juvie and learned what it means to have respect on the yard."

VI. Respect on the Yard

*F**lashback.** "Turn around and face the wall!" Deputy Francisco Guzman De La Fuente, a twenty-five-year veteran of the department of juvenile justice, has given his spiel to new arrivals countless times before. "Listen up! I don't care what set you bang or what hood you're from. In here we run the show!"

A row of six teenage boys, ranging from 13-15 years old, stand rigid and with their noses pressed hard against the wall as De La Fuente lays into them with contempt. The juvenile deputy probation officer is at the point in his career where the only thing motivating him to come to work is getting another day closer to retirement.

"Lucky for you, this is the greatest country in the world, so even in here, you still have choices. You can choose to make your time in here as easy as possible, or you can choose to make it harder than hell." De La Fuente paces back and forth like a border patrol agent terrorizing a group of newly captured illegal immigrants. "I prefer you try to make it hard. We're always looking to put our self-defense training to good use, hah!" He jerks into an defensive stance. "Isn't that right, Deputy Greene!"

A young, athletically built female deputy in training responds with an enthusiastic, "Oh, hell to the yes we are!"

"You see," continues De La Fuente, "So, don't try and test us. Now turn and face me!"

The detainees turn and quickly stare down at the tile floor, avoiding eye contact with the menacing deputy.

"We have the power in here. We can put extra time on your books if we see fit. So, I recommend that you keep your mouths shut, and do your time without any goddam' problems. Is that clear enough for you!" The veins on the side of De La Fuentes's neck coil like an angry viper.

"Yes, Sir!" The teen's pubescent voices echo down the hallway of New Horizons Juvenile Detention Facility. The large skeleton keys attached to De La Fuente's utility belt rattle as he marches the teenagers down the hall with their arms crossed tightly in front of them. One juvenile in particular sports an orange T-shirt, blue sweat-shorts, and tan slippers designating his assigned unit.

Deputy Greene separates from the group, escorting a lone, fourteen-year-old detainee named Leonardo Santiago, or Lenny, to 1200, a housing unit designated for long-term offenders. He is to serve a four-year stint in the hall, at which point he will bounce around like a pinball throughout California's prison system.

"Santiago!" yells out the supervising deputy of the unit. Short in stature, but as vicious as a rabid Chihuahua, Deputy Enana carries raging contempt for young detainees accustomed to degrading women, especially those under her watch.

Lenny stands unresponsive, stupefied that this place will be his home for the last precious years of his teenage life.

"Hey, you! *Pendejo*!" Deputy Enana shouts, coming within several inches of Lenny's face, "Are you mentally challenged or what!?! Room 25, over there!" She points angrily towards a large, blue-steel door with the number **25** stenciled above the door jam.

For months, Lenny has been walking through a maze of confusion saturated in a fog of denial. He hasn't been able to take in the full gravity of his situation, even though last night was his last slumber in his bed.

"Young man, vehicular manslaughter is a very serious criminal offense. You took away an innocent life. But because you plead guilty and accepted the plea bargain which negated the possibility of no parole, it's with a heavy heart I sentence you to serve out a minimum of twenty-five years to life with the chance of parole."

Lenny heard what the judge had said, but he hadn't fully grasped what he was actually conveying. It was probably because of the concussion he suffered from the head-on collision with the cop car.

"Your son may experience some residual cognitive side effects," explained the trauma doctor as Lenny laid handcuffed to the rail of the bed, "Including short-term memory loss, a temporary lack of understanding, and possibly some delusions of grandeur."

"*Ay, Dios mío,* will he be ok?" Deep concern resonated in his mother's voice.

"We didn't see any fractures or signs of hemorrhaging on his scans. He just needs time to heal. He'll be ok in due time," the doctor assured.

Lenny's psychosis still anchors on the illusion he's trapped in a surreal nightmare, and all he has to do is figure out how to wake up.

"*Clank*!" But it wasn't until that steel door slammed shut, followed by the echo of the locking mechanism, that full realization struck him like an overhand right from boxing champ Juan Manuel Marquez himself.

The judge should have put it in terms a teenager could have more easily understood, something like, "You no longer have control of your life, kid. We can now do whatever we want with you for the next twenty-five years, and possibly the rest of your life."

In that moment, Lenny's nightmare became as real as global warming, and if he doesn't come to terms with it, he risks melting away like the forgotten glaciers of old. Tears form as he turns and bangs his head against the steel door.

"Hey, new booty, where you from, homes?" says a voice from behind.

Lenny freezes like an intruder caught in the *click-clack* of a twelve-gauge shotgun. Blinded by hopelessness, Lenny hadn't noticed someone sitting silently towards the back of the cell.

"I said, where you from, new booty?"

Unfortunately for Lenny, the detainee behind the voice resembles more a man in his twenties than a sixteen-year-old kid. His name is Rafael Munguia—but in his hood, one of the oldest and roughest *barrios* in San Diego, he goes by a different name. Lanky yet muscular, his movements are as fluid and calculated as a professional prizefighter.

"I...I don't bang, homes." Not wanting to appear timid, Lenny quickly wipes away his tears before turning to face him. Rafael sets his book down on a desk fixed to the wall and rushes up to Lenny, stopping only a breath away. He glares deep into Lenny's eyes.

"I'm Lil' Boxer, homes," he says, throwing up the sign of his hood right in Lenny's face.

"I'm Lenny." He reach out his hand as a show of respect.

"Lenny, huh?" Lil' Boxer turns, leaving his new celli's attempt at a handshake hanging in the air. "This your first time, ey', new booty?"

"Ah, what do mean?" The crack in Lenny's voice incriminates him.

"Yeah, it's your first time, alright. You ain't gotta bullshit me, homeboy, I don't give a shit one way or another."

"How can you tell?" Lenny says, deepening his voice while trying to bury his fear deep down.

"By that scary-ass look on your face, homes. That same look my *carnalito* makes before catching a beat down from my *jefe*." Lil Boxer reaches out his hand, finally giving Lenny a Chicano-style handshake. "You know what, homes, you kinda' remind me of him." A speck of sentiment slips out of his voice. "You get the top bunk," he says, "It's just a thin-ass cushion on top of hard-ass concrete. You'll get used to it after your back becomes numb." He twists his torso, popping like bubble wrap.

Lil' Boxer likes to impose his dominance on a new celli on the spot, forcing them into a life of servitude—mostly for making his bed and such. Luckily for Lenny, Lil' Boxer does something he usually doesn't do, he takes pity on him.

"Chow in fifteen," announces a voice over the intercom.

"Check it out, homes, I'm gonna give you the rundown on this unit, since you a new booty and all. Things go down the same way every day, homes. I'm gonna tell you *derecho*, straight-up, you're gonna get rushed, but as long as you hold your own, show these *vatos* in here you ain't a *chavala*, you'll be alright, homeboy."

"*Órale*, gracias, homes," Lenny replies graciously, although he can't quite decide for what—for preparing him for what's to come or for not kicking the crap out of him right then and there.

"You'll get down with Chubs, that fat-ass *vato* rushes every new booty that comes to the unit. I'm not gonna' lie, homes, he's gonna' sock you up, he may be fat, but he still got hands. As long as you don't rank out, you'll earn respect on the yard, homeboy."

"Yard? What yard?" Lenny asks.

"Don't trip. It's just something my big homie used to say after he got out the *pinta*. It means you've earned respect from everyone in the unit, homes."

"Oh, ok cool," Lenny responds, gathering up as much determination as he can.

An officer peers in through the little rectangular window on the door.

"They do that every fifteen minutes," continues Lil' Boxer. "Don't let them catch you playing with yourself, homes. That shit can be embarrassing, homes, especially if Enana's on shift. She'll clown you all over the intercom." He points to a small, metallic speaker mounted flush into the wall. "There's one in every cell."

"I don't do that, homes!" Lenny replies, uncomfortable with the topic.

"Look, homeboy, you can keep it real with me. We all do that in here! But on a more serious tip, once you get into it with Chubs, get down, *de volada,* homes, and I mean with the quickness, especially when you see them coming," he points out towards the deputies sitting at the front desk.

"They're gonna' spray you with a gang of OC, it's like mace, to try to teach you a lesson. They sprayed me for like a minute straight for whooping some fool's ass! That shit burned for hours, it's like taking a shower in jalapeno juice, *serio.*"

Deputies pop open each 10-by-12 cell in sequential order—the clatter from the key untwisting the lock to his cell twists at Lenny's guts. The picking sensation coming from the pit of his stomach is as real as it's ever going to get, and in a few minutes, he's going to have to prove that he's worthy of respect in 1200.

Lil' Boxer exits first. "Stay on your guard, homes," he says with a wink and struts to a table in the middle of the day room—the area designated for eating and engaging in free time. Lenny follows closely behind. As soon as he steps out, the heat from the stares singe away any courage he had gathered up. He heads towards a spot next to his cellmate, hoping Lil' Boxer's status will serve as protection.

"You're lucky, homes, we get hot trays today." As Lenny eyes the afternoon meal, he immediately concludes he's not fortunate at all. A hot tray may be a welcomed meal for someone long deprived of home cooking, but it's cruel and unusual punishment for a palate accustomed to authentic Mexican cuisine.

Chow consists of a hot pocket that tastes more like the inside of a freezer and an assortment of vegetables steamed *á la* radiation. Even the chocolate chip cookie resembles the ambiance—hard and dry.

Lenny piles on salt and pepper, trying to give the food some remnant of flavor (you can blame his mother's *enchiladas verdes*, *mole*, and *carne con chile* for permanently spoiling his taste buds). He sighs as his thoughts stir up negative emotions. *It's gonna' take me forever to get used to this crap.*

"I don't want to hear a single word from any of you, or you'll all get a dine-in special. And you all know what that means, no music, no TV, and absolutely no socializing!" Deputy Enana does little to mask her particularly bad mood. Aside from an episode of Looney Tunes playing in the background, the detainees dine in complete silence. They communicate with one another through a series of head nods and facial expressions.

A half-an-hour later, they're ordered to line up in two single-file lines, one at each end of the unit. Deputy Enana heads to the far end of the day room, another deputy positions himself at the opposite end, and another sits behind the control des'k handling the phones.

Chubs moves towards the end of the line. Then, like a demented Pitbull, he rushes up to Lenny.

"Where you from, fool!?!" he comes within Lenny's arm's reach in a flash.

Lenny reacts instinctively, connecting with a straight right hand. Chubs lower lip splits down the center like a ripened plum, stopping him dead in his tracks. Detainees gasp in amazement—*oohing* and *ahhing*—as they're used to seeing Chubs strike first blood. Unfortunately for Lenny, Chubs is skilled at using his two-hundred-and-twenty-five-pound body frame and easily tackles Lenny hard to the ground.

"Ah shit, here we go again. Cover!" Deputy Enana shouts as she and the other officer rush towards the fray. Detainees quickly get down on their hands and knees, covering up their faces. They know all too well what comes next. Lenny takes heavy gasps due to Chubs crushing weight on top of him, but somehow, he keeps swinging, making contact with Chub's rubbery face.

"Ahhh!" Lenny suddenly yells out in agony as a pungent odor invades his nasal cavity, followed by an immense burning sensation all over his face.

Chubs rolls off of Lenny and balls up tightly. Lenny's vision blurs, and his face and hands feel like they're being attacked by a swarm angry fire ants.

It went down exactly as Lil' Boxer had said. Deputies empty a substantial amount of their OC canisters directly onto Lenny's face. He tries to rub off the scorching sensation with his shirt, but the more he rubs, the more intensely it burns.

Deputy Enana rolls Lenny onto his stomach and digs her knee into the center of his spine while another deputy cuffs his hands behind his back. "When will you *pendejos* learn!?!" Deputy Enana says, "Fighting won't get you respect in here, only sprayed."

Lenny lies on his stomach, trembling in pain. He musters all of his will not to cry out in agony. Such a display will only unleash an unending barrage of harassment and ridicule. Once the deputies secure Chubs in his room, deputies haul Lenny off to the showers, where the cold water serves as a reprieve (though only a slight one).

Papi? Mami said your teammates love and respect you. How do you get respect? Lenny's mind blasts him back to his childhood. "Well, *mijo*," his father says, "There are some who think respect comes fighting. If you're the toughest in the *barrio*, no one will want to bother you. But I think that has to do more with fear than respect. Others think respect comes from *poder*, or status. If you're on top, those below you will have to respect you, like how people respect, *El Presidente*.

"I have to be president to get respect?" Lenny asks, surprised.

"No, *mijo*," his father answers with a smile, "But it wouldn't hurt. I think when people see you're not afraid to show them who you are, and I mean who you are inside, *dentro de tu corazón*, people will truly respect you."

"I know who I am," responds Lenny.

"*Ah, si, mijo,* and who are you?"

"I'm an *artista,* like Michelangelo, and I'm gonna paint my own Sistine Chapel one day."

His father whisks Lenny up into and twirls him around and around. "*Si, mijo,* you are, and a great one, so don't ever be afraid to show it."

They gaze out into bay, watching at an aircraft carrier cruising out of the San Diego harbor. Lenny closes his eyes, enjoying the oceanic breeze caressing his face. A smile creeps out as Lenny opens his burning eyes only to find that the breeze cooling his face is coming from a portable fan. His smile instantly turns into a frown.

"Had enough, kid?" asks a deputy with indifference.

Lenny presses his eyes shut, trying to get back to his memory, but it's long gone. He nods, "Yeah, I'm good."

The deputy escorts him back to his cell.

"*Órale!*" Lil' Boxer walks up to Lenny, whose eyes still water from the ordeal.

"I told you that shit burns. You gave a good scrap, homes. I didn't know you could get down like that." Lil Boxer gives Lenny a Chicano handshake. "Now that you showed these *vatos* you ain't a *chavala,* you got respect, homeboy."

Lenny smirks, "Yeah, I guess so!"

The standard juvenile hall mattress is as far from cozy as the sun's warmth is to Pluto, and that's not mentioning the blankets, thin as tortillas. Lenny can't stop shivering as he tries to sleep, another residual effect from the pepper spray.

My first day in the hall, and I hate it. I don't know how long I can take this. Lenny's mind reels long into the night. Finally, an hour past midnight, he falls into a deep, dream induced slumber.

Dazed and a bit euphoric, Lenny opens his eyes and bolts upright. He twists his knuckles into his eye sockets, trying to clear his perception. As he surveys the surroundings, he notices everything has changed drastically. The entire scene is abnormally colorful—waves of emerald green shimmer through the trees, rich hues of royal purple and ruby red sway with the wildflowers in the field, a blue gem sapphire ripples throughout the lake. Even a pale but bright blue color swirls in the sky like a Van Gogh painting.

Am I on drugs or something? Lenny glances at his hands, made up of the refined lines of a brushstroke dipped in adobe brown paint. His skin gives off a glare as he moves slow and animated. *I think I'm...I'm...I'm in a painting!* He rotates his hands. *Oh, snap! I am a painting!* Again, Lenny peers all around, absorbing everything he can from this strange, new dimension.

A ghostly figure materializes on the other end of the lake, immediately catching Lenny's attention. He freezes, spellbound by the hazy figure moving eerily in his direction like a ghost. As it nears, he can make out the shape of a man, but he can't tell who it is. He squints his eyes, then realizes the figure is wearing a familiar soccer uniform— a soccer uniform hanging in his mother's closet still.

Lenny's heart races as the apparition comes within arm's reach and has a blank canvas for a face. Startled, Lenny takes a step back when something appears in his right hand. He looks down and sees that he's clutching the handle of a fine-tipped paintbrush dripping with the same adobe paint as his skin. Without realizing it, his hand moves all on its own. In seconds, Lenny paints the face of his father on the figure exactly as he remembers it, down to the mole above his lip.

"*Ya, vez,*" Lenny's father suddenly comes to life. "It's in you, *hijo.* It's always been in you. So, don't be afraid, *no tengas miedo,*" he nudges Lenny playfully on the shoulder as if he never left, as if they picked up exactly where they left off so long ago. "*Enséñales, hijo,* show them who you are," he says.

"This can't be happening! This is just a stupid dream," Lenny says." You're not real. You're dead. You've been dead a long time." Lenny droops his head, disappointed that even in a dream—where there are supposed to be no limits, where everything and anything is possible—he can't forget his father is gone.

"*Hijo*," his father says, " How can you say that!?! So, you think I'm not real, eh', *tu crees eso?* Ok, if I'm not real, would I do this!" He grabs Lenny and puts him in a reverse headlock (a move they used to practice watching Rey Mysterio Jr. wrestle on Saturday evenings).

"Wait! Is it really you, *Papi*?" Lenny says in his father's clutch.

"*Pues, si, hijo*. It's really me." In one smooth motion, he rolls Lenny to the ground and pins his shoulders down. "Juan, two, tree," he says, tapping the floor with his hand. "*Perdiste, hijo*."

Lenny looks up at his father. "*Papi*, it's you." His eyes gloss over as he embraces him, "It is really you!"

"That's what I'm trying to tell you, *hijo, soy yo!* It's me!"

"But how? You died!" Lenny exclaims.

"*Lo se, hijo, y lo siento mucho.*" he says, "But I'll always be here for you, *hijo, para siempre.*" He places his hand over Lenny's chest, "*Aquí, siempre viviré, dentro de tu corazón.*"

A spasm jerks Lenny back to his cold and colorless reality. "Damn, what just happened!?!" he says, looking around, confused. Then, he quickly realizes he's back in his cell. "Jeez, that was so freakin' real." Lenny takes several deep breaths, feeling as if what had just occurred was more than just a dream. "I'm sorry, *Papi*, but I don't know who I am anymore." He says, the forlorn resonating deep within his soul.

Breakfast in the hall is something the son of a Mexican mother will have a difficult time getting used to—powdered eggs, two radiated pieces of bacon, and a single slice of toast accompanied by a lonely packet of jelly (a tragic contrast to the savory red *chilaquiles* his mother used to prepare for him before school).

"Check it out, looks like Chubs trying to get your attention, homes," Lil' Boxer says, nodding his head in Chubs direction.

Lenny makes eye contact with the heavy-set detainee who's grinding his teeth at him.

"Looks like he wants round two, ey'," Lil' Boxer says.

School in the hall turns out to be a pleasant surprise. Instead of finding a burned-out relic of a teacher condemned to finish the last years of an illustrious career taking crap from America's finest criminal youth, Lenny finds a fairly young, compassionate female teacher. Teacher *Inspiración* has talent for developing innovative ways to engage her rather challenging student population.

"Hello, Santiago, I'm Teacher *Inspiración*, how are you feeling today?"

"I'm alright," Lenny says with a crooked smile.

"I heard what happened to you yesterday." She bends down close to his ear, "You know, there are other ways to gain respect in here." Teacher *Inspiración* hands Lenny a sketch pad and a pack of colored charcoal pencils. "Are you an artist? You strike me as an artist."

Lenny nods, "Yeah, I like to draw."

"I knew it. I have a sixth sense about these things. I don't know if you know, but everyone respects a talented artist. Why do you think people flock to Italy year after year? It's not for the tropical beaches I can tell you that. Think about it, Santiago," she shoots him a wink. "By the way, do you know how to use charcoals?"

Lenny eyes the packet and nods, "Yeah, I think so."

"Let me show you a little trick," Teacher *Inspiración* opens the packet and pulls out a charcoal, "This is what I want you to do. Turn your poster paper over and draw five little boxes right next to each other like this," she says as she draws them out. "Leave the first box white, then shade in each one just a little bit darker. This technique is known as a value scale. That way," she says, shading in the boxes, "You'll know how much pressure to apply to get the right value. You see?" She shades in the last box darkest. It'll set artwork apart."

"Oh cool, I think I got it. Thanks," Lenny says, although somehow he already knew the technique instinctually.

"Now do that for each color that you're going to use, oh, and one last little trick," Teacher *Inspiración* takes her finger and begins smudging each box delicately. "If you rub the charcoal gently, it produces a smooth and subtle finish that'll give your piece an extra dimension."

Lenny nods with approval, "Cool, I got it, thanks, teacher."

Coincidentally, Lenny's first day of school falls on the last day of an art project. Detainees are tasked to create a piece of art that evokes emotion. Although he hasn't produced anything in some time, Lenny still possesses a rather arrogant confidence in his artistic abilities—you can thank his recent victory over Art for that. Even in his delicate mental state, it isn't very difficult for Lenny to conjure up something extraordinary.

Lenny's hand glides across the poster paper, like Ritchie Valens strumming his guitar to *La Bamba*. Random images fill his head, the eyes of a woman in agony, the glimmer of blood under the glare of the moonlight, an infant sleeping soundly in his stroller. Like demons, they torment his creative spirit. He manages to keep them at bay long enough to complete his masterpiece.

The following day, detainees exit their cells with anticipation. Teacher *Inspiración* painstakingly transforms the entire unit into a makeshift art gallery, displaying their art pieces on easel stands throughout the day room. Most turn out to be clichéd prison motifs—Disney characters, cry now smile later faces, caricatures behind cell bars, graffiti pieces and the like, but still done with an artistic touch.

Lenny's gut bubbles, like a freshly poured coke-a-cola (a thing he experiences every time his work is up for criticism). Teacher *Inspiración* makes her way to the center of the room like a talk show host addressing her audience.

"Well, boys, I have to say, I'm very proud of all of you. As you can see, everyone participated in the project, and that's what's most important for me. I have to say, you guys turned out some very interesting pieces. But, there's one piece in particular that completely took my breath away, and I want to showcase it for you all. It's unique and hauntingly beautiful. And what's even more amazing, it was completed in a matter of hours.

Teacher *Inspiración* motions to her aide, "Could you please bring up the artwork." The aide brings up the piece concealed under a sheet of linen.

"Whenever I showcase a piece, I like to place it in the center as a tribute to the artist," she says. "I wanted to keep it hidden to build up the wow factor." She grabs the corner of the sheet and uncovers the piece in one fluid motion. "As I said, this work of art is something truly special. The use of the different values are extraordinary." She makes eye contact with Lenny and winks.

Feeling uncomfortable, Lenny slowly creeps his way towards the back of the crowd. His sketch could have easily been ripped right out of Diego Rivera's art portfolio. It displays the silhouette of a man fused into the trunk of a very large and ancient tree. The man's arms stretch upward, becoming branches stripped of all its leaves. The man's legs stretch downward, becoming a system of roots extending underground at three different levels. The deepest roots pierce through the battered bodies of Native American warriors fused with Spanish conquistadors, the mid-level roots weave in and out of the bodies of Mexican Revolutionary soldiers ridden with bullets and wearing torn *charro* hats. The shallowest roots encase a group of fallen Mexican-American World War II soldiers forgotten from the history books.

The carcasses nourish the tree's tortured soul, filling it with a sense of identity. The face of the tree belongs to a man saddened by solitude. His branches droop, and his leaves have long decomposed, and yet he stands sturdy and strong. He yearns for a ray of light under an impenetrable veil of greyness.

The entire room falls silent as the young inmates take in the work of art that seems to express exactly how they feel.

"I don't know about you guys, but this piece invokes some pretty powerful emotions. Look at the man's expression. It looks like he's in anguish." Teacher *Inspiración* motions for her students to move in for a closer look, "Look at how the artist fused the man into the trunk of the tree by blending in the values. It's subtle, but really sets it apart. However, what I like most of all, is that you can see what gives the tree the strength to carry on, his cultural history. This is what art is supposed to do, to draw out emotion, and it was also the purpose of this project."

"Who did it?" asks a voice from the crowd.

"Oh, I'm sorry, I didn't acknowledge the artist yet." Teacher *Inspiración* clears her throat. "Let's all congratulate," she pauses for a moment, "The newest member to our unit, Leonardo Santiago, for creating this extraordinary piece in only a matter of hours," she searches the crowd for Lenny.

"He's right here, teacher!" Lil' Boxer says, raising his hand.

Lenny glares at him, shaking his head, "Nah', homes, what are you doing!"

"Don't be a *chavala,* homes. Your piece is *firme.*"

The group cuts a path for him. Reluctantly, Lenny makes his way to the center of the room.

"Well, done, Leonardo," says his teacher, "Well, done indeed."

Lenny shrugs his shoulders, "It's all good." A small applause begins in the crowd, and then all thirty juvenile detainees join in. Lenny peers around, feeling surprised and a bit uncomfortable. He makes eye contact with Chubs, who's also applauding. They nod at each other.

Later that evening, Lenny lies on his bunk with his arms crossed behind his head. His mind reaches out towards the emptiness of space when a smile creeps through his mask of self-pity, the one he hasn't been able to take off for months now.

"See, homes, that's what I mean, respect on the yard," says Lil' Boxer.

"Oh, I get it now." Lenny looks up at the ceiling speaking through his thoughts. *Thanks, Papi, you were right! You were right about everything!*

"Hey, homes, I didn't know you were a down-ass artist like that." Lil' Boxer's voice says, interrupting. "You're full of surprises, ain't you?" An idea suddenly formulates in Lil Boxer's mind. "Hey homes, have you ever tatted anyone before?"

"Tattooed? Hell, no!" Lenny says, thrown off by the question.

"*Órale,*" Lil' Boxer hops off of his mattress. "Check it out, homeboy, I'm gonna pop your little cherry." He shakes Lenny playfully. "*Serio,* homes, let me be the first. That way, you can say Lil Boxer from *treinta* was the first *vato* you ever tattooed when you get all famous!"

"No way, I don't know how to tattoo," says Lenny. "Seriously, homes, I just know how to draw, well, and paint, and maybe engrave a little, but that's all."

Lil' Boxer reaches under his pillow and pulls out a manila envelope containing his personal effects—family photos, letters, magazine cut-outs, font templates, lyrics, and the like. "Perfect, homes, if you already know how to do all that, might as well add tattooing to the list. Don't trip, alright homes. I'm the one who's gonna get' inked," he says as he dumps the contents onto his mattress. "Keep an eye out, let me know when they start hall checks."

"What are you doing?" Lenny asks as he jumps off of his bunk and hovers by the door, peering out of the rectangular window for the deputies.

Lil' Boxer shuffles through his items and finds what he's seeking—a paper clip filed to a point. "I'm getting what you need," he says, piling up his effects and shoving them back in the envelope. Flipping over his mattress, Lil' Boxer sticks his fingers through a small tear on the side and pulls out a ball-point pen. Resourceful in his own right, Lil' Boxer snaps off the tip and empties the gooey, black substance onto a white sheet of paper.

"Here they come," announces Lenny.

"Don't trip, chocolate chip." Lil Boxer shoves everything back under his mattress and slips the paperclip in his waistband. "Come over here and hit some push-ups with me so they won't get suspicious."

They get down on their palms and tiptoes as an officer peers inside.

"There he is," Lil' Boxer says, "Follow my lead. *Listo*? I'll count," he says. "One, two, three…" The deputy smirks and then moves on to the next window. They complete twenty push-ups.

"Check it out," Lil' Boxer says without even breaking a sweat and reaches in his waistband. He hands Lenny the paper clip.

"What's this for?" Lenny asks out of breath and already starting to sweat from his brow.

"It's a pick, homes. You heard of picking, right?"

Once again, Lenny's expression reveals his ignorance.

"Look homes, it ain't no big thing. You dip the sharp end into the ink and pick it into my skin." Lil' Boxer animates his movements. "It's like engraving, but skin."

"No way! I can't do that!"

"Why not, you scared of a little blood, homeboy? Come on, give it a try. I'll owe you one."

Lenny exhales in defeat. "Alright, but I don't know what the hell I'm doing, I've never done this before."

"Just pick away, homeboy, even if you mess up, it won't matter, it'll fade in a few weeks, anyway." Lil' Boxer says, trying to put Lenny at ease.

"Ok, but I don't know what the hell I'm doing." Lenny dabs the tip of the paperclip into a tiny bead of ink.

"What do you want me to draw?"

"My hood, homes. Oh, yeah, I forgot!" Lil' Boxer jumps to his feet, lifts his mattress, and pulls out a template of stylized font. "I want it this style, homes," he says, pointing to the sheet, "See if you can add a crucifix. You know, funk it out a little, make it look *firme*."

"Ok, I'll try my best." Lenny takes three very slow, very deep breaths. He cracks every knuckle in his hands and stares at the template, searing the letters into his mind (like when you focus on an image without closing your eyes so that when you do close your eyes, you can still see it clearly).

Lil' Boxer places his hand on the table. Lenny positions the paperclip comfortably in his hand, dips the point into the ink, and then begins picking at the webbing of his cellmate's hand. He digs in for several minutes with short, methodical strokes, then they get down on their palms and tip-toes and do push-ups until a deputy passes by, and then Lenny continues picking again.

After the first fifteen minutes, Lenny finds picking easier than he expected. An hour later, Lil' Boxer washes off his hand in their little metallic sink. He dabs it dry with the inside portion of his shirt and then examines his newly picked tattoo.

"This right here, homes," Lil' Boxer says, pointing at his hand, "Is *firme!*" He rubs a thin layer of lotion in the arch between his thumb and index finger. "The details are ridiculous, homes! The cracks and crevices you put on the cross makes it look real, like the cross Jesus was hanging from, homes, *serio!*" he says, blessing himself. "You're a badass artist. I put that on my hood, Lenny, real talk! "

What Lil' Boxer likes best of all, are the letters of his hood arching over the crucifix in large Old English style lettering.

Present

"So, if I may recap, you did your first tattoo on pretty much your second day in juvenile hall, by a process you knew nothing about, and you were just fourteen at the time?" Lisa peers into the camera, "And it came out perfect no less."

"*Chalé*, I didn't think it came out perfect, but I'm sure Lil' Boxer would've disagreed," El DaVinci says. "I think I just got lucky it came out as good as it did, ey', especially since it was my first time. Shit, I gained some serious status in 1200 because of that tattoo, and that's unusual for a new booty. Even Chubs fat ass wanted a tattoo from me." He looks up and shakes his head, "But you know what, ey', I've been pretty lucky behind these bars, even since back then."

"Oh yeah, what do you mean?" Lisa peers into the inmate's eyes with a sweet, inquisitive look.

El DaVinci clears his throat, enduring a heat flash gnawing at the back of his neck as Lisa's gaze penetrates his soul.

"Well, I was lucky my *jefe* was right. Respect didn't come from trying to be a badass, but from not being afraid of showing who I am, right here, in my *corazón*. I was lucky to have Lil' Boxer as my first celli. He looked after me like a little brother. I was lucky to have a teacher who appreciated art, shit, who made me a better artist." He taps on his chest with a closed fist. "I've always known I wanted to be an artist," El DaVinci says, holding up his tattoo gun, "And check it out, ey', the rest is history, *qué no, mija?*"

"Why, yes! You're right!" Lisa agrees, "It is history, well, television history. I mean, look at us now, in front of these cameras sharing your story with the world. But in all seriousness, I think we're here today because you stayed true to yourself, even in here, even despite all the adversity. Your talent breached the high walls of prison because you didn't give up. And you know what? I have to admit, I completely relate with your idea of respect," Lisa nods. "I've always been afraid of exposing too much of myself to anyone. I guess I've always felt that my friends would lose respect for me if they knew where I came from. The truth is, I'm still a little afraid of what they might think if they find out I wasn't born with a silver spoon in my mouth, more like a plastic one, if you know what I mean. I can't believe I'm revealing this on live television," Lisa looks off to the side, embarrassed. "But talking to you and listening to your story, I'm starting to feel different. And you know what, that fella over there," Lisa points off camera.

Scott whirls the camera around and zooms in on the director.

"That old man over there, ladies and gentlemen. My director, my mentor, my friend," says Lisa.

Scott whirls the camera back onto Lisa.

"He took me under his wing when I was an intern at the network, and it's really because of him," Lisa continues. "I became the hostess of the show. He always pushed me to open up, to not be afraid of showing my true self in front of the camera. He brings out the best in me. He brings out the best in all of us, in our entire broadcasting team."

"Here, here!" The members of the crew shout out in agreement.

"*Órale!*" says El DaVinci. "*Respeto*, homeboy!" He salutes the old man. "You know what, *mija*, you shouldn't feel that way. If your people can't accept you for who you are and where you came from, then they aren't your real friends, and I say fuck em', ey'. They're not worth your time."

"You know what, Mr. El DaVinci, you're right. If they can't accept me for who I am," Lisa repeats, "They aren't my friends, and I say fuck them, too!"

The members of crew glance at each other, shocked.

"Wait! Did she say what I think she said?" asks the lead sound technician.

The director lets out a snort, "She sure did. I wonder what them boneheads from the network are saying," he says with laughter.

Lisa nods at El Davinci as a tingling sensation begins radiating from her shoulders down to the bottom of her back as if a heavy burden just lifted. "So, what became of your cellmate, Lil' Boxer?"

"Yeah, he was killed in a prison riot." El DaVinci blesses himself with the sign of the cross.

"Oh, I'm so sorry to hear that." Lisa falls silent.

"*Simón*, me too, ey', but don't feel too bad for him, that's the life he led, ey'. He knew he was always gonna' be a down as *vato loco* til' the end."

"So, you don't feel bad for him?"

"You're gonna' trip out on this, ey', but I get to see him every day. I painted a portrait of him in my cell. Lil' Boxer will always live on in here," he taps on his chest. "He was one of those one-in-a-million type homies, one you can count yourself lucky to have had, but hey, all we can do is play the hand we're dealt, *qué no*? Real shit, it ain't about the cards, it's about how you play em'. Lil' Boxer played hard, and it was just a matter of time before lady luck had enough. And that's just how the story goes, sometimes, *qué no* Big D?"

Diego nods, "*Simón*. That's how it goes sometimes, *serio*."

"Wow! Again, that was quite a story," Lisa peers into the camera, shaking her head in disbelief.

"Keep it coming, *mija*, I still got lots to tell."

"Well, alright then," Lisa glances at her clipboard, "Let's move on, shall we. I see here on the questionnaire you filled out for us that you listed you won an art contest in middle school. Could you tell us about that?"

El DaVinci sprays Diego's back and wipes it gently. He studies the image of Diego's mother for several moments and then peers at the tattoo. He dips the needle into the ink and continues to outline. "*Simón*," he says with a chuckle. "This is gonna' trip you out, ey', but it was a friendly rivalry over a girl." His memory shoots him back to middle school.

VII. Friendly Rivalry

*F*lashback. "Please don't forget, even though I know most of you will by the time you walk out that door and start your weekend," exclaims Mr. Escanuela pointing towards the exit. "Monday's the deadline for the school's art contest, so if you want to enter a piece and have a chance at winning a pair of movie tickets, it has to be in my hands Monday morning before the second bell." He pulls off his spectacles and blows a puff of hot air onto each lens, wiping off the moisture with the Donald Duck tie his ten-year-old daughter gave to him three months ago on his thirty-fifth birthday. "*Me entienden?*" He turns around and reaches for the eraser, but then pauses. "Oh! I can't forget to mention something about this year's theme."

The middle school Science teacher turns and faces his students. "Save the Amazon Rainforest," he announces it like a dire warning, pointing towards a poster on the wall—the one with an aerial view exposing a patch of burnt and barren land in the middle of the lush rainforest. "You have to incorporate something we've been learning about the Rainforests of South America." He wags his finger at them, "*Por favor*, don't make me look like a bad teacher by turning in something completely unrelated. *Me entienden, mis alumnos?*"

"*Si, Maestro*! You already told us," several of his students answer out with a sigh of sarcasm.

"*Ok, pues, muy bien.*" Mr. Escanuela turns around and erases the old, powder-dusted chalkboard. The final bell fires off just as he is about to wish his eighth-grade class a safe and drug-free weekend. He doesn't get the chance as students hop out of their seats and aim straight for the exit. Arthur Aguilar is first out, followed closely behind by Lenny.

Donning a black, short-brimmed fedora hat, oversized tan Dickie pants held above his waist by black suspenders, a plain black t-shirt tucked in deep, and a pair of black Chuck Taylor shoes with graffiti writing around the edges, Arthur, or Art, is also a fellow artist, and an exceptional one at that.

Lenny, sporting black Ben Davis shorts past the knees, a plain white t-shirt, knee-high tube socks with the three black stripes on them, and a pair of white Nike Cortez's with the black emblems, always seems to be just a half step behind.

Though they're from the same clique, they're bitter rivals when it comes to artistic ability. Their favorite time in school falls on Mr. Escanuela's period, not because they get to goof around together in class, but because they thoroughly enjoy criticizing the hell out of each other's artwork. Their unspoken respect for each other's talent drew them to become homies in the first place. That does nothing to quell their competitive natures, though, it only inflames their desire to find out who's the best.

Art is well known for his wild-style graffiti, and even though Lenny knows in his heart that Art is second best, he still holds the reputation for being the premier artist of the school. And just a couple of days ago, Art struck an even bigger blow to Lenny's ego. He accomplished a feat that propelled him to superstar status around the school.

As of yesterday morning, a reward of $1000 was issued by local law enforcement for information leading to the capture of the vandal who defaced the front wall of Montgomery Middle School (now newly adorned with a larger than life-sized, full-color graffiti piece). Authorities can't decipher the stylized writing, but to those with an eye for such things, it reads, *Esteelo*, Art's street tag. It even got a section in the local newspaper complete with a photograph. Art already has the clipping displayed inside his locker like a certificate of accomplishment. The headline reads, *Graffiti Bandit Strikes Local Middle School*.

Lenny is now compelled more than ever to strip Art of his status, and all that comes with it, like adoration from the girls. All Lenny cares about, aside from demoralizing the hell out of Art, of course, is to get noticed by his elementary school crush, Miriam Kahlo.

"Sup', Lenny, watchu' drawing for the art contest, homeboy?"

"I don't know yet, Es-tee-lo," Lenny says with a hint of jealousy, "But best believe it's gonna be, *mas chingón* than yours."

Art steps forward, squaring off for a friendly tussle. "Nah', homeboy, I'm winning that contest," he throws a quick jab at Lenny, "And I'm taking a fine *heina* to the movies."

"Oh, yeah." Lenny parries and throws a straight-right. "What *heina* would want to go out with a *chavala* like you?

Art jerks his head back, evading the strike to his upper lip. "Ain't no *chavalas* here, and I'm taking that one fine *heina* with the crazy colored eyes."

"What!?! Lenny stops dead in his tracks as if he just got struck by an unexpected blow.

"Ah damn, check it out, here comes, Foo. Let's mess with his little whitexican' ass."

Art quickly turns away and strikes up a conversation with the girl standing closest to him as a chubby little white boy waddles happily in their direction.

"Whatever, foo', I know you guys saw me." David White's extraordinarily round eyes widen, resembling those funny-looking goldfish with their eyeballs ballooned out of their sockets. His dirty blonde hair is slicked back with globs of *Tres Flores* hair grease, and forehead perpetually beaded with sweat (made worse by the black cascade jacket he sports every single day).

David may be the only white kid in the entire school, but inside he's all brown—so much that his favorite meal is menudo, he can sing most of the Mexican *Corridos* playing on the radio by heart, and can throw down the hottest salsa without breaking a smile—courtesy of the Mexican family who adopted him as an infant. But along with his comical features, David also possesses an extraordinary talent, the ability to make everyone around him laugh—and not just any laugh, but a hard, stomach-cramping one. His ability has brought him immense popularity, especially among the girls.

Of course, the Wolf Pack—the small clique of friends consisting of, Art, Lenny, and Sterling—took notice of his status with the *heinas*, and immediately concluded that they needed another member in their pack. They dubbed him "Foo," not because he acts a fool twenty-four-seven (although he does), but because he ends almost every sentence with, *foo'*, a derivative of the word accurately describing his personality.

"What's up, foo'? Whatchu' guys doing?" David nods his over-sized head.

"What up, Foo." Lenny says, returning the nod and then turns towards Art. An overpowering sense of curiosity urges him to find out the identity of the girl Art is referring too, even though a sickening feeling in his gut is telling him he already knows. "Hey Art, what *heina* you talking about?"

Art smiles, knowing Lenny would take the bait. "Damn, I forgot her name, but she's in Mr. Quintero's second period," Art says, snapping his fingers, acting out a case of amnesia. "Come on, Foo," he turns towards David, "You know who I'm talking about, right? That one *heina* with the colored eyes."

"Are you talking about Linda with the big booty, foo'?" responds David.

"Nah', not her, but Linda does have a big booty, though," Art chuckles. "Damn, what's that *heina's* name?" He says, dragging on Lenny's anxiety and relishing every second of it.

"*Órale*! Miriam. That's her name, Miriam, with the green eyes," Art says, acting as if it just came to him.

"What! Hell no! That's my *heina*!" Lenny says, his face crinkling with anger.

"Oh, Yeeaahh'. *La* Miriam. She does have crazy colored eyes. She's fine too, foo'," David says with a peculiar, little whistle between his teeth.

"Oh, so she's your *heina*. Is that right?" Art says, sarcastically, "Does she know that?"

"Ah', not yet, but she will," Lenny snorts back with anger.

"Alright, then, let's bet. Whoever wins the art contest takes Miriam out to the movies. This'll prove once and for all who's the better artist," Art points towards Lenny, "You," and then at himself, "Or me!"

"Let's do this!" Lenny tightens his jaw, accepting the long-awaited duel. "Oh, it's on like Donkey Kong!" He says as they shake hands.

"Let the best artist win!" exclaims Art. They stare each other down, like two prizefighters before the opening bell.

David grabs their hands like a referee. "Ok, guys, I want a clean fight. No kicking or biting below the belt, foo'. And, I can whoop both your asses at Donkey Kong, foo." He releases their hands and pounds on his chest like the character in the video game.

The intensity shatters as Art and Lenny begin laughing hysterically, victims of another one of David's comedy skits.

David looks around suddenly. "Hey, where's Sterl, foo'?"

Art pulls out a palm comb and preens his hair back. "He's probably chasing after some *heina*, which is what I'm about to do, *al rato*. Wolf Pack! Ouuuuuwwww!" Art howls down the hallway, making eye contact with every girl that crosses his path.

"I'm out, too," says Lenny. "Hey, Foo, do me a favor?"

97

"Whatchu' need, foo'?"

"Take off that *pinche* jacket. It's too damn hot out here, man. I'm sweating just standing next to you." Lenny says, tugging at David's sleeve.

"Nah', foo'. I don't want to lose it. My *jefita* won't buy me another one. She says it makes me look like a *cholo*." He brushes off his shoulders and straightens out his sleeves. "And, it makes me look gangster, foo'."

"Whatever," Lenny shakes his head. They give each other a Chicano handshake followed by a fist bump and howl as they stroll in opposite directions.

David suddenly freezes. "Hey, Lenny?"

"What's up? Lenny stops and turns.

"If you see, Sterl, tell him I said, what's up, foo'!"

Lenny nods and then wanders back down the hallway deep in thought—a thought that's quickly turning into a worry. He strolls down National Avenue—a city street crossing through several rough, gang-infested neighborhoods—caught in between the happenings of the streets and the worries of a young heart.

I can't let Art win and take my girl. The thought torments him as an Oldsmobile Cutlass zooms by booming, *Teenage Love* by Slick Rick. *I can't let him win.* He tries to fight the thought, but snapshots of Art and Miriam holding hands at the movie theater flash through his mind like a strobe light in a haunted house. He grinds his teeth, "Forget that! I can't let that happen!"

A voice suddenly calls out from a distance. "Hey, *pen-day-hoe*! *Es-pair-ah-tay*."

"What's up, Hershey squirt," says Lenny, "I swear you speak more Spanish than me."

"Only the cuss words, *pu-toe*." Sterling Jackson, or Sterl, is one of a handful of African-Americans living in a predominantly Latino neighborhood. Tough and muscularly-toned, he keeps true to his roots, even though he's adopted some aspects of Mexican culture, like an infatuation for curvy Mexican girls, an aptitude for dancing *Cumbias*, and an obsession for Mexican food.

"Where were you after school?" Lenny asks with a playful shove.

"Spittin' game to Carla, she let me feel on her *chi chis*."

"Whatever. Why you messin' around with my women anyway, you want some *pedo* or what?" Lenny drops his backpack and takes a defensive stance.

"Cuz, you too afraid to talk to them." Sterling says, shuffling his feet. "You ain't seen anything like this before, Len, float like a butterfly sting like a bee." He throws two quick jabs. Lenny barely manages to duck under them.

"See, there's your problem, Lenny, you need to strike first. Anyways, I got some good news for you, my boy," Sterling says while dodging Lenny's right hook. "You doing anything tomorrow?"

"Yeah, pretty much, *nada*." Lenny's miss-timed attempt at a punch leaves his midsection wide open, "Just gonna' draw something for the art contest. Me and Art got a bet going." Lenny absorbs an uppercut to his ribcage before countering with a straight left, nicking Sterling's jaw.

"Oh yeah, what's on the line?" Sterling asks, jerking his head back.

"Man, you don't wanna' know."

Ah, snap, now you gotta' tell me." Sterling shuffles his feet, like Muhammad Ali.

"Whoever wins gets to take Miriam out to the movies."

"Wait. What!" Sterling stops suddenly, "You don't mean, your Miriam?"

Lenny nods. "Yeah, my Miriam," he says, disappointed.

"Don't Art know you've had a crush on her since fourth grade," Sterling says, shaking his head. "That kinda' stuff makes me mad, Len," he says with an angry breath. "Homies don't steal each other's girl."

"It's all good. I just have to win the contest, that's all." Lenny reaches for his backpack.

"Oh, all you have to do is win, huh? You know that fool can draw. I mean, he's not as good as you, but you saw what he did to the school, right? No disrespect, Len, but that was pretty sick. I mean, his name is all over the freakin' newspaper," exclaims Sterling.

"I know. He already has the clipping hanging in his locker. It's all good, though. I still think I can do better. I just gotta' think of something cool to draw, that's all."

"Well, check this out, then," Sterling puts his arm around Lenny's shoulder, "My big bro is taking me to the car show tomorrow, you down to roll? Maybe you can find something there."

"Yeah," Lenny nods, "That sounds cool. Oh, damn! I almost forgot. Foo wanted me to tell you," Lenny widens his eyes, shifts his weight, and changes the tone in his voice, "Tell Sterl, I said what's up, foo'."

They break into laughter.

"That boy's funny as hell. I'll hit him up, too, see if he's down to roll. Art can stay his ass home for pulling that shit with you. Plus, Foo knows all the fine honeys in the hood. Maybe he can hook us up. Be at my pad at twelve. Laters, Len." Sterling makes a left on 30th, howling as he disappears around a corner. Lenny returns the howl as he continues up National Avenue.

Computer Love plays gently in the background as Lenny lies on his bed, fantasizing about winning the art contest. He visualizes walking over to Miriam, pulling her in close, and whispering in her ear, "You wanna' go to the movies with me?" Then, he goes in for a kiss.

Shit! What if I lose. Like an old vinyl record scratched by the needle of a record player, doubt gouges his thoughts. "I gotta' think of something good to draw?"

Lenny scans his room, not knowing what to look for. He glances at his old wooden desk with stacks of disheveled papers on it. His gaze shifts towards his nightstand with a little lamp absent of its lampshade accompanied by his Mickey Mouse alarm clock radio. He turns towards his half-open closet with a pile of clothes peeking out. Then, Lenny peers back at his desk and heads for the only working drawer. He pulls out a scrapbook made from an old leather document case—modified by his father's hand—now four fingers thick with artwork. "You said it would help me when I needed it," he says, remembering his father's words when he first handed it to him.

"*Hijo,* look what I made for you. I got it at a garage sale. It'll keep your drawing safe so you can look back whenever you need help," his father had said.

Lenny runs his hand over the rough, dark brown covering. His scrapbook has grown significantly over the years and is quite impressive, organized in chronological order according to how old he was when he did each piece. His mother even decorated the divider pages for him.

He skims through the first few pages—a series of whimsical landscapes from the imagination of a preschooler. One, in particular, grabs his attention—a tropical waterfall with a toucan flying above. Though created by the hand of a five-year-old with a pack of Crayolas, the piece resembles more a travel brochure than a child's drawing. On the bottom of the page is written, *Indigo Child,* in his teacher's handwriting. *What the hell does indigo even mean?* He muses over it for a moment, then flips through the next several pages. Another one of his sketches grabs his attention, one he did when he was nine, and it never fails to bring back a sickening feeling in his gut—a soccer player performing the bicycle kick made popular by the Brazilian soccer player, Pelé. The player on the drawing may be faceless, but the number eleven across his jersey leaves no doubt to his identity.

"I'm sorry, *Papi.*" Lenny runs his hand across the drawing, "I couldn't draw your face, I still can't." As he continues flipping through his artwork, a thought intrudes. *I've never had a problem knowing what to draw before. It always just came to me. But now, I don't know what the hell I'm gonna' draw for the contest? All I know is that it has to be better than Art's.*

Lenny tries to shake away the doubt clouding his confidence, but it's as if his imagination hit an obstacle more massive than the Great Wall of China.

He continues flipping through his scrapbook and stops on a sketch of the Coronado Bridge. He closes his eyes, whisking his mind back to where his father's words still echo as clear as the day he said them.

"*Mijo*, how do you come up with ideas for your drawings?"

Lenny looks up at his father, "*No se, Papi.* Sometimes, I look at something, and I feel like drawing it."

"Do you know what that is, *hijo*?"

Lenny shakes his head, "No."

"*Es inspiración divina*, divine inspiration. It means you can look at any ordinary thing, and see something more, something no one else can see, like a true *artista*. You have a talent, *hijo*. To be so young and be able to draw the way you do. It's a gift. Don't ever be afraid to use it."

Lenny jerks back to reality. He slams his sketchbook shut and ambles towards the window. He stands there, peering out, "I don't see anything. I'm just not feeling it." He heads to his bed, lies back down, and shuts his eyes in defeat.

"*Mijo. Mijo, despierta.*" His mother's gentle whispers tickle the hair follicles in Lenny's ears.

"*Qué, ma?*" Lenny croaks, sounding more like an old toad than a young teenager.

"I have to work a double shift today. *Te deje dinero,* on the kitchen counter, *por favor, mijo*, don't get into any trouble. *Te quiero mucho, mi amor.*" She kisses her son on the forehead and tucks in the edges of his blankets, making him into a human *empanada*. She blesses him with the sign of the cross and pleads to Jesus to protect her only son.

Because of her husband's untimely and tragic demise, Dolores Guadalupe Santiago has carried the obligation to better herself financially. So it was with perseverance and hard work she graduated top of her ROP class. She quickly gained employment as a nurse's assistant which brought a steady paycheck, and just as things were beginning to turn around for them (financially at least), hospital management volunteered her (more like made her) to fill the most unfavorable time slots. For the past year, Dolores has been absent on most weekends and major holidays, leaving Lenny unsupervised at a time when the temptation of the streets is becoming all too powerful for a teenager.

Lenny cranks up the volume on his Mickey Mouse alarm clock radio, blaring, *More Bounce to the Ounce* by Zapp and Roger. The speakers vibrate with occasional static as he lays out his clothes for the day's event. He slips on black, starch-creased dickie shorts, a plain white T-shirt ironed stiff, and striped socks pulled up to his knees. He bends down and ties on his favorite pair of black Nike Cortez's. His hair shimmers from the Tres Flores hair grease, and his body emanates from Brut cologne—ready to strut his stuff.

Lenny peers at his reflection, "Mirror, mirror, on the wall, who's the most fine-looking *vato* of all?" He smiles and points at his reflection, "You are, homeboy." He can already picture the hordes of fine *heinas* strolling through Chicano Park in their skin-tight mini-skirts, thick eyeliner, and pompadour hairstyles.

He walks up to Sterling's house exactly at twelve. Sterling is waiting for him on the front porch.

"Are we rolling or what?" Lenny asks as he walks up.

"Yeah, we're just waiting for Foo's chunky ass. Look, here he comes now." Sterling points at Foo, hustling up the block.

"What's up, foo'," David says, arching over, wheezing as he tries to catch his breath, "Damn foo, that was a mean walk, foo'. Are we going or what?"

Jason Jackson, the III, also known as Big Mack, among his homies because of his ability for reeling in ladies, pulls out a marijuana joint and places it in the crevice on the top of his ear. He sports Guess jeans, matching Louis Vuitton shoes and shirt, and a Padres baseball cap twisted to the side. "What's up, lil homies," he says, "Y'all ready to roll in the pimpmobile?"

They enter his maroon 1967 Cadillac Eldorado on gold Dayton wire rims polished to a high shimmer. "I only got one rule, lil homies, take it easy on my diamond-cut interior, I just got it done." Big Mack takes the joint from his ear, lights it, and takes a drag. "Y'all wanna' a hit?" He says, passing it to his little brother. Sterling pinches it with his thumb and index finger and takes a long drag. Almost immediately, his eyes turn bloodshot as he fights the urge to cough. "Hit this, fellas," Sterling says as he passes it to the back.

Lenny's heart races as it comes within hand's reach. He hesitates, his mother's plea still fresh in his mind. *"Mijo, please don't get into any trouble."*

"Nah', I'm cool," Lenny says, shaking his head no.

"What's the matter, Len, take a hit, it's not gonna' kill you," Sterling says.

"Go ahead, lil' homie, Big Mac won't steer ya' wrong. It's the bomb diggity'." He winks at Lenny through the rearview.

"Yeah, hurry up so I can hit it too, foo'," says David with anticipation.

Lenny glances at David, then back at the joint. *She won't be home until late anyway.* He says in his thoughts. Any reluctance he had is subdued as Lenny takes a drag and holds it in until his lungs can take no more. Then, he exhales his mother's plea away with the hardest cough of his life. The effect leaves a twisting sensation deep in the center of his chest. Any guilt he felt fades away like an early morning haze as the herb takes swift effect. Lenny's eyes shut as if weighed down by some unseen force. Time instantly slows as David reaches for the joint.

"Damn, homes, what's in this stuff?" Lenny asks with delayed and exaggerated speech. "I feel, I feel like I'm in a movie stuck on slow-motion, or something."

David also begins coughing uncontrollably. "Damn, foo'," he says in between gasps, "I'm messed up too, foo'. I feel like Batman, and you're my Robin, foo'," he says, nudging Lenny in the ribcage.

Sterling turns, "Batman!? You mean the Penguin." They all break into a hysterical fit.

"It's all good, lil playas', y'all just high." Big Mac pulls the Cady into a dirt parking lot, next to where the Coronado bridge begins ascending into the skyline.

Lenny can hear his heart pulsating in his ears as the excitement intensifies. He steps out of the Cadillac and is immediately awed by a crowd of girls making their way towards the park, like a school of sardines heading towards a feeding frenzy.

On any ordinary day, visitors to Chicano park are rather sparse, but on this day, it becomes a glass jar packed with people marbled with various shades of brown—from *Café au lait* to *Abuelita* chocolate, and everything in between.

Chicano Park Day is a yearly event that hosts a variety of cultural festivities, from indigenous dances, Mariachi performances, political PSA's, booths from various clubs and organizations, to vendors of all sorts. Girls of all shapes and sizes roam the park tantalizing the boys, some tall and slender, others short and robust, and a few that look like they were hand-sculpted by the Goddess of Love herself.

Across the street from the park, next to the handball courts, custom-built lowriders put on mechanical marvels, swaying their half-ton frames front to back, side to side, and corner to corner. Others hop next to a measuring stick over 10ft high, trying to achieve the highest mark. The winner receives a small trophy and a check for a modest sum, but for the owners of these rides, obtaining the title far out values any monetary prize.

For the indigenous enthusiast, a portion of the park is designated for ceremonial dances and reenactments of native rituals. Sage, an ancient and sacred incense, mixed in with the aroma of *carne asada* looms above the park like a thin layer of smog.

For the true Chicano enthusiast, though, the main attraction is the row after row of custom-built lowriders displayed like jewels at a royal gala (some are worth more in sentimental value).

Low-lows are displayed in the most peculiar ways for visual effect, exposing chromed undercarriages, custom-painted engines, luxurious hand-sewn interiors, and the like. Even in Lenny's peculiar mental state, he can't help but to feel a sense of wonder and amazement.

Everything communicates to him in a subliminal language relaying the cultural bindings tied to his Chicanismo. The murals express, *here lies your struggle and artistic potential.* The seed pods rattling on the ankles of the *Chichimeca* Dancers convey, *here lies your past and cultural identity.* Even the lowriders say, *here lies your pride and creativity.*

For the first time in his young life, pride stirs deep within the marrow of Lenny's bones. He takes a deep breath, takes it all in, and then exhales with his chin held high. *Yo Soy Chicano, and I'm down, brown, and proud, y que!*

Sterling taps Lenny's arm. "Snap out of it, Len. Where's your head? Let's go check out the hydraulic show." He says, pointing across the street.

"Yeah, foo', let's go check it out, foo'." David starts waddling in that direction. The three make their way across the street, bumping and smacking each other like they're the stars in an episode of the three stooges.

"Damn, foo', check out how that *ranfla* moves." David wiggles, bobs, and shimmies, trying to imitate the car's movements.

"Man, that's crazy how a car can do that! My brotha's gonna' wanna' get hydraulics on his Cady, fo sho'," Sterling says, astounded.

They're left dumbfounded when a black 1979' Monte Carlo dances to the rhythm of *Heartbreaker* by Zapp and Roger.

The teens make their way to the other side of the handball courts, where the hopping competition is underway. Again, they're amazed at how high a half-ton vehicle can hop with just a flip of a switch. A 1962' Chevy Impala hops with so much force the front axle cracks in half on impact with the pavement. Instead of being devastated for all the time and money put in customizing the car, the owner pumps his fist in celebration, much to the jubilee of the crowd.

"Let's go check out the low-lows," Sterling says. As they snake their way towards the main attraction, a pair of police officers appear directly in their path. Their hearts race as thoughts of being arrested for being under the influence invade their senses. Quickly, they disperse, every man for themselves. Sterling cuts towards the concession stands, Foo makes for the music stage, and Lenny keeps straight ahead towards the lowriders. He brushes against an officer who pays him no mind, scanning the park for bigger fish to fry.

"Damn! Those are some firme lowriders!" Lennys says, eyeing the easily distinguishable vehicles. Some are displayed completely off the ground on engraved jack stands, others tilted on their sides, and others positioned in the most precarious positions. As Lenny strolls through the open-air exhibition, he becomes hypnotized by a 1948' Chevy *bombita* with a brandy glaze paint job. It shimmers back with his reflection—clear and flawless. He nods, a gesture of appreciation for the skill of the painter. "That's it! Forget the six-four. You're the one I want," he says, visualizing the blueish-purple paint job he wants on it to match the color of Miriam's eyes.

Lenny turns into a six-year-old staring up at Mickey Mouse as he gazes at a royal purple 1955' Chevy *Trokita* with 24kt. Gold pinstriping and matching rims. There are vehicles painted with every color you could ever want on a car and adorned with every accessory you could imagine (from mini-bars to movie screens). But what Lenny pays particular close attention to are the murals on these lowriders. Some exhibit voluptuous women and indigenous warriors, while others honor revolutionary heroes or deceased family members. There are all types of images made into works of art by the masterful stroke of an airbrush.

Lenny stands with mouth wide open when he comes across a spectacular mural on the tailgate of a black 1978' Ford Ranchero. Instantly mesmerized, he gazes into the eyes of a sultry, gladiator woman with long, jet-black hair and clutching four leather leashes. Her powerful arms restrain a black panther staring ferociously at you, a stripped Bengal tiger in attack stance, a spotted jaguar growling fiercely, and the king of all beasts—the lion—flashing its menacing canines. What's even more striking is that the woman's purple, almond-shaped eyes reminiscent of Miriam's. Lenny's suddenly jolted with inspiration as if a thunderbolt was thrown down directly at him from Zeus himself.

"That's it! I'm gonna' draw her!" he says, with assertion.

The ride home can't end fast enough as Lenny sits back, conjuring up a mental image for the art contest. Big Mack lights up the unfinished marijuana roach and passes it back. Lenny doesn't even acknowledge it.

"I'll hit it, foo'." David says, reaching forward and pinches the roach with his fingernails. He gasps and pounds on his chest as he accidentally inhales the rest of the smoldering ash. "Damn, foo'!" he says, exhaling out a puff of smoke, "That burned my throat, foo'."

Sterling can't even chuckle, his head leans against the passenger side window, passed out from the weeds after effects.

"Are we almost home?" Lenny asks, his impatience and eagerness growing stronger with every street light they pass.

"Chill out, little homie, we cruisin', what's yur' rush?" Big Mack says, eyeing Lenny through the rearview.

"I'm feeling kinda' sick. It must've been that burrito I ate." Lenny places his hand over his stomach and grimaces.

"What! Hold that shit it in, lil' homie! I don't want you blowing chunks all over my interior!" Big Mack stomps down on the accelerator. The Cady thrusts forward with a screech.

"Yeah, foo', hold it in, I don't want chunks getting all over my jacket, foo." David tries to scoot away only to realize he can't get far enough. He quickly takes off his jacket and stuffs in the corner.

"At least I finally got that *pinche* jacket off you, huh, Foo?" Lenny says content with his ruse.

David shakes his head, sneering, "Whatever, foo'."

Five minutes later, the Cady skids to a halt. Big Mack wastes no time hopping out and pulling the seat forward. He helps Lenny out with a strong yank of his arm. "Alright, lil' homie, I hope you all good."

"Cool, thanks. Later, Wolf Pack." Lenny howls their signature call as he bolts towards his house. David reciprocates half-heartedly, once again intoxicated by the weed.

Lenny rushes into his apartment and shoots straight up the stairs. He rifles through his desk drawers, then shifts through his pile of dirty laundry. Frustration builds as he flips his mattress over. There, under his bed, he finds what he's seeking—a shoebox containing his favorite number 2 pencils, several large erasers, three black, fine-tipped pens, and a packet of brand-new colored pencils.

"Oh, you're done now, Esteelo." Lenny sits on his stool and reaches for a poster-size sketch pad leaning on an art easel—a gift from his mother after his father's death. She had hoped it would help him cope with their loss, as if focusing on his art would help him forget. Lenny's hands shake, but not with fear. He quickly flips through the oversized pages to a blank one. "Ok, I can do this. This for you, Miriam." He closes his eyes and takes three very slow, very deep breaths. He conceptualizes what he wants to draw in his mind's eye. Every detail in his soon-to-be drawing becoming clearer with each breath. As his breathing slows, his hands becomes steady. Then his right hand begins making subtle abstract movements as if he's drawing in the air. As soon as the tip of the pencil touches down on paper, his hand know exactly what to do—squiggling, swirling, and swaying this way and that. After he completes a basic outline, Lenny picks out a black fine-tipped pen and goes over it with smooth, refined lines.

Two hours of painstaking ink work later, he's ready to incorporate color. Lenny breaks the seal on his brand new pack of colored pencils and begins shading with various colors. His shading technique sets him apart from Art, and he knows it, applying darker and lighter shades in strategic places throughout the image. It takes him five and a half hours (including a few bathroom breaks and a couple of peanut butter and jelly sandwiches in between) to complete his work.

Lenny sits back, quietly analyzing his new piece. "It's gonna' win. It has to! It's perfect! Perfect! I hope she likes it," he says, knowing that he has just produced a winning masterpiece. "This has to go up on my wall." He tacks it up and takes several steps back. "Damn, she look just like her. I hope she notices. I hope she'll like me because of it."

The midnight hour strikes, and Lenny still can't find that elusive sheep to bring him much-needed sleep. He closes his eyes, but his mind remains, envisioning tomorrow's events play for play. He can see himself handing in his artwork to Mr. Escanuela before the morning bell, hanging out with the wolf pack during lunch talking about the car show, and then sitting at the award assembly in the afternoon waiting to be announced as the winner. As a virtual cherry on top, his skin chills over as he envisions himself receiving those movie tickets and approaching Miriam to ask her out.

Yes, I'd love to go to the movies with you, Leonardo. It took you long enough to ask me out. I've had a crush on you ever since elementary. He mouths the words as the sweet sound of Miriam's voice plays in his thoughts. An hour later, the last sheep hops over the fence, bringing Lenny much needed rest.

Mickey Mouse chimes at exactly six-thirty in the morning, notifying Lenny of the hour. As usual, he rolls over and gazes at the poster of

Vida Guerra arching over the hood of his no longer favorite 1964' Chevy Impala.

"Good morning, beautiful," he says, staggering to his feet. Lazily, he gazes to the right and eyes his newly completed masterpiece. "Damn, when did I?" For a split second, he experiences amnesia. "Oh, snap! The art contest!" It all comes racing back, like pressing rewind on an old tape deck. His emotions go into overload. "I need some fresh clothes!" Lenny rifles through his drawer, not finding anything suitable for such an occasion. He flings his closet open and to his surprise, finds a black polo shirt and a pair of tan dickies neatly pressed and folded on a hanger. "Thanks for hooking it up, *Mami*." Lenny side-steps, spins, and snaps his fingers to Brenton Wood's, *Oogum Boogum,* remembering the happiness he felt watching his mother and father dancing loving to the same tune so long ago.

"Today's my day! I can feel it!" he shouts from deep within his lungs. Lenny tries to maintain his cool as he makes his way to school. He holds his drawing rolled up tightly in his hand. He can't help but to glance down at it every several minutes as if he's holding the winning lottery ticket and was in route to claim the grand prize. A half-an-hour of mental anguish later, Lenny steps onto the grounds of Montgomery Middle School immediately seeking out his Science teacher.

"Damn, I only got five minutes! Where's Mr. E!?!" Lenny finds his deceptively youthful-looking teacher sitting on a fold-out chair next to his classroom.

"What's this?" asks Mr. Escanuela, reaching for the rolled-up poster paper.

"It's my drawing for the contest."

"Really? You know, Arthur turned his in a few minutes ago. I know how competitive you two are."

"Yeah, I guess," Lenny says sheepishly.

"You're just in time, Leonardo. I couldn't have accepted it a minute later," Mr. Escanuela says, glancing at his watch. "May I take a peek?"

Lenny nods, "Yeah."

Mr. Escanuela slides off the rubber band and unrolls the poster. He stares at it for several moments.

"You did this, Leonardo?" Mr. Escanuela asks with a bit of skepticism.

"Yes, sir. It took me like five hours."

Mr. Escanuela nods his head. "Hmmm, I have to say, Leonardo, I'm seriously impressed." The first bell sounds. "Now, get to class before you're tardy."

During lunch, Sterling recants their experience at Chicano Park to Art. He describes how they split up because of the cops, and how later, he found David dancing on stage with the girls from the bikini contest.

"Yeah, foo'. I even got a little memento." David says, reaching in his pocket and pulling out the top portion of a two-piece Tiger print bikini. "She even signed it for me, foo'." Inside one of the breast, cups reads, *Para mi güerito loquito, Sandra.*

"Did she show you her *tetas*?" asks Art with eyes widened.

"Nah', foo'," David says, shaking his head with disappointment. "She was already wearing her clothes when she gave it to me. She looked fine in her little tight shorts, foo'!" He snaps his fingers, a gesture of amazement.

"Did you at least get her number?" Art asks.

"'Nah', foo'. I tried though. I told her I was eighteen, foo'. She didn't believe me. She did give me a kiss on the cheek, though, foo', and these," he holds up the bikini top.

"Damn, I can't believe I missed that?" Lenny says while sneaking peeks at Miriam. His anxiety shifts into overdrive as time for the assembly finally arrives.

The school auditorium turns into a powder keg of rowdy adolescent boys, gossiping young girls, and overly-stressed teachers. Lenny scans the chaos for Miriam. He spots her sitting near the front of the stage.

Principal Ricardo Carrillo, or better known as Principal Rich, a tall and distinguished Chicano gentleman, attempts to focus the crowd in his unique and surprisingly effective way.

"Alright, alright, how's everybody doing today? *Como estan todos?*"

"Fine!" shouts back the rowdy crowd of adolescent kids.

"Let's see if you can keep up with me." Principal Rich begins drumming a slow melodic beat by clapping his hands and banging on his chest. The group of boys and girls follows along easily.

"Alright, alright. Let's try something a little more challenging." Principal Rich claps his hands a little faster, incorporating his chest and thighs for a livelier beat. This time, about half the crowd follows along.

"Not bad, not bad. It looks like there's still a few among you who can keep up. Now here's one for the musically gifted." Principal Rich maneuvers his hands at a ridiculous pace, clapping and banging on his chest and thighs, creating an impossible beat to imitate. Not a single student even attempts it.

"Hey, that's not fair!" a student shouts from the audience, "You're in a band, and you play the drums!" Silence spreads throughout the auditorium.

"You're absolutely right, and now that I have your undivided attention, I'd like to welcome everyone to this year's special assembly dedicated to saving the Amazon Rainforest!" The crowd of rowdy juveniles erupt with applaud and cheer.

"Even though The Amazon Rainforest is known as the lungs of the earth, and it is home to countless diverse, beautiful and endangered species, it's in great danger," says Principal Rich, "And it's up to you to do something about it. You are the next generation of conservationists, environmentalists, biologists, and scientists. That's why it's important to go to college and become someone who can change the world. Someone who can change the way we think about nature, about the earth," he says, pointing at the crowd to emphasize his point. "I am excited to say that we have a surprise for you today," continues Principal Rich, "We have some of those beautiful and endangered species right here for you to see firsthand."

Time slows as guest speakers bring out exotic animals native to the rainforests of Brazil and Peru. Lenny shows no interest when his teacher selects him to pet a spider monkey. He doesn't even flinch when the thunderous roar of a juvenile jaguar echoes throughout the auditorium, or when a pair of blue and yellow macaws fly around the auditorium and land on boy and girl's shoulder. Lenny remains transfixed on Miriam's subtle movements—how she rocks back and forth, hugging her knees, how she flings her hair back with a roll of her neck, and how her lips curl every time she laughs.

Lenny's infatuation finally breaks when he hears Arthur's name called, along with the names of the other participants in the contest. Twenty-five names are announced, including his.

"Alright, ladies and gentlemen, it's now the moment we've all been waiting for," Principal Rich says. "The runner up to this year's save the Amazon art contest goes to, Arthur Aguilar, for his rendition of a native Yanomami village nestled in the Amazon Rain Forest, which I have to say, will soon become extinct if we continues depleting the earth of its most precious resource." Mr. Escanuela carries out a three-legged easel onto the stage, exhibiting Arthur's not-very-creative but realistic artwork.

"Arthur, could you please come and receive your certificate of recognition." Art stands and struts towards the stage, avoiding eye contact with Lenny. Lenny tracks his artistic rival as he struggles to contain his excitement.

"Arthur," says Principal Rich, "Congratulations on your…"

Art doesn't let him finish his sentence, "Whatever, homes," he says, snatching the certificate from Principal Rich's hand and quickly heads towards his seat. On his way back, Art flings the certificate into the garbage can.

"Well ok," says Principal Rich, "And now, ladies and gentlemen, it is with great pride that I announce the winner of this year's save the Amazon art contest is," Principal Rich pauses for a moment. Lenny was in the process of standing when Principal Rich says, "Emilio Vergara, let's give him a round of applause."

Art's facial expression goes from disappointed to bewildered in a flash as he shouts, "What!!?!" Then, he breaks into a fit of laughter.

Lenny looks around, confused. *Wait! What?!? Emilio! Who the hell is Emilio? It's a mistake! It has to be!"*

Emilio hops to his feet and races towards the stage with his hands held high in triumph.

No way! No, freaking way! Lenny's mind yells out, but he can't seem to verbalize a single word. He stands there in shock, tracking Emilio as he gallops onto the stage.

"What the hell is happening?" Lenny says as his eyes begin fill with emotion. Suddenly, he notices Mr. Escanuela rushing towards the stage. Instantly, he knows something is a amiss because he's never seen his Science teacher move so fast in his life. Mr. Escanuela reaches the stage and places his hand over the microphone, whispering into Principal Rich's ear.

Principal Rich clears his throat. "Ehmm'. Boys and girls, this is very embarrassing. Apparently, there's been some confusion on my part. I mistakenly read the wrong name." He turns towards Emilio, "I'm sorry Emilio, I'll make it up to you, *te prometo*. Please make your way back to your seat."

Emilio stammers back with his head hung low. Realizing what's going down, Art shakes his head in defeat, "Damn it, homes! I knew it!"

Principal Rich taps on the microphone, "Let me try this again. It is with great pride that I announce that this year's winner of the save the Amazon art contest is, Leonardo Santiago."

The auditorium goes silent as all eyes turn towards Lenny. Lenny stands there, looking around, still confused over what just happened. Mr. Escanuela looks around at the student's faces and then begins applauding. In a second, an eruption of applause spreads throughout the entire auditorium. In the mix, the wolf pack release their signature howl. Lenny quickly wipes his eyes and releases a deep sigh of relief. A school assistant carries Lenny's drawing onto the stage with a blue ribbon clipped on the upper right-hand corner. He places it on a three-legged stand in front of the stage for everyone to see.

The piece exhibits a beautiful Amazonian warrior standing at the edge of the rainforest in a protective stance. Her hand is held out, expressing humanity to stop harming the rainforests of the world. Two black, spotted jaguars stand at her side flashing their ferocious teeth. An albino boa constrictor coils around her neck and arm, staring straight at you from the palm of her hand with its sharp fangs exposed.

"Leonardo, will you please come onto the stage and be recognized," says Principal Rich.

Mr. Escanuela walks through the crowd of middle schoolers, grabs Lenny by the arm, and hauls him onto the stage. Lenny tries to look cool as he approaches Principal Rich, making eye contact with Miriam along the way. A hot flash consumes him as she smiles at him.

"So, Leonardo, could you explain to us what inspired you to come up with such a striking piece?" Principal Rich asks.

Lenny shrugs his shoulders, "I got the idea from a lowrider."

Present

"I can't believe you said that," responds Lisa, laughing and smacking her knee. "It's pretty amazing you got the inspiration you needed from a lowrider," she says, nodding in agreement. "But you want to know something? I completely understand. And this might sound a little strange coming from, you know, a diva like me," she says with swagger in her expression, "But I have a lowrider, too. It was my papa's." She smiles at how easily her feelings can convert into words. "It's a 1964' Chevy Impala. He spent years turning it into a show car, and you know what, I love it! I've always loved it! I love that car as much as my papa loved it. Can you believe I thought about selling it," she says, then quickly points to the camera, "But only for a second, don't get it all twisted, people. I can never sell it," Lisa says."

"And you shouldn't, ey', ever," El DaVinci says. "It's *firme* you have a lowrider. It's even more *firme* that it was your *jefe's*. You should be proud of it, ey'." He sprays a misty layer of the antibacterial solution onto Diego's back and wipes away tiny beads of blood. He studies the fine strands of hair he just added to the tattoo.

"Thank you, I won't, ever," says Lisa. "So, let's get back to you. Tell us, did you take Miriam out to the movies?"

El DaVinci sighs, embarrassment escaping from his breath, "I hate to admit this, ey', but I didn't have the *huevos*. Like I said, it's one of my biggest regrets. And you know what people with regrets always say? If only I could go back."

"Oh, I agree," responds Lisa. "I swear, we live parallel lives. Something very similar happened to me, but in high school." She says, staring at El DaVinci, a seed of passion sprouting in her eyes.

"Two of my friends, well," she pauses, "Two of my good homegirls, I mean," she says, smiling. "We won first place in a talent show. For our act, we lip-synced *Baby Love* by The Supremes. My dad loved the Supremes. I think he had a thing for Diana Ross. He loved them so much he had me learn their dance routines when I was a little girl. Geez, I can still remember how hard it was convincing my homegirls to do the talent show with me. But they did. Talk about real homegirls. We even wore tight-fitting dresses with gold sequencing all over them. My *nanay*, that's what I call my mother, it's what she used to call her mom back in the Philippines, she hand-stitched them all by herself." Lisa flings her hair back, fighting back a rush of deep-rooted emotion.

"We practiced almost every day for a month. They were so mad at me when I told them I did it for a guy, a guy I was too scared to talk to, Kenny Williams. Geez, I still remember his name." Lisa shakes her head, "He was a senior, and I was just a sophomore. For some crazy reason, I got it into my head that if I won the talent show, he'd notice me." Lisa's facial expression converts to disappointment. "I was so devastated when I saw him holding hands with Sarah Johnson, all up in the hallway a few days after." She flings her hand in the air as flashes of her old street swagger slips out.

"I'm sorry to hear that, *mija*." El DaVinci's warm smile offers her comfort. "That vato was a fool, ey'. I mean, check you out now, all famous and shit."

"Thank you, but it was all my fault," Lisa laments. "I shouldn't have been afraid to talk to him. Who knows, if I had the courage back then, I could've been the one holding his hand in the hallway that day. So yeah, I know about regrets."

"A teenage love, *qué no*?" says El Davinci. "Slick Rick knew his shit, ey'. It's crazy. We should've listened to our hearts, instead of letting fear get into our heads." El DaVinci reaches for a long tubular-shaped package and breaks open the seal. He pulls out a new sterilized needle and replaces the old one from his tattoo gun. Guards scrutinize his every movement as he places the used needle into a jar on the easel.

"I'm curious," Lisa asks, "What would you say to her if she were watching right now?"

"Who?"

"Miriam," she says.

"Damn, *mija*, I haven't thought about that." El Davinci peers into the camera, and then back at Lisa. "You think she could be watching?"

"Well, why not? We broadcast all over the nation, and we're live, so you never know, she could be watching right now, this minute."

El DaVinci glances into the video camera and then freezes. The thought that Miriam could be watching sends him into another state of shock. Lisa looks at him, and then at the camera, and then back at him. Sensing his panic, she jumps in to save him.

"You know what I would tell Kenny Williams if he were watching right now?" Lisa says, turning towards the camera, "I'd tell him, you messed up, boy, look at me now!" She gives El DaVinci a wink. "I'm educated, successful, independent, and way out of your league, son. You couldn't handle a woman like me."

"*Órale,*" El DaVinci finally says. "*Chalé,* I can't believe I'm gonna' say this, especially on camera, ey', but you just inspired me. I'd tell Miriam that I've had a straight-up crush on her, ever since I was a *mocoso* in Mrs. Lopez's class. I'm talking way back since the third grade. And *dispensa,* from the bottom of my heart, for being too much of a *chavalita* for not letting you know." He clears his throat, dips the needle into the ink, and continues adding facial features to tattoo.

Lisa also clears her throat, "So then, if you didn't take her to the movies, what did you do with the movie tickets you won?"

"You're gonna' trip out on this, ey', but I gave them to Art."

"Wait. What! Are you serious! Did he take Miriam out to the movies!?!" Lisa asks, shocked.

"*Chalé*! No way! He took Linda with the big booty instead. They ended up becoming a thing."

"Geez, you had me going there for a minute." Lisa bursts out laughing. "I have to say, that was another amazing story."

"Thanks, *mija,* keep em' coming, ey'. I got plenty more to tell."

"OK, then, let's keep it moving. If you don't mind me getting a little personal, I've noticed you tend to call on your dad when things get, well, a little difficult. It's evident he meant," she stops, shaking her head, "I'm sorry, I meant to say, it's evident he means a lot to you. I don't have a tattoo of my papa, but I do the same thing. I call on my papa when I need help. It's strange, we should be praying to the Almighty Father, but we asks our dads for help instead. I guess that's what happens to people like us, who lose a parent we love way too early in life. If you don't mind me asking, what happened to him?"

"My *jefito*?"

Lisa nods, "Yes."

"Yeah, he passed away when I was nine, ey', talk about way too early in life. *Pero sabes qué*? Even though he passed when I was young, he's always been a big part of my life. *Chale!*" El Davinci says, trying to find the right words. "I believe things turned out the way they did for me because of him, well, and God too, ey'. I know it's hard to understand because he's not here in the physical sense, and I don't know how to explain it, but he's been guiding me my whole life, ey', one way or another." El DaVinci stops tattooing and peers down at his forearm.

"I know exactly what you mean," says Lisa.

"*Simón,* I do too." Diego jumps into the conversation. "I feel like my *jefita's* watching over me too."

"See! We're not the only ones," says Lisa. "Even Diego feels the same way," she says, rubbing the charm of St. Anthony's around her neck. "Sometimes I swear I can feel my papa's presence, and I mean like he's standing right next to me or something. Sometimes, the feeling gets so strong that the hairs on the back of my neck stand straight up." Lisa caresses the nape of her neck. "I even feel he guided me to find you.

Diego nods, "*Órale,* I believe in that supernatural stuff. That's some real shit."

"*Simón,* I believe in it, too," says El DaVinci.

"So, would you mind telling us a little more about how your father died and how it affected you at such a young age?"

El DaVinci adjusts the pressure on his tattoo gun. He gently dabs the tip of the needle into the ink and continues outlining. His hand moves in short, circular motions, shading with the contentment that only doing what you were truly meant to do can bring.

Diego grinds his teeth behind a smile, trying to conceal a sudden surge of pain from the piercing of the needle.

El DaVinci pauses and wipes down Diego's back. He releases a small sigh of relief.

"*Chalé*, that was a long time ago, ey'," El DaVinci says, "Back when my days as a happy, carefree little *mocoso* changed forever, and it was all because of a bargain my *jefe* made with God."

VIII. The Bargain

lashback. "It's ok if you want to kiss me," Miriam says with her voice fading into the background. Mickey's eyes illuminate as a tune begins playing from Lenny's Disney alarm clock radio. The chance at experiencing his first nocturnal emission (a.k.a wet dream) disappears as the pull of wakefulness grows stronger with each cadence of the beat.

Lenny rolls over frustrated and struggles to sit up. Right at the chorus, *My mind is playing tricks on me* by the Ghetto Boys, he slams his hand down on the power button.

"*Feliz compleaños, hijito,*" a voice as soft as a bag full of cotton balls calls out. Lenny's mother leans against the doorway, gently blowing away steam from a freshly-made cup of *café con leche.*

"*Gracias, Mami,*" he says, yawning with the full contentment of adolescence.

"*Ay, mijo, nueve años,* I can't believe it, *cómo vuela el tiempo!*" she says, shaking her head, the nostalgia of his infancy still tugs at her heart. Dolores sits at her son's bedside, caressing his face as delicately as a mountain breeze.

"Where's, *Papi?*"

"*Tu Papi* left early this morning to practice for the big game," she says in her sweet Mexican accent. "*Pero, no tarda en llegar.*"

Just then, the knob to the front door slowly cranks open. Angel Emiliano Santiago slides the key out of the lock and slips into his home like cat burglar, trying not to make a sound. Slowly, he creeps through the kitchen when he's startled by the sound of his soccer cleats tapping on the tile floor. "*Chingado! Pinche cleats!*" He curses under his breath as he slips them off. With the stealth of a Navy seal on a secret mission, he maneuvers up the staircase, avoiding the spots where the creaks like to give warning.

Aside from being a gifted soccer player, another trait Angel was born with is the ambition for pulling off the perfect prank. And although outwitting a goalie is among the best possible feelings he can experience, pulling off a good prank comes in a close second.

Angel creeps towards his son's bedroom with the mischievous notion of giving his family a loving fright. Slowly, he pokes his head through the door frame. Just as he is about to yell, *La Llorona esta aquí*, in the deepest, loudest voice he can muster, his heart stops (not like a cardiac arrest or anything, but one that still takes your breath away). The sight of his beautiful wife and loving son embracing in the purest form of affection causes him to take a different approach.

"Happy birthday, *mi cabezón*," he yells with his arms held wide open. Lenny looks up and spots his superhero dad standing in the doorway (there can be no higher compliment for a father to be seen as such by his son). His blue and yellow soccer jersey, matching shorts, and pair of blue grass-stained knee-high sports socks are the common fits to many glorified soccer heroes around the world after all. Lenny pops out of his bed and rushes towards his father's embrace.

"*Híjole!* My big boy is nine. I can't believe it, *nueve años!*" He takes an emotional breath. "Soon, you'll have a girlfriend, and won't want to hang around your old *papito* anymore," he says, trying to draw out a little more love from his son.

"*Nunca*! I love you too much. *Eres mi Papi!*" Lenny squeezes his father tight, welcoming the smell of salty perspiration and fresh-cut grass invading his senses.

Though their financial situation is rather dismal at the moment, Lenny's parents make it their absolute priority to spoil their only child with all the love they possess. Lenny may not have the luxuries money can buy, but he's got a treasure trove of love that far outvalues any monetary sum.

"*Oye, hijo*, I want you to come straight home from school so we can go to your favorite place," says Lenny's father.

"What? Seaport Village? Really!?!

"*Si, hijo mío*, I have important news for you and your *Mami*," he says, peering at Lenny with a sudden look of distress causing the butterflies to stir in Lenny's gut. He's never seen his father worried before, not even during one of his beloved soccer matches, although he did see him cry after his team lost a hard-fought match.

"Ok, *Papi*. I will," Lenny says.

"I want you to bring your sketch pad so you can draw me another one of your *dibujitos*." His hairy, mud-caked arm reaches for Lenny's art portfolio on the nightstand. "Remember what your teacher said? You should draw something every time we go somewhere special. *Ay, mijo*, you can't imagine how proud I was when she said you have the potential to be an artist, *como el gran Leonardo da Vinci*."

Logan Heights Elementary is located in the middle of a Mexican-dominated *barrio*. Lively Mexican culture is evident everywhere you look as *dulcerías*, *llanteras*, and *taquerías* openly blast Mexican *Corridos*. The area carries a reputation for being dangerous after dark, and yet, it is also home to a popular cultural zone for the entire Chicano community. Instead of becoming a highway patrol hub, the Chicano community of Logan Heights got together and defeated the City of San Diego by exercising their constitutional right to protest, and turned the area into a park with larger than life murals instead. It is a testament that ordinary people can come together to make an extraordinary difference.

Lenny struts down the halls of his elementary school, trying to look too cool for school when he's shoved in the back.

"What's up, little homie, I heard you were talking smack!" says a young African-American boy named Sterling.

"Ok, chocolate chip, let's do this!" Lenny drops his backpack and takes a boxer's stance, like the renowned boxing champion, Julio Cesar Chavez.

The boys begin throwing wild swings in the air, stirring up a small ruckus. A group of kids quickly encircle them, chanting, "Fight, fight, fight!" A pudgy, little white boy named David encourages them from the crowd, knowing they're simply putting on an act.

"Watch out! Principal Fuentes is coming!" David yells out, jumping into the circle with them. "Hey guys, do what I do."

Student's disperse as Principal Fuentes forces her way into the circle. Instead of a tussle, she finds the three boys dancing like a pair of old school *cholos* in perfect synchrony—their arms held tightly to their chest and stepping side-to-side.

"Alright, boys, what's all this commotion about?" she asks, unamused. "Not you two again. Up to your antics, I see. And now you too, *guerito*?" You know David, your *mamá* and I are good friends. I talk to her almost every day."

"Don't be mad at him," says Sterling, "David was just showing us," he gestures with his hands, "What's the big deal?

"Showing you what, exactly?"

"How to dance, Señora Fuentes," Lenny replies.

"Yeah, Miss Fuentes, I was showing them how to lean like a *cholo*," David says, swaying his body and stepping side-to-side. The three boys break into a fit of laughter.

"Ok, that's enough of that, *niños*. Now get your butts to class before I call your *mamás*!" she commands. "And you, *guerito*, you're lucky I don't call her right now! Now go!" She points down the hallway.

"*Si*, Miss Fuentes! *Gracias*, Miss Fuentes!" David says, wobbling in hurry towards class.

"*Gracias*, *señora* Fuentes!" responds Lenny and Sterling in unison.

Though he's black, or African-American if you prefer, Sterling is Lenny's best friend. The history of their friendship started in kindergarten. Lenny was nice enough to share some of his *pan dulce* with the only non-Mexican kid in his class, and they have been close ever since.

"Hey Len, I got you something you're gonna' love."

"Oh yeah, let me see it!"

"Not right now. I'll give it to you at lunch." Sterling says, bolting down the hall like a racehorse out of the starting gate.

"At least tell me what it is!" Lenny shouts.

"I'll show you at lunch!" Sterling shouts back rounding the corner.

Lenny makes his way to class with the anticipation of a teenager who just got a driver's permit. He thoroughly enjoys Mrs. Lopez' fourth-grade class, especially during social studies hour. Her passion for teaching ancient history keeps him engaged, but something else seems to stir deep inside when he learns something new about the indigenous people of South Americas. Today's lesson is on the Spanish conquest of *Tenochtitlán*. But no matter how hard he tries to focus on his teacher's impassioned lesson, thoughts of Miriam Rodriguez swoop in like an early-morning fog blanketing the sea.

Oh, Miriam, Miriam, Miriam. Why do you look so different today? There's something different about you. Her big, purple cat-like eyes, long, black curly hair and playful smile with a set of perfect pearlies, teleport him to a place he doesn't ever want to leave—a place where the sacred quetzal serenades enchanting melodies.

In the middle of his fantasy, Mrs. Lopez makes an announcement, "OK class, five minutes till' lunchtime. Please finish up your writing assignment." Student's close their books and lift the top of their desks, placing their classroom materials inside. The commotion pulls Lenny back into focus. He eyes Miriam, who is already sitting at attention with her hands crossed. Their eyes meet. Lenny has to touch his cheeks, to make sure they're not on fire—though her smile sure makes them feel like they are.

Lunchtime is the most chaotic time of the entire school day. Kids scurry about securing their favorite spot for eating and socializing. Lenny's go-to place is under a big maple tree a short distance away from the lunch tables. The tree's large trunk serves as good cover so he can eye Miriam from a position of stealth. He enjoys watching her curls dance with the breeze.

"Man, when are you gonna' talk to her?" Sterling asks as he approaches.

"I'm gonna' talk to her, one day, you'll see."

"Yeah, right," Sterling says, shaking his head with doubt.

"I will!" Lenny exclaims, "I just don't' know what to say."

"You should just draw her a picture," Sterling says, "Show her how good you are." He reaches in his backpack, "But for now, she can keep you company." Sterling hands Lenny a poster rolled up tight with a thick rubber band.

"What's this?"

"It's your new girlfriend," says Sterling.

"Girlfriend?" Lenny unrolls the poster, revealing voluptuous lowrider model, Dazza posing next to a convertible, royal blue 1964 Chevy Impala, tilted with one wheel in the air.

"Whoa! That ride is sick."

"I know the six fo's your dream car, but check out the honey, she's bad, too!" Sterling says. "My brother took me to Plaza Bonita Mall to get it for you."

"Thanks, man, it's awesome!"

"It's all good. Happy birthday, boy," Sterling says, bumping fists with his best friend. Lenny rolls the poster back up and secures it with the rubber band.

"So, we gonna' play Nintendo after school, or what?" Sterling asks.

"I can't. I'm going to hang out with my parents at Seaport Village today. You can spend the night tomorrow, though, after my dad's soccer game."

"Cool, I'll bring my Nintendo, so we can play video games all night," says Sterling.

"Heck yeah! So I can kick your butt at Mario Kart."

The last half hour of school arrives, and each student is to share out their plans for the weekend as the last assignment of the day.

"Class," announces Mrs. Lopez, "It's very important when you present, you use classroom talk and with complete sentences."

Lenny zones out, his thoughts shifting to concern. *I wonder what my Papi has to tell us? He looked worried.*

"Ok, Miriam, it's your turn to share out," Mrs. Lopez announces. Simply by hearing her name, his thoughts shift again—this time to matters of puppy love. He sighs from an ache in his heart—an ache only an arrow from Cupid's bow can bring. Miriam stands and takes a nervous breath. Lenny shares her nervousness as their hearts chime with the same beat.

"On Saturday, I'm going to my cousin Rosa's *quinceañera*." As Miriam describes the festivities involved in the Mexican girl's rite of passage into womanhood—the blessing from the church, the procession to the hall, and the waltz—Lenny envisions himself spinning her around and around, holding her tightly in his arms, just like he saw his mother and father doing while they danced lovingly in the kitchen.

"Leonardo, Leonardo, it's your turn to share," says Mrs. Lopez's soothing but commanding voice.

"Huh? What!?!" The synapses in his brain fire suddenly, "It's my turn?" Lenny asks, already knowing the answer.

Mrs. Lopez nods, "Yes, Leonardo, it's your turn."

"Ah, well, I'm just gonna' chill out, you know, kick it at my *papi's partido de fútbol*," he says, trying to sound as cool as the Fonz from *Happy Days*.

"Leonardo, you know we don't speak like that in class. Please use classroom talk." Mrs. Lopez glares at Lenny with the look (that infamous facial expression a teacher gives a student who is doing what he or she is not supposed to).

"*Perdón*, Mrs. Lopez." The embarrassment in his voice makes several of his classmates giggle. It sends a hot flash shooting throughout his body. "Um, this weekend, we're going to my *papi's partido de fútbol*. They're playing Los Diablos in the championship, and they're the meanest players in the league."

"Much better, Leonardo. Thank you for sharing, and please wish your *papá, buena suerte,* on behalf of our class."

"*Si, Maestra Lopez.*" The school bell blows like a cruise ship unloading a hoard of anxious passengers. Lenny snatches up his backpack and maneuvers his way through the tsunami of students flooding the halls. He doesn't even stop and wait for Sterling. He heads straight home concerned with what his father has to tell him.

Of all the collection of little shops and eateries at Seaport Village, Angel chooses Ben and Jerry's ice cream parlor to reveal the most important news of their lives.

"*Mi esposa querida y mi hijo cabezón,* I want to tell you something very important," Angel takes a deep breath and manages his most worrisome face.

Lenny and his mother glance at each other with concern.

"What is it, *mi amor?*" asks his wife.

Angel pauses, staring at his family with deep disappointment etched all over his face. "At tomorrow's game," he pauses again and looks down, exaggerating his distress.

"*No, mi amor*! Don't tell me. Coach Leon is not letting you play?" Dolores tries to embrace him, but he waves her off.

"What is it, *mi amor*, tell us. I can't take it anymore," she says as Angel sits there, shaking his head and taking heavy breaths.

His performance makes the bubbles in Lenny's stomach intensify. A dry heave escapes from his esophagus. "What's wrong, *Papi*?" he asks, fighting back the urge to vomit. "I'm starting to feel sick."

"At tomorrow's game," Angel pauses again as if the words are too difficult to come out. Then, all of a sudden, an enormous smile curls across his face, as if he just took a giant gulp of Kool-Aid. "Scouts from the Major League of Soccer are coming to watch me play. They told Coach Leon they'll call me up to the majors and offer me a contract if I can show them I have what it takes at tomorrow's game. And if that happens, *mi familia querida*, my beautiful family, our lives will change for forever!"

"*Ay, mi amor!* You scared me, *menso!*" Dolores says, punching her husband hard on the arm. "I knew this was going to happen! You've worked so hard for it!" Tears of happiness fill her eyes. Lenny takes a relieved breath, the bubbles in his gut subsiding instantly.

Angel scoops his family in his arms and plants a kiss on his wife's lips and one on his son's forehead. He cups Lenny's face in his small yet masculine hands. "*Hijo*," he says, staring into Lenny's eyes, "I'm scoring two goals for you, and I'm getting that contract for your *mami*!" He says, winking at his wife. "And we're going to get a big house with a swimming pool, and have everything we ever dreamed of."

Rays of hope shine down on the Santiago family as they stroll down the boardwalk, swinging Lenny in between their arms. They stop to enjoy the scenery while Lenny's mother takes in the tiny shops scattered throughout the harbor. Father and son gaze out at the bay watching the USS Nimitz aircraft carrier make its way out towards open sea. The majestic Coronado bridge compliments a fiery backdrop created by the setting sun.

Inspired by the vibrant colors of the approaching dusk, Lenny pulls out his sketch pad and his favorite number two pencil from his backpack and begins drawing. From afar, one would think a kid is simply scribbling on a piece of paper. After about fifteen minutes, Lenny unzips the outer pocket on his backpack and reaches in for a pack of colored pencils. He pauses, peering up at the bridge, taking in every possible detail he can. A magnificent blend of red, yellow, and orange hues coat the skyline.

Angel watches in amazement as his son's tiny hand moves across the page like a young Mozart composing his earliest symphony. He had always hoped what his preschool teacher had said about his son was true, but it wasn't until this moment, that absolute certainty struck him like a superman punch from the famous Kryptonian himself. "*Mijo*, you're going to be a great *artista,* aren't you?"

"*Si, Papi.* One day, I'll be so famous, I'll be on tv, you'll see."

Back at home, Lenny tacks the poster Sterling gave him onto the wall adjacent to his bed, so when he rolls over, he can wake with happy thoughts.

"*Hijo*, that poster, *me gusta mucho,* that car, wow! *Esta chido*, but I'm not sure your *mami* will approve. I'll try to convince her for you," he says with a wink. "You're growing up too fast, *hijo*." He reaches for Lenny's newest drawing, a rendering of the Coronado bridge with a magnificent setting sun highlighting the backdrop. He caresses it as if he drew it himself. Then, he opens the leather-bound portfolio and turns over several pages. When he gets to the end, he places his son's new sketch inside.

"*Hijo*, always keep your *dibujos* inside, so you can look back and remember. Trust me. You'll understand when you get older."

Lenny's extraordinary talent became evident at a young age. His preschool teacher first noticed it when she gave him a pack of crayons. She was expecting to get back some basic looking stick figures or simple shapes, but what she got back completely blew her mind. She began referring to him as, indigo child, or young prodigy. Ever since then, Angel had collected all of his son's art projects as a testament of his ability, hoping one day they would amount to something special.

Lenny lies comfortably in his bed, thinking about how his life is going to change when a sudden rush of anxiety begins twisting inside the pit of his stomach. *What if he doesn't score two goals?* He hunches over in pain as the darkness of doubt stifles his thoughts. *What if he doesn't get the contract?* The darkness spreads all the more. *What if he fails, and our lives don't change after all?* Lenny becomes completely saturated in doubt that the sickening feeling in his gut returns with a vengeance.

Even though his father is the best player on the team, in the entire league in fact, and Lenny has watched him score countless goals, he can't shake the fear—fear that his hopes and dreams will be blocked away by the opposing goalie—fear that he'll resent his father for getting their hopes up so high, they're too impossible to reach.

In the only other bedroom in their little apartment, Angel is experiencing the same kind of anxiety, but with the added pressure pressed upon him from his coach and teammates. His team has never won a title before, and they yearn to feel what it's like to be regarded as the best. As the hour becomes late, Angel strikes a bargain with God. *Dios mio, te pido, grant me two goals for my son, and a victory for my team? Te ofresco mi vida con gusto, if you grant me this.* And with that, he shuts his eyes for the night.

"*Mijito*, wake up. Wake up, *mijito*." Lenny's mother runs her fingertips through her son's hair. "It's time to get ready for your *papi's partido*."

Lenny stirs, stretching out like a cat waking from a long nap. He glances up at his mother and then looks over her shoulder. Her sweet attempts at coaxing him to wake are left in vain as Lenny closes his eyes and loses himself in a not-so-innocent fantasy induced by his new poster.

She turns to look at what her son was gazing at, "*Ay, Dios mio*, I don't approve of that poster, but your *papi* said it was ok because you're a growing boy. *Que alcahuete. Pero sabes qué, mi amor?*" she says with a tinge of jealousy, "I think he likes it more than you. *Ay, hijo*, I think you're too young to be looking at a woman like that. You're still my baby, *mi bebé lindo*," she sighs in a my-son-is-growing-up-way-too-fast type of way.

Then, as if he stuck his finger in a light socket, Lenny pops upright, "Today's the game!" he shouts. A rush of anxiety immediately upends his stomach. It takes all of his mental strength to fight back the urge to vomit.

"*Qué te pasa, hijo!*"

A stomach heave escapes in response. Lenny quickly covers his mouth and sprints towards the bathroom.

"*Ay, mijo*, don't worry," she shouts as Lenny vanishes down the hallway, "I know how you feel!"

To Lenny's dismay, the only bathroom in their apartment is occupied. He was about to kick at door when the sound of heavy heaving echoes out from inside. He presses his ear up against the door, listening to his father puke his guts out. Lenny looks around in panic. *Oh, damn! I can't hold it anymore.* Just as Lenny is about to fertilize his mother's favorite plant with stomach bile, the welcoming sound of flushing seeps out from under the door. The sink runs for a few seconds more, and the door finally opens.

"*Ay, hijo*," Angel says, surprised to see his son standing just outside. "*Son los nervios*, that's all." He places his hand over his stomach. Lenny rushes past him without saying a word and slams the door shut.

Angel presses his ear up against the bathroom door listening to his son vomit. *"Hijo*, don't worry, *vamos a ganar*! Don't tell your *mami*, but I made a bargain with God. I know he's going to answer me. He answered me when I had you," he says.

Sports Arena stadium fills with all types of crazy, die-hard spectators, most of which are passionate, emotionally-charged Latino fans. Even though it's just a semi-pro indoor soccer league game, true connoisseurs of the sport flock from all over to eat, drink, and cause all sorts of mayhem. Rowdy, beer-saturated fans yell, sing, and gyrate to the festival of Latin beats mixed by the stadium DJ.

Today's gladiatorial game comes highly anticipated, the mystique revolving around both teams have garnered mass publicity. The sold-out crowd has come to watch the championship match featuring the two biggest rivals in the league, The Sun Gods vs. Los Diablos, a classic rivalry against bordering cities. The two teams have matching regular-season records, but The Sun God's have home-field advantage because of the goal differential, thanks in large part to Angel himself.

The Sun Gods sport their baby-blue uniforms with gold stripes and matching socks while their opponents don black uniforms with blood-red stripes and socks.

Los Diablos stroll arrogantly onto the astroturf led by their newly-elected team captain, Malicio Satán. Satán holds the record for the most ejections in a season and is known as the dirtiest player in the league— a reputation he makes sure to live up to. Such an incident was captured on a spectator's video camera, clearly showing Satán digging his cleats into an opposing player's hand, fracturing several metacarpals while he was down.

The Sun Gods strut confidently onto the astroturf led by their team captain, Angel Santiago. Adoring fans have dub him, *Número Once,* and he's the top scorer in the league. Even though *Número Once* holds the scoring title, he's also holds another title he's even more proud of, most assists.

Lenny's heart rate jumps several beats as cheers and yells for *Número Once* spread throughout the stands. Fans jump to their feet, waving their team swag as officials head to the center of the field. Players take their positions, communicating with the opposing side through a series of unfriendly body gestures.

The game whistle blows, and the championship match begins. Lenny peers around the crowd, trying to figure out from where the scouts are watching. The first fifteen minutes pass uneventful. Both teams penetrate each other's defenses several times, but neither can attempt a successful shot at goal. When one team nears the other's goalie box, an opposing player steals away the ball, sailing it downfield in a hurry. The game is played as a virtual stalemate, like a Bobby Fischer and Boris Spassky chess match, with neither side giving in.

The game drags on as both teams try to adjust to the other's defenses. Lenny entertains himself by watching several scuffles break out a few rows to his right. Men and woman alike partake in beer tossing and verbal obscenities.

"*Ya vez, mijo*, you see what too much drinking does? It brings out the worst in people," says Lenny's mother.

On the thirty-fifth minute, Satán sends a perfectly angled pass towards a teammate who positions himself through a hard shove unseen by the refs—near the center of the goal. A Sun God player rushes in to defend but trips on his own feet. The Diablo player jumps and twists his body at the right moment, heading the ball towards the corner post and in for a goal. Lenny's stomach drops as the Diablo pulls his shirt over his head and scampers throughout the field with excitement.

The celebratory display doesn't discourage the Sun God's team captain, though, "*Vamonos*! Let's go, team! *Es una nada más*, it's only one. We'll get it back!" shouts *Número Once*. His faith in his team pays off in the fortieth minute. Angel accelerates downfield, putting on a network of faints and jukes that would make any NFL running back bow with respect. The ball sticks, as if the orb is somehow magnetized to his feet as he dances and spins, outmaneuvering two skillful midfield defenders. Satán sets his sights on Angel and barrels full speed towards him.

Número Once can sense Satán's presence bearing down on him and quickly gets rid of the ball by kicking it about forty-degrees to his right. Like a bank shot in a billiards game, the soccer ball bounces off the wall and lands perfectly at his teammate's feet. Satán slides at *Número Once's* with his cleats up, causing his nemesis to lose balance. Satán pops back up and gives chase.

Número Once rolls like an acrobat and also pops back up quickly. He cuts across the field as his teammate makes a couple of sweet juke moves. Right as Satán attempts another aggressive slide tackle, the Sun God player angles a perfect pass to the other side of the field. *Número Once* doesn't let the ball hit the ground as he karate kicks it in midair with such force, it bends around the goalie and in for a score.

Fans explode out of their seats as he sprints towards the area his family is sitting and points at them. The roar of the stadium becomes deafening, but Lenny can still make out the words coming from his father's mouth, "*Uno mas!*"

That's how the first half of the championship game went down, a 1-1 tie. The fifteen-minute half time begins. Lenny and his mother take the opportunity to hit the concession stands.

"*Qué, partidazo, mijo*, what a game!" expresses Lenny's mother as they make their way into a sea of rowdy, overly-excited fans.

"*Si, Mami*, it's an awesome game. I hate Satán! I hope he gets ejected. He's going to hurt one of our players, I know it."

"*Si, hijo. Él es muy malo.* You saw how he tried to trip your *papi*."

The concession booths fill with hordes of hungry spectators painted in their favorite team colors. Some sport blue and gold faces while others black and red, reminiscent of rival Native American war parties ready for battle. Lenny's mother motions secretly towards a man and women in costume. The man proudly dons a white toga with a golden halo fixed on top of his head. The woman flaunts a red she-devil outfit with matching horns and pointy tail. Lenny chuckles over the length people go to support their favorite team. They break in laughter as a ridiculously obese man walks past them shirtless, and with the words, *Número Once* painted across his protruding beer belly in gold-glitter paint.

"We'll have to tell your *papi* about his biggest fan after the game," she says, laughing. They order the classic game-day snacks, large nachos with extra jalapeños, and a large Coca-Cola to wash it down.

The second half begins with Los Diablos driving downfield with pinpoint passing. A little past midfield, Satán swings his right leg forward with such force, it sends the ball spinning straight towards the goal. A Sun God defender manages to get right in front of the ball at the last second, altering the trajectory with a twist of his head. He falls hard onto the astroturf. The game halts due to the player knocked unconscious. The stretcher comes out, a quick substitution made, and the championship game resumes.

The game clock marks the eightieth minute, and Lenny witnesses first hand why Los Diablos earned their infamous reputation. Diablos players resort to what they're know for—dirty tactics. They begin tripping, kicking at shins, and pulling at Jerseys. Satán receives his second yellow card for kicking a player in the knee who didn't even have the ball.

The clock marks the eighty-fifth minute, and both sides refuse to give up a goal. An evil frustration begins to engulf Los Diablos, while the Sun Gods gain confidence as they work more closely as a unit.

On the eighty-seventh minute, a Diablo illegally trips a Sun God just outside the goal zone, giving The Sun Gods an opportunity for a throw-in. *Número Once* takes a position next to the right goal post. A Sun God player named Federico Rodriguez throws the ball high up in the air.

Angel jukes, spins, and rushes in as a Diablo player makes first contact with the ball, using his head to send it straight up in the air. Angel waits and then leaps at the perfect moment. He flips backward with his right leg arching upward. The front part of his foot makes contact with the ball, sending it past a stunned goalie and into the net. The crowd goes wild, chanting, "*Chilena, Chilena, Chilena!*" (the name for the stylistic bicycle kick made popular by Pelé).

The stadium erupts like Mount Vesuvius over Pompeii as fans stomp their feet and shout with the full force, "Sun Gods, Sun Gods, Sun Gods!" Lenny has to cover his ears from the roar rattling in his cerebellum.

Disoriented from landing hard on his back, *Número Once* is hoisted up in the air by his teammates. He looks around, trying to make sense of what's happening, and then he holds up two fingers. *Número Once* is paraded around the field in his teammates arms. Lenny's anxiety subsides, and extreme jubilation takes over. He hugs and kisses his mother, and they join in with the crowd, jumping up and down and shouting.

I have to draw that kick! Lenny makes a mental note.

There is still several minutes of injury time left, and in this game, anything is possible. Lenny glances at the game clock, "Come on, only three minutes left. *Tres minutos,*" he says, taking a deep breath as the sour feeling in his gut returns.

Los Diablos play like demons desperate for souls to take. They kick, push, and elbow their way across the field as time winds down. Defeat becomes inevitable as the crowd—synchronized with the game clock— count down in unison. Lenny and his mother join in, "10, 9, 8, 7, 6, 5, 4, 3, 2, 1, 0."

A referee blows the whistle, and the crowd is left celebrating the victory freely. Again, Lenny jumps up and down, shouting and high-fiving everyone around him. "*Ganaron, Mami!*" expresses Lenny, "They won!"

"*Si, mijo, que golazo de tú Papi!*" She says, jumping up and down.

In their celebration, Lenny doesn't notice a fight breaking out on the field among the players. At first, he assumes it's just part of the celebration that made its way onto the field. What he does notice, with prophesying clarity, is Satán running full speed and jumping into the fray with his cleat pointing outward like a tiger pouncing on its prey.

It takes several, seemingly never-ending minutes for security to subdue the mayhem. After the players are separated, a body is left lying motionless on the field. Sun God player's scream out in agony, dropping to their knees as they surround their fallen comrade.

It occurred as a player was trying to break up the fight. He couldn't have seen it coming. The kick to the side of his head came with so much force that his skull cracked instantly.

Everything moves in slow motion as Lenny tries to seek out his father's number eleven jersey. His guts twist and pull as the feeling of uncertainty grips tighter by the second. He scans the field at every Sun God jersey for number eleven to no avail.

Then, it all becomes a blur. However strange as it may seem, Lenny can remember tasting the bitter stomach acids bubbling up from his esophagus. He can remember feeling the ambulance jostle from side to side as it sped towards the hospital. He can remember listening to the sirens pierce the calm of the evening, the sterile odor of the bandages wrapped around his father's head—blood-soaked on the right side. He can even remember reading the name on the paramedic's badge as he administered CPR (it was Jason Chapman). That's as far as the details of his recollection went at end of that day.

The Santiago family is given the official news shortly after arriving at the hospital. Dolores collapses, wailing with the worst kind of agony anyone can experience. Oddly, Lenny senses go deaf. The only thing that registers in his mind is a faint ringing growing louder and louder until, blackness.

Present

"Oh, my goodness!" Lisa says, wiping away tears from her eyes, "That was," she pauses. "That was incredibly tragic." She peers into the camera with soul-torn pupils.

"As I've been saying, *mija*, I got some stories to tell, ey'." El Davinci sprays Diego's back and gently wipes the tattoo clean. He rolls his chair backward and analyzes his progress.

"*Órale*, Big D, she's coming along nicely. I'm gonna' save her eyes for last, ey'. I wanna' make em' pop, homes."

Diego nods, "*Oralé*, do your thing, homes."

"So, whatever happened to the player who attacked your father, Satán, I believe his name was?" Lisa asks.

"This is gonna' blow your mind, ey'. That *vato* served fifteen-years for involuntary manslaughter, and the court banned him from any soccer field for life, he can't even coach little league. He told me carrying the guilt of killing a good man was the worst and the best thing for him."

"Wait, what!" exclaims Lisa, "He told you that!?! So you spoke to him?" Lisa asks, perplexed.

"*Simón*," El Davinci nods.

"And he said it was the worst and best thing for him?" Lisa asks again, even more perturbed.

El DaVinci rolls his chair forward. "*Simón*, but hear me out, ey'. This is where the story gets real trippy. I talk to him almost every day," he says.

"What!?! Are you serious?" The whites in Lisa's eyes easily become visible.

"Like I said, this gonna' blow your mind, ey'. He's the local Chaplain here."

What do you mean here?" Lisa asks.

"I mean right here, at Donovan." He peers into Lisa's disbelieving eyes. "That *vato* ended up changing his life. He straight up found God in the joint. That's why he said it was the worst and best thing that could have happened to him. Shit, he even changed his name. He goes by Cristóbal Mendez now."

Diego turns his head back, "*Chalé*, do you mean Pastor Cris, homes?"

"*Simón*, Big D, Pastor Cris. That shit's a trip, *qué no?*"

"Damn, that's some crazy shit, homes, for real!" Diego says.

El DaVinci rolls his chair forward, dips the needle of his tattoo gun into the ink, and continues tattooing. "You know what's even crazier, Big D? I used to wish I'd run into him in here. Man, if we ever crossed paths when I was younger, who knows, ey'," he sighs. "I'm glad we didn't. Anyways, when he got out, fifteen years later, the first thing he did was track me down. He found out where I was and sent me a letter, ey'. I didn't open it for months. Shit, I almost threw it away a few times," he says, shaking his head. "When I finally opened it, he wrote me about his whole story in prison. How he found God, how sorry he was for what he did, and he pledged his service to me as repentance, ey'. That's why he moved down here from L.A. and became the Chaplain after I transferred in, so he can make amends."

Diego flinches as the needle penetrates a sensitive spot.

"*Dispensa*, homes," El Davinci says.

"So, you forgave him. then?" Lisa asks, unbelieving.

"*Simón*. But don't get me wrong, it took me a while, but I did, ey'. Most *vatos* probably wouldn't have, but I know what it's like carrying that type of guilt. I know what it's like wanting redemption," he pauses for a moment, "*Chalé*, more like, needing it, ey'. No matter what you do, though, that guilt haunts with for the rest of your life."

"You know what, Mr. El DaVinci, this is all serendipitous," Lisa says, glancing into the camera and then back at El DaVinci. "I swear we live parallel lives. My dad died because of a game, too, well, sort of.

142

When I was a kid, he took me to Staples Center to see the Harlem Globetrotters. He didn't think they were all that because they weren't a professional basketball team like the Lakers, but I still made him promise to take me whenever they came to L.A. I loved the crazy tricks they did. Anyways, he finally took me to a game, and during halftime, three different seat numbers were picked to try a half-court shot and win a basketball signed by the whole team. My dad's seat was one chosen." Lisa pauses, trying to get a hold of her emotions.

"He was so excited when he won the ball for me. He was the only one who made the shot that night," Lisa's voice breaks. "When we were driving home, he was sweating like crazy, and he told me he wasn't feeling well. He died later that night from a heart attack." Lisa wipes the tears from her eyes.

"The doctors told us that the excitement from that night could have triggered it. I've always felt it was my fault. I pushed him to take me to the game," she covers her face, hiding the watery emotion accumulating in her eyes.

"Don't feel that way, *mija*," says El DaVinci, "Those things happen, ey', it ain't nobody's fault. Trust me, after all the shit I've seen in here, everything that happens changes the course of something else, and only God knows why." He blesses himself with the sign of the cross. "Look at what happened to Pastor Cris. He helps out a lot of *vatos* in here, helps them change their lives because of what he did. I know this might be a trippy thing to say, but if you think about, my *jefe's* death saved a bunch of lives in here, real talk."

"Wow! You know, I never really thought about it that way, to see tragedy with a silver lining," Lisa says, wiping her tears. "Things did change a lot after I lost him." She pauses, "Ok! You know what? That's enough of that," Lisa repositions herself in her chair. "Let's move on, shall we?"

"*Simón*. Let's do it, ey'. I still got plenty to tell."

The members of the broadcasting crew wipe tears from their eyes as a little more of Lisa—the part of her they never knew—is revealed.

The director suddenly begins motioning wildly. Lisa cups her earpiece. "Lisa doll, save it for tomorrow. We're out of time," the director says.

El Davinci peers at the tattoo and then at the photograph, and then back at the tattoo. He remains silent for a short time, looking back and forth. Then, he dips the needle into the nearly empty jar of black ink and continues tattooing.

"I'm sorry, Mr. El DaVinci, but it looks like that's all the time we have for today."

Lisa peers into the camera, "Folks, once again, I'd like to thank El DaVinci, Warden Wiesel and his staff of deputies, our network sponsors, and most importantly, you, our beloved audience, for making this special event possible. Please tune in tomorrow for our final segment on the day in the life of El DaVinci, the tattoo prodigy. On behalf of all of us here, have a wonderful night. We'll see you all back tomorrow at four Pacific time, seven eastern time for the conclusion of this special edition. I'm your hostess Lisa Deveroe, signing off." The sound technician cues the show's theme music, and the cameras go black.

Somewhere, out there on the streets of Los Angeles, Lil Playboy loads nine-millimeter caliber bullets into the clip of his pistol. He switches off his television as Entertainment Weekly's theme music plays, and the credits begin to roll.

Tomorrow, huh? Gotta' be back by four, I don't want to miss it. He pops the clip into his Berretta—a gift from an OG for his initiation into the gang—and secures it behind his waistband. He pauses and glances down at the sketch pad lying on his desk. A half-finished and beautifully detailed Aztec calendar awaits completion. His eyes move towards a collection of specialized colored pencils lying in wait.

"Should I just chill, and finish it?" He says, turning and peering at the mirror hanging on his door. His reflection exposes cuts and bruises barely healing from the sixty-second beat down he took not more than a week ago. He takes a glance at his sketch once more, wraps a bandana around his forehead, and heads for the door.

IX. The Sound of Success

Back at the prison, the show concludes for the day. "Cut! that's a wrap, folks!" The director—the same old, overbearing, anal-retentive perfectionist—raises his thumbs high. "One hell of a first day, team! One hell-of-a-show!" The wrinkles on the edges of his eye sockets spread out like fingers eagerly reaching for gold, followed by an uncharacteristic Kool-Aid smile. The broadcasting team shoot each other bewildered looks that instantly convert into smiles. Compliments such as these are too far in between.

Before every broadcast, you'll find the old man prowling about the set, making it his absolute mission to seek out the slightest misstep—an irrelevant misplaced chord, a camera lens slightly smudged over, a spotlight beginning to dim. It's rare for a broadcast to meet his rather unrealistic expectations, let alone surpass them, but today is such a day.

"We'll pick it back up tomorrow, folks." The director points at the security glass, like Babe Ruth pointing out a home run. "Eat your hearts out, gents! We'll be expectin' raises." The crew applaud, high-fiving, and hugging each other.

Though just another show for the network, everyone involved can't help but to feel that they're part of something truly extraordinary. The executives glance at each other, shaking their heads with a combination of defeat and triumph. Though it's their jobs not to show it, they can't help but to feel the same way.

"I have to give it to the old goat, it's turning out to be a little more interesting than I expected," says the lead executive, downplaying his excitement.

The warden stands and joins in the applaud, "Yes, indeed, gentlemen. I have to agree with the man. It is turning out to be one hell of a show."

The director approaches El DaVinci. "Mr. El DaVinci, I wanna thank ya', man to man, for allowing us to share your story, I know it can be a damn hard thing to do, putting yurself' out there like that." He motions towards the large video camera on his right. Scott notices them glancing in his direction. He smiles and gives a thumbs up.

"I'm sure I'm speakin' on behalf of my team, when I say, your story's the most captivatin' we've ever filmed. You expose a perspective I'm sure most aren't accustomed to. It's damn inspiring, how you're staying true to the gift God gave ya', even in a place like this. And I wanna say, your tattoos are truly amazin'. I'm not at all afraid to admit, they're the most amazin' I've ever seen, son, and that's coming from a fella who don't fancy tattoos much." He bows in a show of respect.

"*Òrale*, I appreciate that, homes." El DaVinci returns the gesture. "*Pero sabes qué*? You're gonna have to let me change your mind on that," he says jokingly, but meaning it. "I already got an idea for it, too, homes."

The director smirks. "Whoa, slow it down, son. I don't think this old, epidermis can hold ink anymore, but I'll tell you what, I know where to go if I change my mind." He turns towards Lisa. "Lisa doll, all I gotta' say is, atta' girl! That's how you captivate an audience," he says with open arms. "I've always told you, you can't be afraid to let them in, make the audience feel like they're part of the story, like they're part of the show. I just don't know why it took you so long to do it.'"

"Oh, stop it, and get your old butt over here," Lisa says, embracing the old man. "Thank you for that, pops, but I really didn't have to do much." She throws at nod at El DaVinci. "He did all the heavy lifting."

"Yeah, he's quite a character, no doubt about that." He cups Lisa's chin in a fatherly way. "But don't cut yo'self short, honey. You're part of this, too, opening yourself up like that, sharin' your vulnerability. Just keep doing it, this is your show as much as it is his."

He releases her chin. "We were right there with the both of ya'. This is your best performance to boot, and if them bone heads at the network can't see it," he says, pointing at the glass. "Then da' hell with them! Da' hell with the whole lot. They don't deserve you, Miss Lisa Deveroe," he says with a bow.

"Ah, thanks! That's sweet, pops." Lisa kisses him on the forehead.

The director grabs Lisa by the hand and twirls her around, "Move over Barbara Walters, and Oprah Winfrey, phenomenal y'all ladies are, there be a new hostess in town, and she goes by the name a' Lisa Deveroe."

El DaVinci runs his index finger across his forehead, guiding off a trickle of sweat. He pulls off his gloves and tosses them in a wastebasket. Then, he wipes his hands with a towel and pulls out a small, rectangular shaving mirror from his waistband. "Here, homes, check it out. It's a work in progress, ey', but she's coming along nicely," he says, handing Diego the mirror.

"*Órale*, gracias, homes." Diego grunts as he stretches out the knots in his back. He heads towards the security glass and turns his back towards it. Holding up the shaving mirror, he peers at the reflection. A half-finished but hauntingly beautiful silhouette of a woman's face stares back at him. All of her facial features are perfectly outlined and symmetrical, but lacking the realism only expert shading can provide. Her eyes are eerie—empty and soulless—as El DaVinci has yet to fill them with life.

An executive leans up against the glass, getting a closeup. "Extraordinary," he says. "Look at her lips, they're outlined perfectly, just perfectly! The strands of hair are so vivid and refined, I mean, it's coming out better than the photograph. It's ultra-realistic."

"Yes, it is. Much better than the photograph," says the warden, glaring at the team of executives. "And he isn't finished, gentlemen. Wait until he adds shading and color enhancements. Your minds are really going to be blown, then. He blows a puff of hot air on his Stanford University ring, polishing the cushioned-cut garnet gem with a handkerchief. A reddish glimmer sparkles in his eye. "Inmate Santiago is the best I've ever seen, and I've seen my share of talented artists come and go in these institutions." He walks over to a small table and pours himself a gulp full of expensive brandy. "I think it's safe to say this venture is turning out to be quite a success, wouldn't y'all agree?" he asks with a sly smile.

"There's still one more day of filming," counters back the lead executive. "Let's wait and see what the numbers have to say. They decide the measure of success, after all." His cell phone suddenly goes off. "Excuse me, warden, I have to take this in private," he says, covering the receiver with his hand.

El DaVinci ambles towards to Diego. "When I add shading tomorrow, homes, she'll really come to life, ey'. She's gonna' look like she came down from heaven, you got my *palabra* on that, homeboy."

"Cool, homie." Diego lowers the mirror and stares down Deputy Smith with a look that'll make anyone think twice. Deputy Smith reciprocates with the same look as he makes his way towards the inmate with shackles in his hand.

"Inmate Martinez, time to get you back to your cell," says Captain Briggs, motioning towards Smith. "Search him thoroughly, Deputy."

"Yes, sir, Captain." Deputy Smith scans Diego with a hand-held metal detector and then frisks him from head to toe. He snaps the restraints on Diego's wrists and ankles. "We're good to go, Cap."

"Open up twenty-one," Captain Briggs says into the walkie attached to his vest. On command, the door hisses to life.

"Hey, Big D, make sure your celli washes your tattoo, homes. Then tell him to put some of that ointment I gave you the other day. Just a thin layer, homes," instructs El DaVinci.

"*Simón,*" Diego says as the deputies escort him back to his cellblock.

El DaVinci reaches for his tattoo gun, and with slow, precise movements, pulls out the needle and places it in a jar half-filled with alcohol.

"That's good, Santiago, you know the drill, nice and slow." El Davinci looks up at his own face reflecting back from the captain's mirrored sunglasses.

"*Simón, Capitán,* I wouldn't want you to think I'm some kinda' criminal, ey'." He studies the captain's face for a reaction—a smirk, a head shake, a smile creeping through the corner of his mouth—but he gets nothing.

"I create not destroy. You know there's a lot of vatos in here with that kind of talent," he says, wiping down his tattoo gun and sealing the ink container.

"Yeah, well, with all due respect, Inmate Santiago," the captain of the guard scans the surroundings, "Even with all you have accomplished in here, impressive as it is, the bottom line is, you're still a convict, and you know what they say about convicts, right, Inmate Santiago?"

"What's that, *Capitán*?"

Captain Briggs crosses his muscular arms. "Never turn your back on them."

Lisa approaches the men. "Well, he just might be an exception to the rule, captain," she says with a wink.

"Hmmm," the captain of the guard smirks, doing little to mask his skepticism.

Lisa turns towards El Davinci. "You know, you're a natural in front of the camera. You should consider a career in show business."

"*Gracias, mija*, but what good will that do for me in here," he says, returning the wink.

A hot flash consumer Lisa unexpectedly. "Yeah, but you never know, someone may want to make a movie about all of this someday."

"Hmmm," El DaVinci smirks. "Wouldn't that be something.

"So, tomorrow's our last shoot," Lisa says. "I'm looking forward to what else you have to say. It's amazing how you've overcome the tragedies in your life. I mean, considering," Lisa says, looking around.

"You can go ahead and say it, *mija*. Considering I'm serving life behind bars, right? But you know what, I don't think I overcame anything, ey', I more like learned from them. Shit, I'm still learning from them. I mean, I'm still behind these bars, *qué no*?" He peers into her honey-glazed eyes, noticing the sympathy hiding behind them.

Lisa averts her gaze. "Actually," she says, shifting her mood, "I completely understand. I'm going through a kind of difficult time in my life right now, and you know what, you're helping me learn from it."

Deputy Smith and Deputy Jones approach with handcuffs. "Captain, we're ready for Inmate Santiago," Smith says, unstrapping the hand-held metal detector from his utility belt.

"Proceed, deputy."

"You know the drill, Santiago." Deputy Smith waves the wand at him.

El DaVinci places his hand behind his head and spreads his legs. Deputy Smith commences to scan El DaVinci from head to toe.

"Well, *mija*, I guess it's back to reality, ey'," he says with a wink. "To my little cage. You know what? I just might be an animal, after all."

The pair of deputies escort El DaVinci out through door and back to the honeycomb of cells of his cell block. As they make their way down the tier, something happens—something very unusual that some would say is unbelievable. It starts slowly as a single applaud echoing down the hallway. But in a matter of seconds, a thunderous roar of applauds consumes the cell block like a rogue wave consumes a ship. Minutes later, the entire facility becomes engulfed in whistles, cheers, and clanking on cell bars coming from hundreds of inmates in their little concrete confinements.

"What the?" Officer Smith looks around with his eyes as wide as they've ever been in his life.

"What's that?" asks an executive as the commotion reaches behind the one-way security glass.

"That my friends, is the sound of success." The warden pours himself another gulp full of expensive brandy and takes it down with a smile.

"You hear that, Lisa, doll?" The director shoots her a toothy smile. "You hear that team?" he shouts it through his megaphone. "That's the sound of something truly significant!"

Captain Briggs stands stone-faced, listening to the strange phenomenon, "Well, I'll be!"

The lead executive approaches Lisa. "Excuse me, Miss Deveroe, may I have a word with you in private?"

"Sure. Is there a problem?"

The executive motions towards the door, "It's better we speak in private." They make their way out.

"So, what's the problem?" Lisa asks with a bit of anxiety growing.

"I just got off the phone with the network." The lead executive says, taking a heavy breath as if what he's about to say is too difficult for him. "Mr. Blunt wanted me to express his congratulations. Preliminary indicators are in, and well, apparently, they're the highest we've ever seen. We've also been monitoring chatter about the show on various social media outlets. What can I say? Today's show is already trending. We're probably going to go viral." He nods his head, expressing genuine respect and gratitude. Well, done, ma'am."

"Thank you," Lisa says, relieved. "I needed to hear that, but I think I'll keep the champagne on ice, until the official numbers are in."

The youngest executive of the network, a twenty-four-year-old Yale graduate, maneuvers his way through the bubble of video equipment towards the director.

"Wow," he says as he reaches him, "It's turning out to be quite a show, huh?" The young executive reaches out his hand for a congratulatory handshake.

The director slaps it instead. "You damn right, sunny boy. It is quite a show. You best go run and tell your bosses that we'll be expectin' raises after this, ya' catch my drift?"

X. Eyes of Despair

El DaVinci enters his cell—the place where he balances sanity with anguish. His single-man cell is unlike any other in the entire prison system. Fresco-like paintings adorn all three walls of his tight living quarters, including the ceiling. He often refers to it as his own little Sistine Chapel. It's a regular thing for inmates to stop and stare like one would do a Banksy on the streets or a Monet in a museum.

The wall against El Davinci's bed looms with his stylized version of The Creation by Michelangelo. The only difference is Adam is brown-toned, with a goatee and prison tats all over his face and body. If you look up at the ceiling, you'll get a bird's eye view of the Aztec empire of Tenochtitlán in all its splendor, complete with beautifully painted pyramids and causeways spreading out like the legs of a spider across a vast lake. If you look through the bars of his cell, at the wall directly in front, you'd see a small, square recess containing several books, a metal sink, and a large image of the Virgin Mary, painted with eyes so striking they pierce deep into your soul.

But of all of what could be considered masterpieces in El DaVinci's cell, he spends most of his time staring at the wall opposite his mattress. Imagine walking through an entryway of an old Victorian-style home with walls crammed frame-to-frame with portraits of family members long departed. That's kind of what it resembles. El Davinci's portraits even resemble the style of photograph before the invention of the camera, painted by a master artist. Even the frames were painted to resemble wooden frames with imperfections and all.

Most of El DaVinci's portraits aren't of family members, but of who have left a lasting impression on his life. Of those who have made his wall—his mother, father, the Wolf Pack, El General, Lil Boxer, *Pelón*, Joker, Pastor Cris, Charles, The Pitt, and others—the portrait of the nameless woman affects him the most. She's not an exact likeness, probably not even a sort-of likeness, but more of what he imagined she may have looked like under happier circumstances. What is accurate, though, is the despair reflecting back from her eyes, a despair seared permanently into El DaVinci's soul.

To combat those long nights of emotional strife, El DaVinci painted his childhood crush near the center. Miriam's Elizabeth-Taylor-like, purple eyes uplift his spirit when guilt stabs deep—like a shank penetrating his chest.

Today has been another significant moment, and he's already picked out where his next portrait will go. El DaVinci closes his eyes, etching Lisa's soft, angelic facial features into memory—her long, straight hair, high exotic cheekbones, and perfectly defined lips.

Back at her Hollywood home, Lisa gulps down her last sip of wine and tosses the empty bottle into the trash bin. It seems like the bottom of a bottle did reveal what she so desperately needed. She slips on a silk nighty and turns her Bose stereo down so it's barely audible.

"What a day! What a story! What a show! It wasn't by coincidence, how I remembered what the intern had said, how the posts about him intrigued me, how his story happened to be one I've always wanted to do my entire career. Oh, no, there are no coincidences at all!"

Lisa glances at her dresser, where the red, white, and blue basketball signed by the Harlem Globetrotters sits. She thought it would have been difficult to find, especially because she hasn't held it in years (it never failed to bring back the pain of losing her father). But when she stepped into the garage, somehow, she knew exactly where it was. And when she held it, this time, it brought back the indescribable excitement she felt when he made the shot.

"I know it was you. I know you helped me, papa. You were right. I just needed to keep my feet moving forward." She looks up at the ceiling, "Tell Grams, I miss her." An epiphany strikes suddenly, like a jolt of electricity. Quickly, Lisa reaches for her cell phone. "It might be too late," she says, tapping in a phone number, "But the hell with it." She lets it ring. After a minute, the voicemail activates.

"Hey *nanay*, it's me, your Lilyboo. Gosh, I don't know what to say right now. I just picked up the phone and dialed your number," she pauses for a moment. "No, *nanay*, that's not true at all, I do know what I want to say. I know it's been a long time since we spoke, and I know it's all my fault. I've been going through some things lately. Things that are helping me realize what's really important. So, I'm calling you at 10:30 on a Thursday night, to say, I'm sorry. And even though it's totally out of the blue, I want you to know, I finally understand, I understand why you married Jon, and I'm not mad at you or him anymore. I'm just so sorry it took me this long to see things this clearly. Anyways, I'm doing a live show, and I'd like for you to see it, same channel as always. It airs tomorrow at 5. Let's talk soon, I love you, and I miss you so much, *nanay*."

Lisa ends her call and places her cell on the nightstand. She lies in her Queen Elizabeth inspired bed looking up the ceiling. "Keep my feet moving forward." Those were her last words before closing her eyes for the night.

"Lights out!" El DaVinci is pulled back from his thoughts as a deputy activates the power shut-off on a computer screen. He reaches in a rip on the side of his mattress and pulls out a small book of matches. He lights a small candle, nearly depleted of wax. The flicker from the flame serves as a tiny refuge against the overwhelming darkness he has inside.

"Our Father, who art in heaven, hallowed be thy name..." He whispers the Lord's prayer. It dissipates into the void like a pebble thrown into the ocean. El Davinci looks up at his wall of portraits. Each face represents a distinct moment in his life—some moments he remembers as they were, others he alters in his imagination so that things would turn out different. His eyes stops cold on the woman's face—the woman with no name. How he wishes things would've played out differently. Many times, he closes his eyes and sees himself shaking his head, no, at Sterling, and instead of getting in the car, he turns around and walks back to his house. But every time he opens them, he has to relive the guilt of his actions.

"If only I could take it back, I would, I fuckin' would!" he grinds his teeth, the bitter taste of enamel lingers. "But I can't, all I can do is keep praying for your forgiveness. You've been haunting me ever since that night, as you should." The anxiety rumbles in his stomach like an unceasing tremor. "I better crash out before I lose it," he says and blows out the candle.

El DaVinci tosses and turns stuck somewhere in between sleep and wakefulness. Tomorrow's final interview weighs heavy. He won't be able to avoid it. Lisa is going to ask him, the one question he's been dreading. He'll have to reveal everything, in honest, brutal detail. He owes it to her. He especially owes it to him. Hopefully, he'll be watching. Hopefully, he can forgive him.

El DaVinci's mind spins like a reel at the end of its film, with nobody there to change it. *Maybe some good will come out of this. Maybe my story will help some little vato out. Help him understand that choices come with consequences and that one wrong choice, one little misstep, one tiny lapse in judgment, can affect the rest of your life. Hopefully, that'll be enough to make him turn and walk away, like I should've done, instead of getting into that damn car!* This was his last thought before succumbing to a deep, gut-wrenching, slumber.

"Sterl, where are you!?!" Lenny stands and looks around." Sterling!?! Where are you!?!" He calls out again, now realizing he's a lone prisoner in a cell of regret. His heart speeds as the fight or flight response kicks into overdrive. Fighting to keep his soul clean, Lenny darts towards the figure lying motionless on the asphalt. The only thing he's sure of is that a terrible sensation stabs deep into his chest. A sensation that feels more like guilt than fear.

Lenny reaches the figure lying face down in a flash only to take a step back, shocked by a puddle of blood the size of a small fist leaking from the person's skull. He's never seen blood that looked like that before, like an oil puddle—thick and reflective under the glow of the moonlight. "Oh shit! It's a woman!" Lenny kneels and struggles to roll her body over. The cowboy's words from earlier replays in his mind, "Ju' be careful, ey', *la luna está llena.* Bery' dangerous!"

Lenny looks up at the moon, and then drops his head. His eyes gloss over as he tries to wipe away the coagulated blood from the woman's forehead with his long sleeve shirt.

Suddenly, an electric jolt rushes down the length of his spine when her eyes open to meet his—the desperation reflecting back sears into his soul. She groans as she tries to speak, but the only thing audible enough to hear is the gurgling of blood in her throat. With all the life she has left, the woman lifts her hand and points—her finger trembles towards the darkness. "*Mi hijo.*"

Just as Lenny is trying to comprehend what she's saying, death strikes with his scythe. Lenny turns towards where she was pointing and notices a baby stroller standing near the side of the curb. He looks back down at the woman, confused, but she stares back with the eyes of doll—haunting and lifeless.

El Davinci convulses. His chest heaves, and his back drips with sweat. "Mami…mami? Where are you?" he calls out to his mother in a state of delirium. His eyes open, but his mind remains clouded. It takes him several minutes to come to his senses.

"Shit! I'm in my cell," he realizes, still feeling discombobulated. "What the hell just happened!?!" He gazes at his wall of portraits, trying to catch his breath. His eye fixate on the nameless woman. "I don't know how, and I don't know when, but I'll find him. I'll find your son, and I'll beg. Do you hear me? I'll beg for forgiveness."

He glances at the portrait of his mother, but turns away. "If you only knew, *jefita*, this pain I have inside." El Davinci pounds on his chest, "But you can't. This is my pain to bear, not yours." He pounds harder and harder on his chest until he reaches full might. It takes three more powerful blows for him to hit the floor. Within seconds he regains consciousness. Gasping for breath, he continues ranting.

"I was too young, too stupid." El DaVinci struggles to get to his knees, "I shouldn't have gotten in that damn car." He looks up. This time he gazes at the portrait of his father. "I needed you! But you weren't there!" Guilt stabs instantly. "No! I'm sorry, *jefe*. It wasn't your fault. This was all me! I did this to myself, and I gotta' get myself out!" He looks up again and gazes at his mother. "It's time. It's time for you to know you still have a son. It's time for that little vato to know, I owe him a debt and I'll pay it for as long as it takes." El DaVinci crawls onto his mattress and lies back down.

"Thirty-minute wake-up call," a voice announces through the intercom.

"A new day. A good day for redemption."

El DaVinci starts his morning like any other. First, he douses his face with cold water. He takes several deep breaths, stretching his arms upward as high as they can reach, and then letting them hang loosely.

He snaps, cracks, and pops his back with every trunk twist and side bend, and then begins his exercises.

On his thirtieth burpee, a thought invades. *Why do I deserve all this?* His mind asks as his breathing increases. *Is it because of all the crazy shit I've been through?* He does five more burpees in perfect form.

"That ain't it," he says out loud, taking heavier breaths. *Is it because the gift God gave me?* He does another five burpees still in good form, clapping his hands as he jumps and then dropping back down for another push-up.

"No, that ain't it," he says again. Five more burpees and the answer becomes clearer. "It's because I have a chance," he says as his form begins faltering. "To get a message out, to my jefita, to the little vato, to all the little vatos out there like him, like me." His breath labors as he pushes through five more. "To let them know not to waste their talent, not to waste their only shot in life, no matter what!" His chest burns, and his legs feel like Jello as he struggles through his last five burpees. On the fiftieth push-up, he pops up to his feet and claps with finality.

El DaVinci leans up against his wall of portraits, catching his breath. He looks up at all the faces on his wall, and it hits him like a flash flood—all the memories, all the feelings, all the emotions of his life ignite a feeling so powerful his knees buckle. He falls back on his mattress. "That's it!" he say. "That's why Lisa found me! So I can tell my story!"

Breakfast arrives just as El DaVinci is pinching a crease down the length of his pants. He eats in isolation, like a celebrity in hiding, except in here, the public may want to take your life instead of your picture.

The captain of the guard arrives exactly at four o'clock and pops open El DaVinci's cell door. He waits patiently, a gesture reserved for only a select few. El DaVinci leaves the sketch pad open and places it on his mattress. The Captain eyes it with a curious expression. At first glance, it looks like little circular scribbles covering the entire page, but with closer inspection, you can tell they are eyes of different sizes.

"*Listo, Capitán*, let's finish it, ey'," El Davinci says as he walks out of his cell. "

"Yes, inmate Santiago, let's finish it indeed."

The men maneuver their way through the tier when a trustee, a man quite advanced in years and with Nordic symbols tattooed all over his forearms, stops directly in their path.

Officer Smith quickly reaches for his mace canister, but Captain Briggs blocks his hand.

"Give em' hell, El DaVinci," says the trustee as he raises his fist in the air.

"Geez, cap, he's lucky you stopped me. I was about to spray his ass." Officer Smith snaps the canister back onto his utility belt.

They continue on their way when another inmate grabs El DaVinci's arm through his cell bars as they're passing. The man's right arm displays a striking portrait of Tupac Shakur, and his left forearm is tattooed with the image of Olympic gold medalist Tommie Smith with his gloved hand raised high.

Officer Smith quickly eyes Captain Briggs, hoping for a command, but the captain shakes his head, "No."

"Represent, El DaVinci," says the inmate, "Represent for all us up in here. Let them muthafuckas' know what's up!" he says, raising his fist also.

Deputy Smith sighs, "This is getting a little ridiculous, ey', Cap?"

They make their way to the end of the tier. As they approach the last cell, an inmate places a book entitled, The Alchemist in the rectangular recess in the wall. Aztec glyphs adorn his entire arms down to his hands. He carries the mark of leadership on his shoulder, tattooed by El DaVinci himself. Captain Briggs pops open the door.

"*Jefe*, you wanted to see, me?" asks El DaVinci

"*Simón*. I wanted to let you know, *El General* was right about you," says the new leader of the carnales. "Let the *gente* out there know what we're capable of. Show them we're meant for more than just killing each other and filling up cells," he says, raising his fist.

El DaVinci nods, "*Simón, Pelón*. I will." They give each other a Chicano handshake and embrace.

Officer Smith shakes his head, "Seriously!?!"

Pelón nods at the Captain. The Captain returns the gesture and locks his cell.

Outside, on the mean urban streets of LA, three teenage gang members huddle in an alleyway smoking a joint. "Damn, Lil' Playboy, I can't believe you capped at them fools the other night. Their lucky none of them got hit."

"I know. That's my bad," says Lil' Playboy, shaking his head with disappointment. "It won't happen again. Hey, what time is it, boy?" he asks, suddenly remembering about the show. He takes a drag and passes the joint.

"It's about to be four, homes," Lil' Scrappy says.

Lil' Playboy exhales with an unexpected and painful cough. "What! Four! I got to bounce!" He says as he bolts down the street.

"Hey, where you going, Playboy?" shouts Lil' Scrappy.

"I gotta' catch a show!?!" he yells back and disappears around the corner.

"Did he just say he's gotta' catch a show?" Lil' Scrappy glances at his little homie standing next to him, "This must be some good weed."

Back at the prison, Warden Wiesel walks towards the door in the security room and opens it. A man in his late fifties, donning all black and clutching the Bible, enters the room.

"Well, this is quite a surprise. To what do we owe the pleasure?" asks the warden.

"You know what? For some reason, I woke up with a powerful sense of purpose, like our Lord and Savior was talking to me. When I opened my eyes, the first thought that came to my mind was the show. I don't know what my purpose is here yet, but here I am."

"Well, we're glad to have you all the same." The warden says as he turns to face the executives. "Gentlemen, I'd like to introduce to you Pastor Cris, our local Chaplain, and may I add, a very good man."

"Wait, is he the one who…"

"Yes, I am," Pastor Cris says before the lead executive can finish his sentence. "But please understand, that was a long time ago, and I'm still trying to make up for it with God's guidance."

"I…I didn't mean anything by it, father," responds the executive.

"I know you didn't, brother." Pastor Cris walks past the men and leans against the one-way security glass. "He's got quite a story, doesn't he?" he says, staring at El DaVinci.

"He sure does," answers back the young executive.

"Welcome back to Entertainment Weekly, and the final segment of our special edition, a day in the life of El DaVinci, the tattoo prodigy." Lisa winks with the excitement of a surfer about to ride a huge wave.

Before we begin, I'd like to say, on behalf of our network, and the crew of Entertainment Weekly, we again would like to thank those who have helped to make this extraordinary event possible, especially you," she gazes into the camera with her mesmerizing honey-glazed eyes. "Our beloved audience. Without your support, none of this would've been possible. We also would like to thank Warden Wiesel and his crew of correctional deputies for allowing us to conduct this show within the confines of a maximum-level penitentiary, which by the way, has never been done before by our network. Finally, we'd like to thank the star of the show, El DaVinci, for allowing us to share his life story with all of you."

The sound technician cues a switch, and the sound of applause reverberates throughout television sets all over the nation.

"Alright, folks, that's enough of that, now on with the show." Lisa sits and scans through her clipboard. Scott pans out just enough to reveal the three of them in the center of the room.

"Let's see here," Lisa says, sliding her finger down her clipboard. "Ah, yes! Here we go. I've had the opportunity to speak with several officers about your reputation, and they shared with me that you're the only inmate in the entire prison system allowed to tattoo anyone you want, that is, without race being an issue. They also said that such an act against prison norms can result in some serious consequences."

El DaVinci nods his head. "Damn, girl, you're starting kinda' heavy, ey'." He smiles, trying to make light of the unspoken rule.

"But, *simón limón*. In this place, people gather with their race," he says. "It's just something that happens. And crossing those lines without permission can bring some serious consequences, ey'."

"I see," says Lisa. "So prison is just naturally segregated by race. I imagine it must be under the rarest of circumstances that an inmate can intermingle."

"Something like that, ey'."

"So then, my question to you is, prison norms being what they are, how is it that you can cross those boundaries without any, how should I say it, repercussions?"

El DaVinci adjusts his tattoo gun, rotating the nob to increase the velocity. "This might sting a little Big D." He sprays Diego's back with the antiseptic and gently wipes the tattoo clean, still tender from yesterday's session. Diego winces, the rawness burns against his flesh. El Davinci studies the tattoo as he dabs it with a clean cloth.

"Everything's a risk in prison, ey'," he says. "Some vato may wake up one day and decide to take me out just for a rep. But I don't live that way," he says, slipping on latex gloves and cracking his fingers.

"Alright, Big D, let's bring your *jefita* to life, ey." He cracks his neck from left to right and then dips the needle into red ink, and begins shading. He makes small circular movements and then stops to wipe the tattoo.

"So, Ms. Deveroe, to answer your question, I guess I'm able to cross those racial lines because of what happened to me way back at Corcoran." He places his tattoo gun on the easel and lifts his shirt, exposing a 10-inch scar on his lower left side. "You can call it my race pass. And this is gonna' trip you out, ey', but I got the pass from a race riot."

XI. Sacrifice

Flashback. "Sit back and enjoy the ride, felons." Sarcasm resonates in Deputy Goodspeed's voice as he secures a 12-gauge shotgun and locks the security gate in the notorious Grey Goose with a twist of his herculean wrist. Bald, rugged, and with a physique worthy of last year's runner up to the Mr. California bodybuilding tournament, he vows to dedicate himself even more, so he can achieve the elusive title.

Shackles clatter with every pothole in the road, tinkering with the minds of the passengers, as the bus transporting prisoners throughout California's correctional system rumbles on towards its inevitable destination. Ten uneasy faces peer out of barred, smoke-tinted windows, catching glimpses of what will soon become an alien world to them.

Life in incarceration can slow to a state of perpetual stagnation, while the outside world continues to flow in a dynamic state of change. Oddly-shaped, electric cars will cruise the streets, new avant-garde fashion will clothe society, and architectural wonders, rivaling the Roman Colosseum in Italy, the pyramids of *Chichen Itza* in Mexico, and the Great Wall of China will soon decorate an evolving urban landscape.

A freshly turned twenty-one-year-old inmate donning a white jumpsuit with the label, TRANSFER across his back in bold lettering, is among the group pondering what's to come. El DaVinci, who is becoming known by reputation, hopes the rumors about this particular prison are way over-blown.

The word around Cali's prison system is that Corcoran State Pen is renowned for having the most violent race riots in all of the West Coast, and this is where El Davinci will spend the next several years.

Barely old enough to purchase a can of beer, but already a seasoned veteran of prison life, El DaVinci is no stranger to violence. He's witnessed the savagery that contributes to prison lore, and he's learned to suppress any fear of violence because of its high probability. The only thing he does fear is risking his God-given talent over a dispute he wants no part in.

"Look at the man's soul, *hijo*, not the color of his skin," El DaVinci's father used to tell him when he was a kid, and he's tried to live by that principle ever since, even as prison politics demand you associate only with those of your race.

El Davinci has crossed that racial divide before. Had he not had permission from those at the top of the prison hierarchy, he would have caught a serious beat-down or even a puncture to the kidney, but he's El DaVinci the tattoo prodigy, and he carries insurance from one of the most feared and respected men in the entire prison system in his back pocket. This being a new prison for him, though, and reputed for its racial conflicts, he's unsure how the *carnales* at Corcoran will receive him.

The Grey Goose squeaks through the triple-layered, barbed wire fence of the prison, leaving behind a dust bowl in its wake. Placed strategically out in the middle of a barren landscape, Corcoran is well isolated from mainstream society. Not many would-be escapees find their way to civilization before succumbing to such the harsh environment—scorching heat in the summer, frigid temperatures in the winter, venomous rattlesnakes, and deadly scorpions are but a few of the hazards awaiting any soul desperate for a temporary sense of freedom.

Like most prisons, designated cell blocks house inmates according to their crimes and propensity for violence. Short-timers are housed in generally low-level security, mid-level offenders tend not to be the most violent, but still merit stronger security measures. Then there are the lifers. They serve what's commonly referred to as hard time and tend to be the most violent of all. These inmates are housed in the maximum-security cell blocks.

On occasion, some white-collar criminal condemned to live the rest of his life behind bars finds he can't cope with the absence of amenities he's become accustomed too and opts for an easy way out. It's both unsettling and remarkable the ingenious ways inmates try to off themselves in times of absolute desperation—light fixture electrocutions, toilet drownings, and knee-high hangings are but a few of the ways that have been attempted within the confines of their single-man cell. It's also well known throughout the prison system that that Corcoran holds one of the highest suicide rates in the entire state.

The door to the Grey Goose folds open like an accordion, but there's no Mexican folk band playing a hero's ballad, just armed deputies gripping stun guns and itching to use them.

A deputy enters the Goose with a barrage of profanity, ushering the transfers out into the desert heat.

"Give me a reason, please!" A deputy ignites a blue streak of electricity from the tip of his baton-like weapon, followed by the crisp crackling of a million volts. "Come on, just one," he says, offering a challenge to the new inmates, "And I'll show you what it feels like to get struck by the lightning god himself!"

They can sense the crosshairs of high-powered rifles aimed at their foreheads from elevated watchtowers as they're instructed to stand in a single file line. They endure the midday heat until a tall, slender gentleman somewhere in his mid-sixties, and decked out in an all-white suit, strolls towards them without a hint of fear. A stereotypical portrait of a Southern plantation owner of the 1800s, Colonel, as he likes to be called, is constantly confused as the identical twin of the late Kentucky Fried Chicken icon, Colonel Sanders—with the same glasses, white hair, funny-looking goatee, and white suit to boot. He's won many costume parties in his day.

"Gentlemen, you may refer to me as, Colonel," he says, sliding out a silver pocket-sized case from the inside pocket of his suit jacket. The inscription on the case reads, *Colonel Sam Vietnam* in military script. Slowly, he opens the case and pulls out an elegant cigarette with a gold filter.

"And I am the warden of this fine institution." He places his hands behind his back. "Well, not quite that fine, as ya'll soon learn for yourselves. My wonderful prison has been suffering. It's been suffering from a pandemic of racial disputes," Colonel says, eyeballing the new prisoners without a glimmer of fear. "This disease, has claimed the lives of many inmates here at Corcoran, and to be quite frank," he says, tapping the butt of the cigarette against the case and lights it with a Zippo lighter. "I never had a problem turning a blind eye while y'all do society a favor," he says, taking a slow drag of his cigarette and blowing out perfumed smoke into the desert breeze. "But politicians in our fine state are starting to take notice of all the carnage. Hell, some of my colleagues refer to my prison as, The Plague. As morbid as it may sound, it does have a kind of a ring to it. However, now, I have no choice but to take action. I have been directed, by the governor himself, to quell these disputes effective immediately." He stares at each prisoner, comforted that the trained eye of a marksman is targeted on every inmate that comes within his arm's reach.

"Now, I'm trying to explain the situation here because I don't want any of you adding to my dilemma, you understand? Rather, I'd like for y'all to become part of the remedy. Maybe there's someone among you who will be exactly what the doctor ordered." He says, walking past El DaVinci. Their eyes meet briefly. "With that said, I'm going to partner you up with a cellmate of a different race. Think of it as a social experiment, and ya'll my test subjects," he says with an odd-looking smile on his face. My hope is that y'all bond, like civilized human beings, and help put an end to these so-called prison politics and the cycle of violence they create."

The new inmates glance at each other, wondering with who the warden will partner them up. Most of them pray they won't have to share a small cell with the freakishly-large African-American man standing among them.

"Can I asks a question, boss?" says the abnormally large man, his voice resonating like a low, deep growl of a lion.

The warden turns and looks up at the menacing figure, "Why yes, my huge fellow, you may."

"What if things don't work out? With our cellmates, I mean."

"Well then, my huge friend, there's always solitary confinement." The warden turns without saying another word and walks away.

"But..." The giant is cut off by a deputy knifing him with a sharp stare. "You heard the warden," he points the stun gun at the giant's chest, "Question time is over."

The new inmates walk in single file towards a holding area where they strip and put on their new prison attire. El DaVinci enters his cell first and places his effects on the bottom bunk, taking stock of the situation. Several moments later, the enormous man, the same the others were praying to avoid, enters his cell. He so large he has to bend down and twist sideways to get through the entryway. El DaVinci glances up at the man and then goes back to his thoughts. Anyone else would have experienced a chill run down to the base of their spine, followed by a spike in blood pressure, but not El DaVinci. He's witnessed men nearly as big fall at the hands of one much smaller.

The giant stands quietly, observing El DaVinci with a curious look. He's never met a man whose eyes did not reveal fear. Even most correction officers exhibit a glimmer of apprehension whenever they have to interact with the giant.

"Look, homes, it don't matter to me what bunk I take, so I'll leave it up to you." El DaVinci says, looking into the man's eyes.

The giant nods. "I's prefers the bottom on account a' my size."

"*Simón.*" El DaVinci grabs his belongings and places them on the top bunk. He hops up and lies on his back, crossing his arms behind his head and returning to his thoughts.

"Hey," says the giant as he places his personal effects on his mattress, "What type of Mesican' are you?"

"Whatcha' mean, homes?" El Davinci still has to look up from his bunk to meet the man's eyes.

"I mean, are you dos' types that hate us black folks jus' cuz' the color of our skin."

El DaVinci breaks eye contact and stares up at the ceiling, pondering a response. He knows the answer will determine the kind of relationship they will have from now on. He lifts his forearm, eyeing the tattoo of his father. Immediately, his voice echoes in his ears.

"*EL corazón, hijo*, that's how you judge a person. If his heart is good, you can see it in his eyes." El Davinci turns and looks back up at the giant. He stares in his eyes for just a moment, but long enough for him to see it. "Look, homes," he says, "I don't have anything against anybody, unless they got something against me, ey'."

The giant groans, "Mmm, hmm." He sits down on his bunk—it squeaks with the complaint.

"I'm not racist, homes, if that's what you really wanna' know. What about you, ey', you got something against us brown folks just because the color of our skin?" El DaVinci asks back.

"Don't know, I ain't never know'd one," the giant says.

"*Órale*! Then, I guess I have the honor of being the first." El DaVinci hops down from his bunk, straightens his shirt, and slicks back his hair.

The giant looks down at him, surprised.

"My name is Leonardo Santiago, but people call me El DaVinci," he says, reaching out his hand. The man takes El Davinci's hand and squeezes.

"People call me Charles," responds the giant.

EL DaVinci nods his head, grinding his teeth behind a smile from the strength of the man's grip.

Charles shakes El DaVinci's hand without any aggression, although it might not feel like it. "I'm from Brighton, in the good ol' state of Alabama. I used to play football der'. I was damn good, too, til' I got throw'd in jail. I just came in from Kilby Correctional."

"*Órale*, Alabama, huh? That's a long way from here, *qué no*? Why'd they transfer you way down here?"

"On account of my kin, my mama, and my baby sister. They done moved down here to Califonia' for a new start. So, I requested a transfer so I can be closer to dem', else I'd turn into a serious problem if ya' know what I mean."

"*Órale*, you being such big *vato*, they didn't want the hassle, *qué no*?"

"Yeah, they didn't want da' hassle," Charles says, laughing with deep satisfaction.

"Well played, homes. So, football, huh, what position, ey'?"

Charles takes a deep breath, his chest rising like a rogue tidal wave."I was startin' defensive end at Alabama State. Shoot, woulda' gone pro, too, if things didn't get all messed up."

"Damn, homes, what happened?"

"I killed a man' wit' my bare hands," Charles glares down at his palms with a confused look on his face. "I don't know how, but I done strangled the life right outta' him with these," he says, balling them up tight.

"*Chalé*! That wasn't too smart of him, messing with a big man like you. What did he do to you, homes?"

"He done shot my pa' in da' head. He was undercover police. Dey' said my pa' was transportin' drugs and resisting arrest, but my pa' ain't never broke no law. Dey' said he was reachin' for a gun, but my pa' ain't never owned no gun, either. When I came out da' house cuz' I heard the gunshot, I saw my pa' lying on floor, dead. A cop was rolling his body over, putting handcuffs on him. That's when I lost it. When I came to, my gramma and my sister were around me, protecting me because his partner had his gun pointed at me. I didn't realize I had my hands around the cops throat. When I looked down, his eyes were popping right out of his head. I let go, but it was too late. "

"Damn, I'm sorry to hear that, homes. But, I know how you feel, my *jefito* was killed by the hands of another, too. Well, more like by the foot, "El Davinci says. "He got kicked in the head." El Davinci takes a breath. "Anyways, you know, cop killers get some serious respect in here."

"I's don't care about that none. I's just wanna' be close to my baby sister and my ma' is all," says Charles. "They's all I got. What bout' you, why'd you end up in here?"

"Vehicular manslaughter, homes. A mistake I've been paying for since I was fourteen, ey'. I just came in from Folsom."

"Foe-teen'? Man, you was just a youngin'? I'm sorry to hear dat'. Why'd they send you down to these parts?"

"Ah, you know, we're just leaves in the wind, ey'. I think I was getting too popular back at Folsom, homes," says El DaVinci.

"What'd ya' mean, popular?" Charles gives him a curious look.

"I'm a tattoo artist, homes. I practically tattooed my whole cell block at Folsom, and I got to know a lot of people, the powerful kind if you know what I mean. I guess the warden didn't like that too much, ey'," El DaVinci says with a smirk. "He told me I was becoming a dangerous man because of my associations, and that he was doing me a favor by transferring me out."

"Is that fer' real?" Charles asks, amused.

"*Simón*, it's for real. I did something that's not allowed. I tattooed whites and blacks, and some of them were main heads. I guess the warden didn't like that too much. He said things are the way they are for a reason, and he wanted to keep it that way. I think that *vato* was just racist, ey."

I's glad he don't work here, or else I woulda' never met you," Charles says.

"*Simón*."

"Chow in fifteen," announces a voice over the loudspeaker.

"I ain't never had no tattoo, befoe'," says Charles.

"What, *serio*? I can do you a *firme* piece if you want. That's what I do. I need to find out who can get me what I need in here."

"I ain't too fond of needles, and I wouldn't know what to get," Charles says, shrugging his shoulders. "That stuff's on fo' life."

"That's the point, homes. Portraits are my specialty, but I can tattoo anything you want. I have a pretty light hand, too. You won't feel a thing, homes, well, it won't hurt that bad is what I'm trying to say. You have any kids, homes?"

"Nah', I ain't got no kids, no woman, either."

"Whoa', homes, you serious? No woman? You don't have a thing for *vatos*, do you?" El DaVinci says, jokingly taking a step back.

"What's a *va-toe*?"

"It's a way of saying, you know, dudes, *vatos*."

"Wait, is you asking if I's gay?"

El Davinci shrugs his shoulders, "No, but are you?" he asks again, now starting to feel a bit uncomfortable.

"No sir, ain't nothin' like that," The giant breaks into laughter. "I jus' ain't never had no time for no woman, been too busy trainin'," he says. "But I's got plenty time now."

"I'm just messin' with you, homes," El Davinci says, relieved. "What about someone close to you. Is there someone in your *familia* you want to honor? Your mom or little sister, maybe?"

The giant smiles. "My granny, she done' raised me on account'a my mama was drugged up most of the time. And my pa', he was always out driving his big rig. I hardly ever seen him. My granny was always der' fer' me. She and my baby sister went to all my games. Man, I miss that old woman," he says, shaking his head, emotion filling his eyes. "She got the cancer and died a year back." Charles clears the emotion from his throat, "I's never got to say goodbye."

"*Chalé*, I'm sorry to hear that. I know how that feels too, ey', losing someone close to you sucks, homes! My *jefe* was killed when I was a kid. Check this out. I tattooed his portrait myself." El Davinci shows Charles his forearm. "That pain never leaves, homes, especially in here. It only gets stronger. All you got is time. Time to relive all the bad things you done, and wish you would've done them different."

"Ain't that the truth." Charles points at El Davinci's forearm, "That tattoo is amazin', he looks so real. You got skills, man."

"*Gracias*. If you want, I can try to get what I need so I can do you a *firme* portrait of your granny. Do you have a picture of her?"

Charles nods his head, "Sure do." He digs through his personal effects and pulls out a photograph of an older woman with glasses, and smiling happily (a typical portrait of a strong, grandmother with the weight of her family on her shoulders).

"Oh, yeah. I can get down on this for you. Your grandmother will look like she never left, homes."

Charles nods, "I'd be much obliged."

"Hey, the warden did say he wanted us to get along, right homes."

"Ain't that the truth," Charles says, laughing.

"Line up in front of your cell and keep your mouth shut!" Shouts a deputy as he paces down the hall. The locking mechanisms echo as the steel bars pop open automatically. Inmates line up in single file and march quietly towards the chow hall. As they enter, they immediately separate according their race. The blacks, the browns, and the whites are the majority, and then there's a mix of all other races gathering in a smaller category all their own. El DaVinci has no choice but to separate from Charles.

"Ey', homes, you're the *vato* they call El DaVinci, *qué no*?" asks *Flaco*, the hardened leader of the *carnales* at Corcoran. "I hear you're a *firme* tattoo artist.

"*Simón*, how'd you know?" El DaVinci asks.

"Word gets around, homes, every *carnal* in here knows about you. You're a protected *vato*. The order comes straight from *El Mero Mero*."

El DaVinci nods, relieved by the supreme leader's far-reaching influence.

"Check it out, homes, let me give you the rundown on this cell block. You came just in time. Shit's about to pop off with the *tintos*."

"What do you mean?" El DaVinci asks.

"A *tinto* stole some commissary items from a browns cell without permission. That shit can't fly in this *torcida*. You know the code we live by, we can't show weakness. We're settling up after chow."

"Hey, homes, I don't have anything to do with that, ey'," exclaims El DaVinci, "I just got here."

"*Chalé*, I know you're not a *carnal*, homes, but you're brown like us. You can't deny the color of your skin. This ain't just about the *carnales*, homes. This shit's about all the *Raza* in here, and you're *Raza*, homes, that makes you part of it, whether you like or not."

They make their way to a metal table at the end of the chow hall. El DaVinci sits and was about to dig into a dried, meatloaf-like substance with a side of steamed vegetables when *Flaco* nudges him with his elbow.

"Here, homes, you'll need this." He hands El DaVinci an object under the table.

"What is it?"

"Hard candy, *vato*, what do you think? Trust me, you're gonna' need it," *Flaco* says, staring El DaVinci square in his eyes.

El DaVinci takes it and runs his fingers down the length of it. He's seen many crudely made prison shanks before, fashioned out of an uncoiled bed spring and wrapped tight with cloth for grip. He quickly conceals it under his leg. "*Chalé*, homes, what do I need this for?"

"Don't act a fool, homeboy. You know exactly what it's for. I tol' you, ey'. Shits goin' down. It's for your protection. You'll need it for that big ass *tinto* you came in with."

"*Chalé*," El DaVinci says defiantly, "He has nothing to do with this, either. Shit, homes, we just got here."

"Look, *vato*, in this *torcida*, it's the browns against the *tintos*, whether you like it or not. We back each other up, homes, just like they do." *Flaco* scans the chow hall. "Check it out. They're telling that big-ass *tinto* you came in with the same fucking thing."

El DaVinci looks across the hall and eyeballs his cellmate. The distressed look on Charles's face confirms *Flaco* is telling the truth. El DaVinci drops his fork and pushes aside his chow. *Damn prison politics. Charles is a good vato. I can't shank him. I won't!* He grinds his teeth at the thought. El DaVinci takes slow, deep breaths, searching his mind for a solution. He looks down at his forearm, hoping to hear his father's voice in his mind again. Oddly, he hears the warden's instead, *Maybe one among you will be just what the doctor ordered.*

"It's almost time, ey', *ponte trucha*. We're gonna' rush them when the guards call for line-up," *Flaco* whispers.

A deputy walks out onto a platform overlooking the chow hall and lifts his megaphone, "Chows over! Line up!"

"*Listo?*" *Flaco* reaches inside his waistband. "*Vamonos!*"

When adrenaline hits, there's no time to think, only to react. That's how the race riot at Corcoran went down that day, real fast. Conflicted, El DaVinci does the only thing he can. He grasps the shank tightly. All the browns rush the black inmates in a flash. The fight is vicious, like a

National Geographic documentary, showing a pack of wild dogs attacking another pack of wild dogs in the Serengeti. Food trays fly, bodies are bludgeoned, and blood spills as shanks stab into human flesh.

Once again, El DaVinci finds himself frozen. He glances to his right, and what he sees quickly snaps him into action. He catches the sight of *Flaco* and two other *carnales,* and they have Charles backed into a corner. His face shows mad desperation as he throws huge, wild swings, keeping the *vatos* at bay. EL DaVinci rushes into the fray just as *Flaco* lunges in with his shank. In that moment, El DaVinci slips in between them, taking a puncture just above the hip. *Flaco* digs in with his shank and slices several inches upward. El Davinci falls back into Charles's arms.

"Why the fuck you do that, homes!?!" *Flaco* says, peering down at the blood on his blade, realizing he stuck the wrong person.

"I told you, homes," El DaVinci says, grasping his side, "We don't got nothing to do with this." *Flaco's* eyes inflame with rage, and he was about to take another lunge, but a *carnal* quickly grabs his arm.

"*Cálmate,* homes! He's protected. You don't want to answer to *El Mero Mero*! You'll get us all put on the *leva,* homes."

The thought of backing off is unbearable, but the thought not following a direct order from their supreme leader is unfathomable. *Flaco* lowers his shank. Just then, a hornet's nest grenade explodes in the air, sending small orbs of solid rubber ricocheting throughout the chow hall like bomb fragments. The blast sends combatants scrambling to the floor.

The melee goes from chaotic to controlled in a matter of seconds, as a specially trained task force surrounds the hall in full tactical gear. Not a single inmate makes a sound, not even those writhing in pain.

El DaVinci lies on his stomach in a painful daze, with one hand behind his head and the other clutching his side. He's coaxed back to awareness by a pair of eyes staring directly at him. As he regains focus, he realizes it's Charles, and he's nodding with a slight tilt of his head. It's enough for El DaVinci to get the point. El DaVinci squints, fighting not to yell out from the burning in his side as he nods back. The distant echo of footsteps gets closer and closer until the warden appears.

"None of you seem to understand. I cannot allow this madness to continue." Colonel says as he steps in between the inmates on the floor. "Y'all left me no choice," he says. He eyes the captain of the guard. "Lock this place down, six months, no sunlight! Let's see if a lack of sunlight will get through to them."

The captain of the guard jumps into action. "You heard the warden, full lockdown!" he says. "If anyone makes a move, if anyone twitches a muscle, if anyone makes a sound, you will be shot!" The clicking sound of bolt action rifles loading their chambers with ammunition echo from above. The warden lifts his hand. The room falls silent again.

"Gentlemen, I advise you to take this time to reflect," Colonel says, "Think about whether you want the privileges I afford you in my prison, or continue this animalistic behavior and stay in your cages until you rot, where dangerous animals belong. I won't lose one wink of sleep keeping y'all confined in your cells for as long as it takes, even if it is permanently. And just in case y'all are thinking about your constitutional rights, I'm here to tell ya', safety and security overrides any rights y'all think you have in here."

Months pass extraordinarily slow for the inmates at Corcoran. Showers are reduced to once a week, inmates eat chow in their cells, and nobody's allowed in the yard for fresh air and exercise. Even with the extreme lockdown, inmates still communicate through an intricate system of hand signing and fishing for wires. An unusual message is passed throughout the facility—a brown saved the life of a black.

El DaVinci couldn't have known that his actions would spark an idea, a rather revolutionary idea for a prison—that blacks and browns can coexist without killing each other, and even crazier yet, they can become friends.

El Davinci lies in a bed in the infirmary pondering what's to come once he hits the cell block tomorrow when the warden enters unexpectedly.

"Mr. Santiago, how are you feeling?"

"I'm cool, sir," El DaVinci says, "My back aches from being in this bed for a month, and my side is a little sore, but other than that, I'm cool."

"Well, you took a pretty good wound in your side, fractured a part of your hip from what the doc told me. He also said just few centimeters higher, and your kidney would've suffered a severe puncture wound. He said that could've been the end of you."

"*Simón*. He told me the same thing," El DaVinci says.

"You might walk with a limp, but at least you can count your blessings," the warden says. "I have to say, Mr. Santiago, when I first saw you, I knew there was something about you, something I couldn't quite pinpoint."

"What do you mean, sir?"

"I couldn't tell ya', I just had this feeling. After what occurred, I did some research on you, Mr. Santiago. Apparently, you're quite the talented artist, aren't you? It seem you're developing quite the reputation. According to my sources at Folsom, you had significant influence among the inmates there. Inmates of status from what I hear. And based on what the warden told me, you're considered high risk because of it."

"I knew it," El Davinci says confirming his suspicion. "I'm not a risk, ey'. It was no big deal, I just tattooed some people, and they were cool with me," El Davinci says.

"They weren't just some people. They were influential people, and of different races to boot. You can imagine my surprise when I heard that bit of news. It seems that fate brought us together for a reason."

The warden tosses a package at El Davinci.

"What's this?" he asks, catching it.

"Open it."

El DaVinci unwraps the box and opens it. To his surprise, he finds a prison-made tattoo machine, several needles, and a jar of ink. He looks up at the warden. "Why?"

"You know, tattooin' is highly prohibited in all state-run facilities, but the word is out. It seems you saved the life of your cellmate, a black cellmate. Not that the enormous fellow needed any saving, but the fact that you intervened and sacrificed yourself is significant in my eyes. Now, there's some rather unusual talk going around, talk of a peace treaty among the races," he say with a smile. "Because you did something rather bold, I'm willing to do something bold as well, something that goes against my better judgment, not to mention against policy, but I am willing to turn a blind eye to your tattooin' on one condition."

"Oh yeah, what's that, sir?" asks El Davinci.

"As I said, I am willing to turn a blind eye only, and only if you tattoo different races as well, not just the browns, like you did a Folsom. Now, look here, Mr. Santiago," the warden's tone turns serious, and he points his finger menacingly. "If I get wind that you're tattooin' only those of your race, I'll take away all your privileges, and throw you in the solitary as a bonus. If your tattoos can help to keep the peace around here, so be it. Do we have an understanding, Mr. Santiago?"

"*Simón.* I mean, yes sir," El DaVinci says.

"Well, alright then, and please, call me Colonel, son. I hope you have a pleasant homecoming." The Warden turns and walks away without saying another word.

"*Gracias*, Colonel," El Davinci says, out loud.

The following day, El DaVinci enters his cell. Charles welcomes him with a strong embrace.

"That's a little tight, ey'. I'm still sore.'"

"I's sorry, I just wanted to thank ya' for sticking up for me, I means, for getting stuck for me," Charles says, pointing at El Davinci's side. "Aint' nobody ever done something like that for me."

"It's all good, homes. We're cellies, and cellies have each other's back."

A week passes by.

So, what'd you think's gonna' happen when they let us out?" Charles asks.

"I don't know, homes. I'll probably be an outcast," El DaVinci says, wiping down Charles's shoulder. He shuts off the tattoo gun—the one the warden gave him—and seals the ink jar. "That's good for now. We'll let it heal for a couple weeks. Then I'll shade in some more."

"I's owe you a life debt, El DaVinci. On my name, Charles Bufford Lewis, I'll have your back, no matters what anybody says!"

"*Órale*, I appreciate that, homes. You know, once I finish this tat, I wanna' let it heal for few more weeks so I can go over it again. That way, the ink'll stay in."

"It's all good, my frien', we ain't got nothin' but time, and this ain't nothin' compared to being blindsided by a four-hundred-and-fifty-pound lineman."

"Yeah, that don't sound too fun at all, homes."

"It ain't, let me tell you. That kinda' ringing stays in your head for days." Charles says, bursting out laughing.

El DaVinci spends the next several months, reading, drawing, and tattooing Charles.

"There, she's done, and she ain't going nowhere, homes, she's with you forever. You're lucky, homes, this tattoo machine the warden gave me works way better than I thought, ey'. The *vato* who put it together really knew what he was doing, ey'."

Charles walks over to a small mirror fixed to the wall of their cell and analyzes his shoulder.

"Damn boy, you truly are a great artist, El Davinci. That's my granny, right there." He fights back the sentiment. "Hey granny, I miss you," he says, "But now you're with me forever."

"Thanks, homes. I'm glad you like it."

"I don't like it. I loves it. Where I'm from, we kinda' have a tradition," Charles says. "Whenever you want a friendship to last, y'all become blood brothers." He grabs the needle from the tattoo gun and stabs it into his hand. El DaVinci stares at Charles's outstretched hand curiously. Then, he takes the same needle and makes a small gash on his palm. They shake hands and their blood mix.

"Now we're brothers, and I means it with all my heart."

"*Simón*, me too. Trip out, ey', I've always wanted a big brother, homes," says El DaVinci, "I just never thought I'd have me a big, big brother!" Charles breaks into a fit so hard, he hunches over from the strain in his gut.

At the end of the six month, a message is communicated between the leaders of the browns and the blacks. It calls for a gathering on the yard. One of the leaders of the blacks requests El DaVinci sit in on the negotiations.

A week later, the groups congregate on the benches. Officers keep a watchful eye as the groups near each other. The warden orders a tactical squad on stand-by just in case. Even though he's uneasy about it, Colonel allows the gathering, hoping it'll put an end to the violence at Corcoran.

Flaco, Smiley (his second in command), and El DaVinci step forward to meet the leaders of the blacks.

"So, you're the one they call El DaVinci, huh?" asks a muscular black man with two long braids.

El DaVinci cocks his head to the side, "You look familiar, do I know you, homes?" He says, noticing something vaguely familiar hiding behind the man's facial hair and deep voice, especially in the eyes.

"Yeah, you can say that," says the man. "You can also say I owe you one big-ass solid, *pen-day-ho*." El DaVinci squints his eyes, and then a big smile crosses his face.

Present

"That was unbelievable!" says Lisa as she gazes into the camera with a look of disbelief. "So it was Sterling?"

El DaVinci chuckles. "*Simón*, it was Sterling, alright!"

"What an extraordinary coincidence, that one of the leaders of a rival prison gang happened to be your childhood friend."

"*Simón,* that was crazy, *qué no*? And he wasn't just any friend. Sterling was my best friend back in the day. After the racial tension cooled down, I tattooed a portrait of Big Mack on his calf." El DaVinci points to the back of his leg. "It was hilarious. You should've seen him. For such a strong-looking *vato*, he squirmed like a baby." He wipes Diego's back and dips the needlepoint into the ink, continuing to shade with small, circular strokes.

"Yeah, Sterl is serving life without parole for premeditated murder. He shot the crackhead who killed his brother over a piece of rock. That's how he ended up at Corcoran. He got into that prison gang life with full force, ey', ended up becoming a made man. He told me it ain't easy being a shot caller because there's always a young lion trying to overthrow the king. Life's a trip, *qué no*? Anyways, the racial riots stopped, at least while I was there, and the word spread. After that, wherever I went, race wasn't an issue. Black, White, Brown, Indian, Asian, I tattooed whoever I wanted, and no one could tell me anything. *Chalé*, I even tattooed that Koi over there on a Yakuza." He points to the drawing of the iconic fish taped to the wall. Scott zooms in on the image.

"You've heard of them, haven't you? The Japanese mafia?

Lisa nods, "I see, and so that's how your popularity spread throughout the prison system, I imagine."

"Something like that. I've tattooed some down-ass *vatos* over the years. *Vatos* from different races and backgrounds with some crazy-ass stories of their own."

"I bet. And Charles, what became of him?" Lisa asks.

El DaVinci peers at the scar on his palm. "I got love for Charles," he says. "He was paroled just last year. I knew that was gonna' happen. Charles may be a big, intimidating-looking *vato*, but he's got a big heart. And it was just a matter of time for the parole board to see it, too."

"That's amazing. Have you heard from him since?"

"*Simón*, I get to see him every day. I painted a portrait of him on my wall. He wrote to me a few times. He's living with his sister in San Francisco, and this is gonna' trip you out, ey', but he ended up finding a woman after all."

"That's wonderful. You know, your story just brought back another memory," says Lisa. "If you didn't already know, I'm half black and half Filipino. Back when I was a kid, I associated more with my black side. It's because my mother's family are all in the Philippines, and I grew up with nothing but my dad's family around me. Anyways, Sasha, one of my best friends from elementary school, was full Filipino. All my black friends didn't like her too much. They'd always make fun of the way she talked. It was hard getting them to accept her, but eventually, they did, and we all became close in high school. She was one of the girls who did the talent show with me, the one I told you about the other day. She always said I'd be famous one day. It's been over twenty years since I've heard from her, since I've heard from any of them. And to tell you the truth, I really miss them." Lisa looks off to the side, the nostalgia hitting her like a lowrider hitting the switches.

"You should give her a call, ey', invite her to one of your shows," El DaVinci says.

"You know what? I might just do that," Lisa says, glancing into the camera and shaking her head in agreement. "I know this is starting to sound a little cliché, but that was another amazing story."

"*Chalé, sabes qué*?" he says, chuckling, "I'm running out of stories to tell.

Lisa brushes her hair back with a wave of her hand. "There's one thing I still don't quite understand. And it happens to be my next question? How exactly did celebrities like Drake, Lil Wayne, and Anthony Kiedis, a hardcore rocker for goodness sake, get your tattoos?"

El DaVinci pauses. "I owe that to The Pit."

"The what?" Lisa asks.

El DaVinci stops and studies Diego's tattoo. Then, he continues maneuvering the tattoo gun in small, circular motions.

"The Pit. I met that crazy *paisan* back in the day." El DaVinci's mind rewinds to when he met one of the most influential people in his life.

XII. The Pit

Flashback. A tattooed hand glides across a sketch pad creating life on a lifeless sheet of paper. Like the Big Bang, the charcoal moves in a series of small, swift explosions, resembling the artistic technique of a five-year-old. Two-hours later, El DaVinci polishes off another masterpiece by taking his index finger and delicately smudging the ashy residue. What began as random circles and lines that could be displayed on a proud parent's refrigerator door, evolves into an elaborate ancient Mayan ruin veiled behind a lush, tropical rainforest, worthy of exhibition in any upscale gallery.

"*Qué onda*, El DaVinci? I'm still trippin' out how *El General* got you back down here to Folsom," Joker says, entering their little two-man cell. "I didn't think I was ever gonna' see you again, homeboy, especially after what you pulled down at Corcoran. *Chalé, Flaco* took some serious heat because of what he did to you, ey'." Joker blows out a bewildered whistle, "*Serio*, though, I know *El General* knows people in high places, but damn, he's got some serious pull to get you back down here. The only way he could've done that is by knowing some big shots up there in corrections ey', especially since the last warden ran you off like that."

Simón, says El DaVinci, "I'm glad they changed wardens, homes. The other one didn't like me too much at all, ey'."

"I know. *El General* might have had a hand in getting that fool out of here too." Joker's mood suddenly turns serious. "You know what, though, that's the way it's supposed to be, homes. That's why he's *El Mero-Mero*. We should start calling him Benjamin Franklin, put his face on a hundred-dollar bill, ey'," he says, laughing out loud.

"That's a *firme* idea, homes! That's gonna' be my next piece, a big hundred-dollar bill with *EL General's* face right in the middle." El Davinci says as he smudges the top portion of his new piece, creating a hazy sky.

"Either way, I'm glad you're back down here, homes, I've been wanting some more of your ink, ey', although, I think I don't have any more space. Oh, snap!" Joker says suddenly, "I forgot to tell you, the Goose just pulled up. Let's hit the yard and clown the new fish." Joker's expression carries the enthusiasm only one truly gifted in the art of ridicule can possess.

"*Órale*. I remember when I first got here, shit, about twelve years ago now, and how you *vatos* messed with me when I got off the bus. Time to experience it from the other side, ey'." Now a thirty-year-old prison *veterano*, El DaVinci blows away the excess residue left on the paper.

"Are you done with your new piece, homeboy? Let me check it out," Joker says, reaching for the drawing.

"*Simón, limón.* I just finished it right now." El DaVinci relinquishes his artwork with a bit of anxiety. Even after all the compliments, all the favors, all the gifts he's received for his extraordinary ability, he still gets the butterflies whenever one of his pieces is up for criticism.

"Damn, *vato*, you're never gonna' stop hearing this, but you're one talented *artista*, homes. You're like a genius, ey', a straight-up Einstein or like that one *vato* in the wheelchair. You know who I'm talking about, right? That science *vato* who talks with a computer." Joker releases another bewildered whistle. "Seriously, homes, you can burn any artist out there. When they hear about you on the outside, homes, you're gonna be big-time, homeboy, big time."

"I don't care about that, homes. I need to get out, ey'. I got too many wrongs I need to make right."

"I hear you, homes. It's just crazy, ey', it's like society imprisoning a real credit to society." Joker smiles, "Damn, that sounded *firme*, like it should be in a rap song or something."

El DaVinci laughs in agreement. "*Órale.*"

The two *vatos* stroll down the tier, making their way out towards the prison yard. The sun beats down as they snake their way through a crowd, once again segregated by the unyielding power of prison politics. They receive head nods, a show of respect, from each inmate they make eye contact. This simple non-verbal form of communication can carry a multitude of meanings depending on how it's given (or how it's perceived), from a simple greeting to an outright declaration of war.

The two inmates lean up against the perimeter fence, looking out towards the sand-beaten Grey Goose. The sun continues its relentless barrage as they hang their shirts over their shoulders, exposing their jailhouse tats like human art exhibits.

Joker, the taller and slimmer of the two and several years older, is covered with ink from his neck down to the soles of his feet. He slips on pitch-dark sunglasses. "Damn, homes. This heat is killing me. It feels like I'm getting shanked with a curling iron, ey'." Joker shoots up a murderous glare. "I'm never eating *chorizo* again, homes, now that I know what it feels like on the frying pan, my *grasa*'s leaking, homes." Joker wipes the sweat from his brow.

El DaVinci laughs hysterically.

Joker joins in. "That shit was funny, huh?"

"I'm not laughing because of that." El DaVinci places his hand on Joker's shoulder, "I'm laughing because you're never are eating chorizo again, homes!"

Joker stops laughing suddenly. "Wait, you saying that because I'm never getting out, homes?"

El DaVinci nods, "*Simón*."

"You're right, ey', I guess I am never eating chorizo again!" Joker breaks into a fit.

Several yards away, twelve men stand in the desert heat, restrained by chain leashes like a team of Alaskan sled dogs, except there's no snow around here, and the masters carry lethal weapons instead of whips.

"*Washa'*, check out the fresh fish, homes. That vato right there's gonna' crack for sure." Joker points out a pudgy, wide-eyed inmate emanating with fear. "Fresh bait for the sharks." He says, whistling and yelling out sexual innuendos.

"*Simón*, he looks like a straight momma's boy, ey'." El DaVinci says, forcing out a chuckle, knowing he was once a momma's boy, too. The thought only inflames the struggle raging within. He can never forget the day he pushed her away—a day that stings his soul still. "Ma', don't visit me anymore," Lenny had said to her, "Seeing you suffer like this is too hard for me. It shows weakness, ma', and I can't show weakness in here. I have to train my mind for the kind of life I'm gonna' have in here with hardcore prisoners."

"*Mijo, pero como me puedes decir esto*?" she said. "How can you ask me that? You're all I have, *no puedo hacerlo, mijo*. I can't do it. I'm going to be here for you for as long as it takes until you get out," she said.

"If you love me, ma', don't visit me, don't write me, don't look for me anymore. Let me do my time by myself, or else I'll die, ma'. *Me oyes*, do you hear me, I'll die." He knew she did it for him. She made the ultimate sacrifice when he never heard from her again.

"*Simón*, forty-year-old virgin, and shit," Joker says, releasing his signature high-pitched laugh.

El DaVinci smirks as he studies the others in the group, reminiscing how it felt when he was in their jumpsuits. He notices one man in particular who seems oblivious to his surroundings, where the others try to mask their fear with hardened faces. Slim but with an overly muscular neck, the man wears a constant smile accentuated by an emerging beard with a hairstyle swirled to the side.

El DaVinci shakes his head, "Check that fool out, ey'," he says, pointing the man out. "It looks like he don't know where he's at. I guess he'll learn the hard way like I did."

Oddly, the guards seem to ignore the man while the others catch a serious dose of verbal abuse for the slightest twitch.

"*Simón.* That *vato'll* learn the real hard way. You know what I'm saying." Joker says, squeezing his crotch.

"Damn, *paisan*, this is some scary-lookin' place, huh?" expresses the man as he elbows the inmate standing next to him. "Check out those guys over there," he says, "They look like they want to do terrible things to you, *paisan*."

"Chill out, man, people die in this place," whispers back the inmate from the corner of his mouth.

"Whoa, relax, *paisan*, show a little heart. You can't be afraid to grab your *cannolis* every once in a while," expresses the man as his expression turns serious, "Hey," he says whispering, "Seriously, if it comes to that, make sure you die on your feet like a man, and not on your knees like a mook." He tries to contain his laughter.

"Are you crazy or something, man?" whispers back the inmate.

"Yeah, I'm crazy," says the man. "I'm one crazy-ass, American-*Italiano*, and I'll chop your balls off and shove em' down your throat if you mess with me, got it."

"Sorry, I…I didn't mean anything by it," the inmate stutters back.

"Hey, relax, I'm just busting your balls, *paisan*."

Officers conduct a thorough search of the Goose as the new arrivals are reminded to remain silent with the crisp crackling of a stun gun.

"Anyways," continues the man, "I got them pearls of wisdom from this Mexican rapper I used to promote. He'd always quote this cat named Zapata, you know who I'm talking about, right? That Mexican fella with the big sombrero and thick mustache printed on practically every Mexican's T-shirt."

The inmate acknowledges with a subtle nod.

"He'd always say, I'd rather die on my feet like a man, than live the rest of my life on my knees like a slave. Now there's some wisdom for you, huh? Especially in a place like this," says the man known as Jimmy The Pit Santino (or just simply, The Pit)—a classic example of a fully assimilated first-generation born American. Though he's proud to have been born American, The Pit's cultural roots took hold long ago in a land he's never known. His parent's story is the same as the countless who have left their beloved homeland for a better life in a foreign country—a country known for its freedom and opportunity.

Vitto and Antonia emigrated from a little Italian province in their teens. They met and fell in love on the boat bound for Ellis Island.

Unfortunately, tragedy struck the young couple during the happiest time in their lives. Vitto Santino—Jimmy's biological father—met an untimely and freakish demise working the docks of New York when a two-ton shipping container broke free from a crane and fell one-hundred feet directly on top of him. He left his twenty-two-year-old wife, Antonia, widowed, pregnant, and alone in the city that never sleeps (or also known as the Big Apple).

Antonia had to leave her New York lifestyle, the only one she has ever known in this country, and moved to Los Angeles to live with her only other relative in the states. Even with a four-month baby bump, Antonia was still exotic and very beautiful. Her mesmerizing blue eyes attracted the attention of a small-time movie producer. The two fell in love and married quickly.

Jim Walker—the only father Jimmy has ever known—became extremely successful after several of his movies became major blockbusters. And because of his success, Jimmy grew up in the glitz and glamour of Hollywood. Even as a teen, he experienced all that Hollywood had to offer, mingling with famous actors, popular musicians, and CEO's of multi-million dollar companies. His stepfather tried to etch out a career for him in acting, but it wasn't for him. Jimmy, however, did display an aptitude for networking, and with his extraordinary social skills, accumulated powerful connections. He smooth-talked a few of them to invest in a music label of his own making, and under his leadership as CEO, Santino Corleone Records became ultra-successful.

Prison in the early morning hours transmits an eerie frequency, like an empty house yet full of ghosts imprisoned in a limbo of regret. El DaVinci sits on his bunk hunched over, fixated on the glow coming from the candle of the Virgen De Guadalupe. The flame projects a distorted figure on the wall that seems to dance with each flicker. He keeps an ear open for Joker's loud and irritating snore. As the *carnal* takes a nasal breath, El DaVinci lets his guard down.

"I'm sorry, *pa'*. I'm sorry I turned out to be such a disappointment," The sound of El DaVinci's voice doesn't make it past the bars of his cell. As quietly as he can, he reaches for his metal box and pulls out a red charcoal pencil. He stares at it, conjuring up images that involve his mother—a single red rose he picked from her garden to give to Miriam but was too shy to do it—her favorite shade of lipstick that she always wore before for his father's soccer games—the blood left on her hands when she corralled his father's head on the field that terrible day.

El Davinci flips through his sketch pad to an empty page. He closes his eyes, seeking out the perfect image—one that'll express what he's feeling inside. It appears suddenly, big, bold, and painfully beautiful. His eyes open, and his hand begins outlining a shape. The tip of the red charcoal moves with the fluidity of a gentle stream. Several minutes later, a heart takes shape, not the typical one encapsulating the names of young lovers with the promise of forever, but an actual, anatomical heart. Even in the candle's low flickering glow, he sketches it textbook, complete with ventricles. He adds a master's touch by weaving in a spiderweb of bluish-green capillaries, a true testament to Leonardo da Vinci himself.

El DaVinci then reaches for a brown charcoal pencil and imprisons the heart with a wreath of thorns. He stabs the heart in various places, adding droplets of dark crimson where the prickly spines penetrate. The paper softens as the blood turns to a lively red from the emotion that rolled off his cheek. He dabs the translucent droplet, creating a watercolor effect.

"That's for you, *jefita*, a stinging thorn in my heart for every time I've hurt your sacred heart." He closes his sketch pad and allows the anguish to consume him. The wetness on his cheeks reminds him he's still alive, and that hopefully, there's time.

Four days pass, and Jimmy happens to stroll right into the maximum-security wing, escorted by a pair of correctional officers. They usher him through the bottom tier towards a single-man cell.

"*Washa'*, who does that *vato* think he is, strolling down the block like his *caca* don't stink!" exclaims Joker.

"*Simón*. That's the *vato* from the other day," says El DaVinci. They lean against the third tier railing looking down. Jimmy glances up as he passes.

"*Washa'!*" Joker's eyebrows curve with surprise. "They're giving that *vato* a bottom cell! Who the hell is this fool, the Godfather!?!"

"He must have some serious *clecha*, homes. Lucky *vato*! He don't have to deal with your snoring ass all night!" El DaVinci turns and walks back into his cell.

"I know, huh. It wakes me up sometimes, too. *Serio, pedo*, homes, I gotta' find out who this *vato* is, *al rato*." Joker disappears down the hall like a bee in a honeycomb.

El DaVinci scans through his book collection, all given to him as tokens of appreciation. He glances over several titles—Mexico's Great

Muralists, Art of the Renaissance, Leonardo da Vinci, Michelangelo's Sistine Chapel. "Michelangelo's Sistine Chapel it is," he says and sprawls out on his bunk with his book in hand—every page illustrated with full-blown frescos. El DaVinci sits with his back against the wall, admiring *The Creation of Adam*, the famous painting portraying The Creator reaching out ready to impart Adam with a soul. He lowers the book and notices for the first time how blank the walls in his cell are. He glances up at the ceiling, then at the book, and then at the walls again, and then back at the book. An idea formulates.

"*Washa*', I'll turn this cell into my own Sistine Chapel, ey'!" A rush of excitement hits him like the asteroid that killed off the dinosaurs. "I'll even have Joker help out. Even Michelangelo had his assistants." He reaches in his bookshelf and pulls out a wooden box cleverly painted to look like an ordinary book. It serves as his keep-safe, concealing various items of value—new playing cards, sealed cigarette boxes, green raffle-like tickets, all acceptable forms of currency in the bartering economy of prison.

El DaVinci has amassed what you could call a small fortune from his tattooing, and he makes sure to save a portion for friends in need. He's learned long ago money can never out value friendship, especially in prison, where a friend can end up saving your life. The other portion he reserves for his vice—art supplies. Whenever he gets the inclination to work with a new medium or to replenish a charcoal pencil or sketch pad, the man to see is none other than Freddie The Magic Man Johnson.

The Magic Man has a reputation for making the most difficult to obtain items appear on your bunk when you least expect it, like magic. Not exactly what you would expect of a hardcore prison veteran—a balding, middle-aged man of average height with a pudgy belly, and most taboo of all, an out-of-closet homosexual. Constant ridicule sprinkled with beat downs can be everyday life for an inmate with unusual sexual preferences, but because of the powerful connections he's accumulated over the years, The Magic Man enjoys the kind of respect and status on the inside that no amount of money can buy for him on the outside. He has become so accustomed to prison life that he has developed a dependency on it.

The Magic Man should have been granted parole five years ago, but year after year, he assures his preferred way of life by threatening the members of the parole board. Though no strangers to such occupational hazards, the only difference when it comes to The Magic Man is that his threats come with very real and very personal information (home addresses, names of living relatives, social security numbers, and the like). He was even brazen enough to have a bouquet of red roses delivered to the residence of a female parole board member, with a note thanking her for denying his release. Like El DaVinci, The Magic Man isn't affiliated with any prison gang and yet protected by all. Within the walls of the prison, he's a bona fide Donald Trump, but on the outside, he's just another Joe Shmoe.

El DaVinci strolls the tiers searching for this highly sought-after inmate. He finds him on the fourth tier with his companion, an attractive twenty-three-year-old serving a twenty-five-year bit for bludgeoning a man to death over a homosexual insult.

"*Q-vo*, Magic Man, I need to get my hands on some goods, ey'," says El Davinci

"Hey, hey, *qué pasa mi amigo*." For some unknown reason, The Magic Man is always compelled to practice his limited Spanish with El DaVinci. "Anything for the best tattoo artist in the world. Are you gonna' finally put in an order for a hot *chica*," he says, batting his eyebrows, "Or something a little more exotic?"

"Nah', homes, nothing like that, ey', but check it out, I do need something a little heavier than usual, and to tell you the truth, I'm not sure you can deliver." El DaVinci knows how to play into The Magic Man's ego.

"Oh, come on now, my young Chicano friend, you should know me better than that, what'd ya' have in mind, *amigo*?" His eyes widen, "You have me, *muy in-tere-sado*."

"Well, just a few paintbrushes, some oils, and…"

The Magic Man cuts him off, "What! That's it, oils and paintbrushes? You had me going there for a minute, *amigo*."

"You didn't let me finish, ey'," El DaVinci says, smiling, "And a few cans of spray paint."

"Whoa!" The magic man raises his hands. "You know those are flammable, right! I can smuggle in things no one else can, I can even arrange an occasional rendezvous with a good-looking lady or guy, but spray cans, *amigo*. That's damn near impossible. You know the warden will go flippin' *loco* if he were to find out."

"Don't worry about him, homes," responds El DaVinci. "I got him covered, ey'. Can you do it or not, I mean, you are the Magic Man, *qué no*?"

"Well, *amigo*, I do love a challenge, but you're asking a lot." He stops to ponder for a moment. "Let me see what I can do. And, uh, you already know if anyone were to ask about…"

"Whoa, come on now, Magic Man," El Davinci cuts him off, "You gotta' take it there, homes? You know me better than that, too, ey'."

"My bad, *amigo*. We'll discuss price, if and when I get the goods."

Four men make their way up the stairs towards El DaVinci's cell. *Pelon* and *El Gallo* position themselves just outside, crossing their muscular arms like a pair of secret service agents. *El General* enters, followed by Jimmy The Pit.

El Davinci stands and greets the leader of the *carnales* with an embrace. He quickly eyes Jimmy.

"*Qué onda,* Villa, to what do I owe this unexpected visit?"

"No need for that, homes," says El General, "This *paisan* right here knows who I am."

El DaVinci shoots him a perplexed look, his eyes express, *he must be someone important to know that.*

El General places his hand on Jimmy's shoulder. "Lenny, this is man right here, is a good friend of mine, a man of many powerful connections, Jimmy Santino is his name, but he's known as The Pit. He runs the music label that produced one of my nephews on the outs." *El General* steps aside. "The Pit came down from E-block just to meet you."

El General places his hand on El DaVinci's shoulder. "Jimmy, this *vato* right here is also a good friend of mine, Lenny Santiago is his name, but in here he's know as El DaVinci. And I know I already told you, but I'll tell you again, he's the most *firme* tattoo artist you'll ever see in your life. His hands are a straight gift from God, homes. *Serio*, check it out." *El General* displays the tattoo on the inner portion of his forearm and kisses it. "He got down on this portrait of my little girl."

El DaVinci and The Pit, two men with growing reputations, shake hands for the first time, reminiscent of Pancho Villa and Emiliano Zapata shaking hands in the capitol at the end of the Mexican revolution.

"Well, I'm happy to meet this man. So, El DaVinci, huh? You have quite a reputation, *paisan*. I hear your name mentioned everywhere I go in this prison." Their hands maintain a firm hold. "A good strong handshake, I like that. You can tell a lot about a man by the way he shakes your hand," expresses The Pit.

"*Simón*? What's it telling you right now, ey'?

"It tells me you're confident in your abilities, *paisan*." They maintain eye contact.

"*Órale*. So The Pit, huh? You must be pretty big-time, homes, to have *El General* introduce you himself."

"Oh, I don't know if you can call me big-time just yet, *paisan*, but as the man said, I do have some big-time connections in my back pocket. If you know what I mean." He gestures towards *El General*.

"*Órale,* I do. Good friends are hard to find, even harder to keep, ey'."

"You got that right, *paisan.*"

"Well, it's *firme* to meet you, homes, what can I do for you?"

The Pit moves towards several sketch pads lying on a small desk.

"May I take a look?"

"*Simón.* Be my guest."

The Pit picks one up and opens it. "These you?" he asks with a bit of skepticism.

"*Simón.*"

"Damn *Paisan*, these sketches are impressive!" He flips through several pages and stops on one in particular. That's one badass Koi," says The Pit. "You did this for someone in the Yakuza organization, didn't you?"

El DaVinci nods, "*Simón*, how'd you know that?"

"I've had dealings with them in the past. No doubt the real deal. This Koi represents loyalty, *paisan*, you can tell by the color patterns. The rumors about you must be true," The Pit says, "They only get tattoos from a true master."

"Damn, homes, you know your stuff, ey', I did that up at Corcoran several years back," El DaVinci says, "That *vato* was straight-up gangster, ey'. I learned the art of *Irezumi* for him. You've heard of that, right? That crazy Japanese tattooing technique. *Chalé*, that goes way back, I'm talking ancient times, homes."

"That's crazy, *paisan*! I heard it takes years to learn under a master. How'd you learn it in here?" he asks.

"From a book, homes." El DaVinci reaches in his bookcase and pulls out a book titled, *Irezumi: An Ancient Art Form.* This is might sound trippy, ey', but it only took me eight months to master."

The Pit shoots him a perplexed look, "Come on, seriously?"

Serio, homes. I practiced every day. It's crazy what you can learn when you got nothing but time."

"Get outta' here! No way it only took you eight months to master, and from this book," The Pit shakes his head. "Please don't take me for an assole'!" he says, gesturing with his hands.

"*Serio, homes*, I wouldn't bullshit you, ey'. He got everything I needed. He even brought me a *vato* to practice on." El DaVinci says with a laugh. "I can tell you that *vato* took a hell of a lot of pain, homes, but it only took me his upper torso to get good. It's like surgery. You gotta be precise, homes, precise."

"No way, *paisan*!" The Pit glances at *El General* in amazement.

"He's for real, homes," responds the leader of the *carnales*. "I transferred to Corcoran for a few days to see how it came out. I'll say we have a strong association with the Yakuza because of that tattoo. It covered his whole back, homes. They are a committed people," he says.

The Pit nods, "That they are, *paisan*. It must hurt like hell."

"It ain't too bad in the right hands, homes." El DaVinci says, "It's all about the motion, you gotta' find the right rhythm."

"Well, damn, *paisan*, it seems I found the man I've been looking for." He closes the sketch pad and places it back on the desk. "I think we might be able to help each other out," The Pit says.

"*Simón*? What do you have in mind, ey'?"

"I can get the word out, *paisan*, help spread your reputation way beyond these walls. I'm talking worldwide, my friend."

"That sounds *firme*' homes, but what good will that do for me in here?"

"If all the talk about your skills are true, which I'm sure they are, people will come for your ink, no matter where you are. Shit, *paisan*, look at me, I'm in this cellblock with killers so that I could meet you."

"Yeah, but the only way anyone's gonna' see me is if they commit a 187, homes."

"You forget, *paisan*. I came to see you, and I'm gettin' out in six months. I'm not supposed to be in this cell block, but here I am. Nothing's impossible with money and influence," The Pit says, rubbing

202

his thumb and index finger together in a circular motion. "And believe me, Jimmy 'The Pit' Santino has friends with more money than you can imagine."

"*Órale*! You what, know, I'm curious ey', why do people call you The Pit?"

"It ain't because of my muscular neck, *paisan*, I can tell you that. I got my name because when I set out to do something, I put a lockjaw on that shit, like a pit bull in the ring."

"*Órale*, I like that," responds El DaVinci.

"What about you, why do people call you El Davinci?"

"I'm guilty of that," answers *El General*. "It's because he wields a tattoo gun like Leonardo da Vinci wields a paintbrush," he says, nodding at the tattoo artist.

"That's good enough for me, *paisan*."

You know what, homes?" says El Davinci. "I had you pegged all wrong, ey'. When I first saw you, I thought you were just another hard-headed *vato* about to learn prison life the hard way, homes. I was wrong, ey'. You know wassup', homes."

"No worries, *paisan*. Most people don't know to take me seriously at first. It must be because of this handsome mug." The Pit says, caressing his cheeks with the back of his palm, "But once you get to know me, you know to take me as serious as a fuckin' heart attack."

"*Órale*, homes. So, where's all this heading, ey'? What do you want from me?"

"Isn't it obvious, *paisan*? I want you to do what you do best, my friend. I want your ink."

"A tat? Is that all? No problem, homes. Just say when and where you want it."

"No disrespect, *paisan*, but it ain't gonna' be that easy. I haven't gotten ink because' I haven't found the person with the right skill set. I was considering Mr. Cartoon, he did 50 cent's tat, but now it's you. It's crazy, *paisan*, I had to come to the maximum-security wing to find the man I was looking for."

"*Órale!*" responds El DaVinci, "Didn't you know? Some of the most talented *vatos* are all locked up, homes. Don't trip, ey'. I got you. It'll be my honor. When do you wanna' start?"

The Pit slips off his shirt, showing off his deceptively muscular physique. "There's no better time than the present. Think you can do half a sleeve for me, from my elbow to my shoulder," he says, pointing to his right arm.

"Half a sleeve, huh. Do you have something in mind?

"I'll leave that up to your creative genius, *paisan*, but it has to rep who I am, a proud, Italian-American."

An image immediately flashes in El DaVinci's mind. "You know what, homes, I just thought of something. Have you seen *The Godfather*?"

"Whoa, come on, *paisan*, that's my all-time favorite movie. That's like asking a Chinaman if he's ever seen, *Enter the Dragon*."

"*Órale*, my bad. I got this, then, homes." El DaVinci closes his eyes and preens his goatee, conceptualizing an image in his mind.

"Yeah, I got something real *firme* for you, homes, you want to hear it?"

"No thanks, *paisan,* I like surprises."

"*Órale*, then let's get this party started." El DaVinci begins with the preparations.

El General, who was sitting off to the side flipping through one of El DaVinci's sketch pads, stands. "Well then, homeboys, now that the deal's done, you'll have to excuse me. I got some business to take care of. Oh, and Jimmy," El General places his hand on The Pit's shoulder. "Don't forget about our arrangement. I told you he's the real deal."

"Don't worry, *paisan*, I'm as good as my word. Just remember, I'm the best at what I do, you know that, but I'm not God, my friend. Your boy's gotta' be able to lay down some tracks. I'll produce him, but I can't do anything if his music don't sell."

El General nods and then turns towards El DaVinci. "And you, *vato*. Once again, it looks like your tattoos can advance the organization. Do what you do and make us proud, homes. I'm counting on you. And don't worry, I'll talk to the warden about those spray cans."

El General turns and walks out. Three members of the notorious prison gang stroll down the tier as inmates cut a path.

That's one serious man, *paisan*. I wouldn't want to let him down.

A feeling, similar to what he felt when he lost the poker game so many years ago, suddenly consumes El DaVinci. He shakes it away as he snaps his knuckles and slips on a pair of black latex gloves. With an old, dirty toothbrush, he scrubs the components of his prison-made tattoo machine. The Pit sits cross-legged on the floor as El Davinci settles down on the bottom bunk. He pulls out a black bandana and blindfolds himself.

"What's up with that, homes, you don't like needles or something?" El DaVinci asks.

"No, nothin' like that, *paisan*, as I said, I just like surprises."

"*Órale*. Are you gonna' do that every time, homes?"

"Absolutely, *paisan*, I don't want to see it until it's complete."

"*Órale*, I get it. As I said, too, homes, I'm gonna' get down on this for you, so don't even trip!" He rests The Pit's arm on a pillow on his lap and wipes it with a damp cloth.

"Alright, homes, *listo*?" El DaVinci says, switching on his tattoo gun.

"Ready when you are, *paisan*."

"Here we go, homes." El DaVinci dabs the needle into a jar of black ink and begins tattooing The Pit's arm. His hand vibrates as he outlines a shape.

Three month and a half later, El DaVinci completes the final phase of shading. He wipes the sweat from his brow and switches off the prison-made tattoo gun. It's astonishing the kind of artistry a simple pen casing, guitar string, and a battery pack from a dismantled radio can produce.

"*Órale*, that should do it, homes." El DaVinci directs The Pit to the faucet. "My bad for taking so long, homes. I had to wait for it to heal so I could go over it a few more times, that way the ink'll stay in permanently. What can I say, I don't have access to the best equipment in here."

"We'll have to fix that, *paisan*," The Pit says as he douses his arm with lukewarm water. It's a slight reprieve from the residual burning effect. "I can't wait to see it, *paisan*."

El DaVinci dabs the tattoo dry with a towel and squeezes Neosporin onto his finger, "Apply a little of this every day so that it can heal faster," and then he rubs it on The Pit's arms.

"*Órale*, it's ready. Check it out, tell me what you think." El DaVinci slips off his latex gloves and hands The Pit a shaving mirror.

"I have to tell you, *paisan*, it was hard as hell not looking at it these past months. I'm glad *EL General,* sent one of his men to bandage up my arm every day. I held out because I wanted to see it for the first time in all its splendor. Man, you got my heart pumping, *paisan*. I think I'm excited."

Jimmy reaches for the mirror and begins examining his arm. He angles the mirror this way and that, soaking up every detail of his new tattoo.

El Davinci sits patiently waiting for his critique, but his mind moves with the anxiety of a child at the dentist office.

Five agonizing minutes later, The Pit finally speaks.

"Man, *paisan*. This right here," he pauses to shake his head, "Is mindblowing! I'm gonna' put your name on the map, my friend."

"So, you like it then?" El Davinci says with an exhale of relief. "You had me going for a minute, homes."

"Are you kidding me? Are you kidding me right now?" The Pit puts on his best Italian accent and gestures with his hands. "I love it! Bada' bing, bada' boom!"

The Pit's tattoo displays a vintage 1930 Ford Model A—the kind old school gangsters like John Dillinger used as getaway cars. The details on the car are as exquisite as the concept. EL DaVinci even tattooed a pit bull for the hood ornament. The Model A isn't even the best of it. A Perfect likeness of The Pit stands on the car's running board sporting a feather in his Fedora-style hat. He glares at you with intensity in his eyes as his Tommy gun spits out fire. You can even make out the forty-five caliber casings bouncing off of the sleeve of his incredibly detailed pinstripe suit.

"I had no doubt you were gonna' do me badass tattoo, but this surpasses all my expectations, *paisan*." He walks over to El DaVinci and kisses him on both cheeks.

"*Órale*, homes, relax with that, ey', I don't want these *vatos* getting the wrong impression. I'm glad you like it, though."

"Oh, hell yes, *mi amigo*, I like it very much. You can say I owe you one big-ass solid for this, my friend and Jimmy The Pit Santino always returns a favor. You can take that to the bank." He say, shaking El DaVinci's hand.

The Pit's release arrives faster than expected. He strolls out of the maximum-security wing, much like he did when he arrived—with a big smile on his face

"*Al rato*, Pit. Don't forget about me when you're sippin' on Dom Perignon, homes."

"Are you kidding me, *paisan*? How can I forget about El Davinci, the best damn tattoo artist in the freakin' world? Plus, I got your ink on my arm, so don't you worry, my friend. We'll see each other again real soon." With a nod of his head, The Pit heads out of the cellblock.

El DaVinci hangs on the rail, watching The Pit walk away. He turns and enters his cell. His eyes widen when he finds a package lying on his bunk.

"What the!" Mystified, he quickly looks out of his cell in every direction. "*Chalé*, I was just in here a minute ago." He tears open the oddly-shaped package and finds several new paintbrushes and some oils. "*Órale*, you are the magic man, homes." He reads the note on the package. *You were right, amigo. I couldn't acquire the spray cans you wanted, well, sort of. Talk to the warden about it.*

P.S. you owe me a tattoo, amigo.

El DaVinci folds the note and places it in one of his books. "Talk the warden? Why do I have to talk to the warden?"

Three weeks later, El DaVinci is escorted to the warden's office by Deputy Taylor, a respected deputy of the cell block.

"Hey Santiago, my kid loved the Donald Duck drawing you did for him. Thanks for that." He looks around and then reaches in his pocket. "Here's a little token of my appreciation. Don't tell anyone," he says, handing El DaVinci a Snicker's Bar."

"*Órale*, thank you, Taylor. I've been craving some chocolate."

You know, we're gonna' miss you around here."

"Miss me? What do you mean, Taylor?"

"The warden will explain." The deputy opens the door and ushers him into the office.

"Ah, inmate Santiago, so good of you to stop by."

"*Qué pasa*, Warden Goldstein, I heard you might be holding something for me."

"Oh, is that so? Are you referring to the items that were confiscated by my deputies several weeks back? The kind that break some serious regulations. You know how things work around here, inmate Santiago. I know what to allow and what not to allow into my facility, even if you do have a man like *Villa* vouching for you. Don't think for one second I don't know absolutely everything that goes on in this prison, because you would be sadly mistaken. And since we're on the subject, why in God's name would you want spray paint in here anyways."

"I didn't mean any disrespect. I just wanted to turn the walls of my cell into an art gallery, that's all."

"Well, that's highly prohibited, Inmate Santiago. Oils are one thing, I can appreciate the classic style, which is why I allowed you to paint one of your walls, but what do you think will happen if I allow every inmate in here to decorate their walls with spray paint? This place will end up looking like the New York Subway, with graffiti all over the damn place."

"With all due respect, Warden Goldstein, I just want to create art, that's all. You have my word, ey', no graffiti."

"You'll have to excuse me if I don't take the word of a convicted felon all too seriously," The warden says with sarcasm resonating in his smirk. "Look, I genuinely like you, Inmate Santiago. I can't say that about the majority of the inmates in here. You speak to me with respect, and I like that, not to mention you are one hell of an artist. Truth be told, I'd be inclined to grant your request, but unfortunately, you're getting transferred out in a few weeks."

The warden shuffles through some papers and begins writing something down. "What I will do for you is speak to the warden at the facility you'll be transferring. It so happens I know the man well, and I have to say, he's a rather ambitious man. We've been doing a lot of communicating lately. I'll see if he's open to the idea. That's the best I can do. Now, the reason I called you into my office is to inform you that I had some guests over at my home recently, people of significant political influence."

"*Simón*, what's that got to do with me, ey'?"

"Funny you should ask. Needless to say, they were very convincing. It seems that we're getting a significant endowment to fund certain programs I've been wanting to institute in here for some time now but never had the financial backing, until now that is, and it's all thanks to you."

"What do you mean?" El Davinci shoots the warden a curious look, "What did I do?"

"Well, the deal is, as long as I allow you to tattoo on a more legitimate basis, with proper supervision, I'll get the funds I require. Or I should say, we'll get the funds. Since you'll be transferring soon, the warden at Donovan will also get a significant portion of the proceeds for his facility. I've already spoken to him about it, and he's open to the idea. As I said, he's an ambitious man."

"*Órale*, but I still don't know what this has to do with me. I didn't ask for any of this, I just wanted to decorate my cell with art," says El DaVinci.

"Maybe this will enlighten you. One of those guests asked me personally to hand-deliver this message to you." The warden hands El DaVinci a note. It reads,

Like I said, paisan, I know some pretty powerful people. Here's to keeping my word. Because of an agreement I made with the warden, I have to keep your identity a secret from the public, but be expecting visits from some high-profile guests. The word's already getting around, my friend, discretely, that is. I hope you like your new equipment. Good luck at Donovan.

-The Pit

Before you go, Mr. Santiago. Some equipment was delivered to this facility. Tattooing equipment I believe, and top of the line from what I understand. I'll make sure it gets transferred with you along with the other items. That's it. You may leave now."

"*Órale*, thank you, Warden Goldstein." El DaVinci walks out of the office with a strange feeling inside, as if he was granted a wish he didn't know he wished for.

Present

"Nice! So, The Pit had that much influence, huh? He got you this equipment and secretly spread your reputation throughout the celebrity elite?" Lisa asks, amazed.

"*Simón*. That *vato* has a serious mouthpiece. He can straight up sell scripture to a pastor, ey'."

"Did ever you see him again?" asks Lisa.

"Check this out, *mija*, the day before I got transferred, the Warden sent for me again. This time, three important-looking *vatos* were waiting in his office. I didn't recognize any of them at first, ey', because they were all clean-cut and professional looking. I thought they were lawyers or something because of their suits, and whenever a lawyer comes to see you in prison, it's usually to give you bad news. So, this clean-cut *vato* walks right up to me and kisses me on both cheeks. That's when I realized it was him, The Pit. He told me he had a proposition for me and handed me some letters."

"What were they about?" Lisa asks.

El DaVinci points to them on the wall. Scott zooms in. The letter head's read, Nike Graphic Studios, Walt Disney Animation Studios, Google Designs.

"They're Job offers, ey'. He told me I have a future waiting for me whenever I get out," he pauses, "I mean, if I get out."

Lisa nods her head. "Geez, those are major companies. The Pit does have a serious mouthpiece, doesn't he?"

"*Simón*. He's got *clecha*, alright. That's how I came to tattoo in here, like a career or something. Beats the hell out of making license plates."

"And that's how celebs like Drake and Kobe Bryant were able to get your ink and keep it low key," Lisa says.

"I guess so. Life's a trip sometimes, *qué no?*"

"You know what, it really is. Your story reminds me when I first started out in this business. People used to tell me that I had to sleep with the right people to make it in show business. Lucky for me, I didn't have to do that. I found the right connection early on. This man took me under his wing, showed me how to move up in the industry, and not to compromise. I won't mention his name, but he knows who he is." Lisa blows a kiss into the camera. "I want him to know how much I appreciate his help throughout my career. I'll always love my dad, but I have a special place in my heart for him, too."

The sound technician's assistant notices the director wiping his eyes. "You ok, boss?"

"What are you looking at, son? Yeah, she's talking about me alright, but don't you go flapping your gums about it, or it'll be your little ass!" the director says.

"You know, It's pretty amazing how friendships can make or break you. As the saying goes, tell me who your friends are, and I'll tell you who you are'," Lisa says.

"*Simón*, one good connection can change your life, just like one bad one can send your life in a downward spiral."

"I agree. You know, you can take this opportunity to thank the Pit if you want," says Lisa.

El Davinci remains silent, shading in Diego's tattoo. "He already knows how I feel, but you know what, I do want to say something to someone very special to me, someone I love, someone I've hurt."

"Really? Who?"

"My one real connection to happiness in this life, my *jefita*."

"You mean your mother, what happened?"

"I hate to admit this, ey', but I pushed her away. Like I said, the dumb shit you do when you're young. Back then, I couldn't bear seeing her suffer because of what I did. Every time I looked in her eyes, it reminded me how much I messed things up."

"Wow! I'm sorry to interrupt, but we share too many crazy coincidences. I did the same thing with my mother, well, sort of. I pushed her away because she remarried after my father died. She did it ten years after he died, but I couldn't let it go. Every time I would see them together, all I felt was that she was betraying my papa's memory. Now I realize I was wrong. Goodness, this is all just too strange. I'm sorry for interrupting. So, what do you want to say to her?" asks Lisa.

El DaVinci turns and faces the camera. "Dolores Guadalupe Santiago, if you're watching, I want you to know, you still have a son, and I haven't stopped loving you. I've missed you every day since I pushed you away. Wherever you are, I want you to know, I'm here, waiting for you if you ever want to come look for me."

Lisa clears her throat. "That was sweet. Well, it looks like we're finally down to my last question, and I'm sure it'll probably be the most difficult for you to answer. I hope you don't mind."

"*Chalé, mija,* at this point, I revealed my whole life story, *ey'.*"

"Almost," Lisa says, peering into the camera. "I'm sure our viewers are interested, as am I, in knowing how someone with your personality and artistic talent ended up in prison?"

"*Órale,* I knew this was coming. I've been dreading it ever since I agreed to this interview. It looks like you saved the best for last, *qué no?*" He squirts antiseptic onto Diego's back and wipes the tattoo clean. He dips the needle into the ink and then pauses. "You know, when I was a youngster, I didn't care too much about learning things the hard way. Funny thing is, I do now. Life has a funny of teaching us these little lessons." El DaVinci steps on the footswitch and continues tattooing.

Her eyes—those eyes of despair that have been haunting him ever since—flash in his mind as that night rewinds like an old, discarded VHS tape ready to be played over again.

XIII. Redemption

*F*lashback. *"Mijo,* I have to work a double shift tonight,"
Dolores says, running her fingers through her son's
hair—misshapen from an all-nighter with the pillow. Lenny
stirs and squints up at his mother through sleepy eyes.

"Por Favor mijito, don't get into any trouble while I'm gone."

"Ay, ma', frustrated with her usual plea, Lenny turns away. "Why do
you always tell me that, *no soy un pendejo,* you know," he says, taking
an angry breath. "I won't mess up, ok, stop worrying about me so
much!"

"I can't. I'm your mother. It's my responsibility to worry for you.
Por Favor, mijo, promise me, *perdimos a tú papi,* I can't lose you too."

Even though she lost her husband five years back, it still grips
Dolores's heart whenever his memory encroaches her thoughts, which
seems to be happening lately. Something as simple as a melody, a whiff
of Jovan Musk cologne, an unexpected glance at his soccer jersey still
hanging in the closet, can bring it all back, the fond memories followed
by a scourge of pain.

The sentiment in her voice softens Lenny's heart. He takes a deep
breath and turns to face her. *"Ma',* I'm sorry. Don't worry, ok," his
tone now gentle, "You'll never lose me, I won't get into trouble, *te*

prometo." He kicks off his blanket, the one his father got for him at the Tijuana border because he liked the Aztec legend it represented—the image of *Popocatepetl* carrying the dead body of his beloved *Iztaccihuatl* up the mountain, a work of art woven onto fabric.

"*Gracias mijo,* you don't know how hard it is for me to leave you all alone, *todo el santo dia. Me preocupo mucho por ti.*" Dolores fights back the tears and sighs in relief instead.

Lenny puts on a plain white tee, oversized black Dickie shorts, white knee-high socks, and black Coaster house slippers. He escorts his mother to the front door to see her off, as has been his tradition on weekends for over a year now. Their bond has remained strong, even through this turbulent time in his life, a time when a teenager tends to rebel against authority, especially parents (and then add the lack of a father figure to that).

Dolores kisses Lenny on the forehead, gives him *La Bendición,* and walks out the front door. Fear tugs at her insides as she leaves her only son to fend off the temptations of the streets without anyone in his corner. She paces forward, towards the bus stop where she will be taken to a job where she is underappreciated, and on her feet for the next sixteen hours, just so that they can make ends meet.

Lenny leans against the door jamb of their little two-bedroom apartment, watching his heartbroken mother stroll away. He hasn't noticed, until this moment, how quickly she's aged, worn by their tragedy. He struggles to fight back the feeling bubbling up in his stomach as he recalls how lively and beautiful she looked when their family was whole.

Another memory invades, coaxing out hard-fought tears—his parents dancing lovingly in the kitchen, staring into each other's eyes without a worry in the world. It rips at his guts. Lenny jerks his body in an attempt to fight it off, but anger consumes him all the more. He slams the front door shut and dashes up towards his room.

Lenny has become quite adept at shifting his emotions, from utter sadness to uncontrollable rage in less than ten seconds flat. With heavy breaths, he acts out, reaching for his art portfolio and ripping out the pages. After a short release, calmness shifts back into gear. Lenny takes in the aftermath, eyeing his torn artwork all over the place. He takes several breaths and begins picking up the pieces—pieces of his childhood—pieces of his happiness—pieces of his soul. The sudden ring from the phone distracts his anguish, and he rushes towards his mother's room.

"Hello? This is the Santiago residence," he says, putting the phone to his ear.

"Yes, hello, is this Leonardo Santiago?" asks a muffled voice on the other end."

"Yeah, it's me," Lenny answers with apprehension. "Who's this?"

"This is the San Diego Police Department. We're contacting you because you have been identified as the prime suspect in a murder case. I have to inform you that you may not leave the country for any reason."

Wait! What the hell! Is this a joke! This was Lenny's immediate thought, but the voice on the other end sounds legit.

"Whoa! You must be *loco*, man," Lenny's heart races, "You have the wrong guy!"

"Ha! I got yo' punk-ass!" says the voice on the other end

Lenny lowers his head, letting out a long, slow sigh of relief. "Sterling, you asshole!"

"What up, sucka'!?! I had you scared like a little *chavalita*, didn't I!?!" Sterling says. "Check it out, I came up on a bottle of Captain Morgan from my brother, you down to get faded today?"

Lenny peers around the room, suddenly consumed by an eerie feeling, as if someone is listening. With his promise to his mother still fresh in his mind, he was about to reject Sterling's offer, but then his gaze stops dead on a picture of his father in his soccer uniform. The image pierces deep into Lenny's chest. The anguish comes flooding back.

"The hell with it, let's do it. I got a two-liter of coke to mix it with, cruise over," Lenny says, grinding his teeth.

"Cool, it's on like Donkey Kong, boy! I'll bring my PlayStation."

"Yeah, ok. What up with Art and Foo?" Lenny asks, "Are they coming, too."

"Nah', I already hit them up. They got something going on today. It's just you and me, bean dip."

"Whatever Hershey squirt." Lenny slams the phone down, inadvertently knocking down a picture frame from the wall. He picks the image up and stares at it—his mother looked so beautiful in her wedding gown, and his father looked clean-cut in his brown tux. "I'm sorry, *jefita*," he says, caressing the picture and placing it back on the wall, "But I can't handle it sometimes. I need something to help me forget."

Two-hours later, the doorbell sounds. "What up, Len!" Sterling holds up the bottle of spiced rum, the one with the Pirate on it. "Time to get faded'!" The young teens let loose like two freshly turned eighteen-year-olds cruising the Tijuana strip on a Saturday night.

"I bet I can take a bigger swig," wagers Sterling.

"Put your money where your mouth is, homeboy." Lenny slides the bottle across the kitchen table.

"Check this out." Sterling snatches up the bottle and takes an enormous swig. He coughs uncontrollably as the liquid burns his throat. Gimme' soda, quick!

Lenny releases a laugh from deep within his gut.

"Forget you, Len! Let me see you try and do better," Sterling snaps.

"Gimme' the bottle!" Lenny places the bottle to his mouth and tilts it up. He puts a herculean effort trying to subdue the burning in his throat, but his eyes completely water over anyway. The liquor prevails as he too begins coughing so hard, snot shoots out from his nostrils. Sterling

218

breaks into a fit as Lenny slams the bottle down on the table and wipes away the snot.

"Yeah, you won, Len, but you looked like a clown doing it."

"Forget you," Lenny says in between coughing fits, "Give me some of that soda!" He takes a drink from the 2-liter and puffs out his chest, "You ready for a throwdown." Again, they break into laughter. The camaraderie serves as a reprieve from Lenny's tormented heart (now succumbed by drunken euphoria).

Like a pair of lion cubs, they pounce on each other, knocking down furniture as they wrestle throughout the apartment. They stagger and sway as the alcohol takes control of their central nervous system.

"Damn, I'm buzzin' hard," Lenny says, trying to keep his gaze steady, but the room spins like a merry-go-round.

"Hell, ya! I'm tore up from the floor up!" Even though his balance is questionable, Sterling performs a perfect rendition of the running man dance craze.

"Hey Len, I dare you to call Miriam." Sterling zig-zags towards the kitchen, picks up the phone, and aims it at him.

"What for?" Lenny says, waving it away.

"Man, because you wanted to get in her panties since third grade. I still can't believe you didn't ask her out when you won those movie tickets, chicken!" Again, Sterling directs the phone towards Lenny. "You know, you're lucky Art got with Linda, or he would've snatched her away from you."

"Hell nah', she wouldn't have gotten with him. And she probably woulda' told me, no. I didn't want to look like a fool in front of the homies."

"You looked like a fool regardless," Sterling says.

"Man, if I wanted her, I woulda' had her."

"Yeah, right! You've always been scared to talk to her. You know what, you've always been scared to talk to any girl!" Sterling slams the phone down on the hook. "Remember when Maria and her friend hit us up during lunch. Her friend was all over you, and you didn't say anything to her. Look, Len, I'm gonna' ask you, real talk, you'll always be my boy no matter what, so be real with me, are you gay?"

"What'd you say!?!" Lenny rushes past him and picks the phone back up. "Forget you Sterl! You're always talking smack! You want me to talk to her, watch this!" Lenny punches in the musical tone—a familiar melody he's played many times only to hang up when he hears Miriam's sweet voice on the other end.

Like she always does, Miriam answers her little Hello Kitty telephone with a sweet, "Hello?" Expecting an immediate response, she gets only laughter in the background instead. "*Hola, quien habla*?" she says in a Spanish accent.

"Ah…hello?" Lenny tries to deepen the sound of his voice.

"Don't hide your voice, fool, just tell her who it is, Lenny," Sterling shouts in the background.

Flustered, Lenny quickly hangs up the phone. "*You* burned me out, punk!"

"See, I told you. You're scared to talk to her," Sterling says. "Look on the bright side, Len, now you have a reason to talk to her on Monday."

"Shut up, fool, and hook up the damn PlayStation." He says, shoving Sterling hard towards the tv.

"Like I said, chicken!" Sterling labors as he turns the large, cumbersome television set around, careful not to disrupt the makeshift antenna made from a twisted clothes hanger. He connects the audio and video cables and turns the knob to correct the auxiliary channel.

They play video games for hours before succumbing to a long slumber brought on by the alcohol's after-effects.

It takes several rings for Lenny to get up and stumble tiredly into the kitchen to answer the phone. "Hello," he says, the grogginess in his voice making him sound odd.

"*Hola, mijo, estas bien*? It sounds like you were sleeping."

"*Si, Mami*, I was taking a nap."

"*Mijo*, I called to tell you that I'm picking an extra shift tonight, that way I can have the next five days off. I promise we'll do something fun, just you and me. We'll go visit your *tios* in LA, and check out Hollywood, *que te parece?*"

"*Si, Mami*, sounds fun," Lenny says, genuinely meaning it.

"Ok, *mijo*, remember your promise, and please don't stay up too late. I love you."

I won't forget, I love you, too, *Mami*." Lenny hangs up the phone.

"Who was that?" Sterling asks.

"My *jefita*, she said she won't be back till' tomorrow morning."

"Damn, what time is it?" asks Sterling.

Lenny peers at the clock, "Damn, it's 8:00 already."

"What!?! It's Saturday night, too! Let's find something to get into." Sterling says, popping up to his feet and stretching out.

"I'm down, but what?"

"Do you have money, Len?" Sterling digs into his pockets.

"I got ten bucks my *jefita* left me."

"Cool." Sterling dumps a candy wrapper and an empty zig-zag dispenser on the table. "Cuz' I ain't got nothin'. At least we got enough for a couple of forties of Olde E with that ten spot. Time to go fishing."

"Fishing? I don't have any fishing poles," says Lenny.

"Not for fish, dummy, for alcohol. A forty of Olde E is like four bucks. It'll bring our fade back real quick."

"A forty of Olde E, huh?" Lenny eyes the cash his mother left for him on the entry table and then looks up at the clock. *Eight hours until she gets home*, he smiles at the thought. "*Órale*, Let's do it! We can hit up Hahn's down the street," he says with an uncomfortableness in his gut.

An occasional lowrider cruises down the block blaring, *La Raza*, by Kid Frost as the teenagers stroll down Logan Avenue. Mr. Hahn, a Chinese immigrant, has lived in the Mexican dominated community for over ten years. His liquor store has been the target of arson, multiple armed-robberies, a murder in the parking lot, and is the most popular spot in the neighborhood for beer runs. Throughout all the adversity, though, Mr. Hahn has kept his store open year after year. The locals have come to respect his tenacity and refer to him affectionately as, "*El Pinche Chino*."

Sterling and Lenny creep in the alleyway behind the liquor store keeping in shadows, like Pancho Villa and his band of revolutionaries before a midnight raid. They lurk in the darkness, waiting for a patron to score them some beer. They don't have to wait very long. A Mexican cowboy pulls into the parking lot with his lifted Dodge truck blaring *música Ranchera*. The accordion rips a catchy tune accompanied by vocals by, *Los Tigres Del Norte*.

"Go ask that Mexican cowboy," Sterling says, handing Lenny the money.

"What!?! Why me!?! I thought you were going to do it. That's why I gave you the money.

"Because he's Mexican, fool," Sterling says.

"That don't mean anything, you know Spanish, too!"

"Just go ask him, Len, damn it!" Sterling groans with frustration.

"Fine!" Lenny snatches the money from Sterling's hand. The cowboy steps down from his truck and straightens his Stetson hat.

"Hey?" Lenny approaches as the cowboy he's dusting off his green, alligator-skin boots, "Can you buy me two forties of Olde English?"

The cowboy studies the teen for a moment. "Ju' say ol enlish, huh?" He says in his thick accent, "Gimme' da' moonie'."

Lenny hands over the cash. Within several minutes, the cowboy emerges from the store carrying two little brown bags with bottle caps peeking out. He hands them to Lenny along with the change.

"*Gracias*. You can keep the change," Lenny says.

"No *gracias*. I no need it." the cowboy says, opening a brand new pack of Marlboro cigarettes. "*Oye,* little *vato*, ju' be careful, ey'. *La luna está llena*," he says, pointing up at the perfect pearl of a moon in the night sky, "Full moon, *muy peligroso*, bery' dangerous." He nods and pulls himself up into his truck. He reverses out into the street with his *Rancheras* blaring.

Lenny peers around nervously and then rushes back into the darkness of the alley.

"Hell yeah, Len, let's take em' to the dome!" The bottles hiss as they twist open the caps. Lenny takes the first swig. Though cold, the liquid burns going down his throat. In less than a minute, the teenagers empty the bottles.

"*Damn*! Brain freeze!" Lenny says massaging his temples

"That's what I'm talking bout', boy, I got my buzz going again!" exclaims Sterling.

"Hell yeah, me, too."

"Let's go look for some honeys or something," Sterling says, peering around the corner, scheming for a means to cruise the boulevard.

"I'm down to kick it with some *heinas*." Lenny chucks the bottle down the alley. It shatters in the darkness.

"Yeah, whatever. Just don't freeze up when you have to talk, like always." Sterling's attention diverts when he hears a 1979 Buick Regal pulling into the parking lot blaring, *heartbreaker* by Zapp and Roger. A man quickly hops out and dashes into the liquor store, leaving the car running.

Sterling stares into the car, "Oh shit, I can't believe it, nobody's inside, and he left it on! Let's go, Len, hurry!" Sterling dashes towards the Regal and jumps into the driver's seat. Lenny stands frozen, caught off guard by the situation. He snaps into action as Sterling quickly shifts the car into reverse. Lenny pulls open the passenger-side door as the car's moving backward and hops inside.

Sterling shifts the car into drive, and the Regal bounces over the curb and screeches down the street. The owner darts out of Hahn's and draws out a chrome-plated .32 caliber revolver. He begins to squeeze the trigger but thinks better of it. Instead, he pulls out some change and rushes towards the payphone, dialing 911.

"Oh shit! Oh shit! We jacked a car! We jacked a freakin' car!" Lenny says, feeling more alive than he has in a long time.

"Hell yeah, we did! Now we can scope out the honeys in style. This low-low is sick!" Sterling says.

They cruise the neighborhood, sticking to side streets and locations where the cops are less likely to patrol. They hit several small neighborhood parks where transients camp in their makeshift tents. They pass by Arthur's pad, but it's as dark and empty as the night. They cruise by Foo's, but his house is void of any life.

At 11:57 p.m., Sterling turns into a narrow street where two police officers are conducting a vehicle search.

"Damn it, *la jura*, what'll we do!?!" Lenny asks, panicked.

"Chill out, Len," Sterling says, his blood pressure rising quickly, "We'll just drive right by like nothing's wrong." As they pass, an officer casually glances into the car. Something causes him to pull out his flashlight and direct the beam through the passenger side window.

"Damn, we're caught!" exclaims Lenny as the beam of light brightens up the side of his face.

"Hell no, we're not!" Sterling stomps down on the accelerator and races the Regal down the street. The police officer dashes to his patrol car and radios in the description of the vehicle.

"Are they chasing us!?!" With panic kicked into high gear, Sterling jerks the steering wheel to the left, branding the asphalt with a crescent moon as the midnight-black Buick Regal screeches wildly around the corner of Logan Avenue and 28th street.

"I don't freakin' know! You keep turning too damn fast, homes! I can barely hold on!" Lenny's brown, fourteen-year-old hands turn pale as he gouges his fingertips deep into the dash. "Ughhh! Damn, Sterl! Slow the hell down or we gonna crash!" he says, grunting, not like he's in excruciating pain, but more like he knows he's about to get tossed like a rag doll in a hurricane.

Hold on tight, little vato! You about to get tossed! Hold on tight! A chorus to an original rap song forms in his thoughts.

Another 95-mph tail-whip around a corner easily loosens Lenny's grip on the dash. He's pressed hard against the passenger side door as the Regal narrowly escapes plowing into a life-sized mural shared by Roberto's taco shop and Maggie's *Dulceria*.

"Damn it, Sterl, I said watch out! We almost hit Cesar Chavez and Rosa Parks, man!"

Lenny's thought remixes, *Survive the night, little gangsta! Or you won't live to see eighteen! Survive the night!* He recites it in his mind like a prophecy come to pass.

Even though he's never driven on his own before, Sterling steadies the steering wheel like a professional Nascar car driver. Aside from a few wanderers willing to brave the notorious *barrio* after dark, the streets of Logan Heights can be as treacherous as an ex-girlfriend ravenous for revenge.

"Don't be a scary-ass Mexican! Check if they're chasing us, Lenny!" Sterling shouts as his eyes engorge with panic.

"Forget you, Sterl! You're the one driving all crazy! You look back for the *jura*!" Lenny returns the shout, clinging to the dash as if his life depends on it. His head joggles from side to side, mimicking the bobblehead figurine fixed to the dash. Tony *Scarface* Montana's over-enlarged head wobbles to and fro with every turn, while the base inscribed with, *The World is Yours* remains stuck in place.

Time seems to slow as another obscure thought flashes in Lenny's mind, *will I get to see my dad, if I don't make it through the night?* He grinds his teeth, building up the determination to take a look, "Whatever! I'll look back for the *jura*, alright, Sterl!" he yells out. Lenny's chest expands with a deep breath as he releases hold of the dash and twists his body back to peer out the rear window. "I think we're good!" he says, exhaling. "I don't see no one chasing...!

In that moment, Sterling quickly yanks the steering wheel to the left, making another hard turn. The lowrider reacts unexpectedly, tail-whipping out of control towards the opposite side of the street. "Shit, Len! I lost it!"

Lenny can't finish what he was about to say, tensing as the sidewalk invades his peripherals in a flash, "Watch out, we're gonna hit!" Sparks ignite as the rear Dayton rim warps like a busted lip against the curb. Lenny's tossed again, this time twice as hard. The passenger side window shatters instantly against his skull with a deafening burst. "Ahhh! My head!" The rush of cold, night air instantly numbs his senses.

Sterling stomps down on the gas pedal and tightens his grip on the wheel, somehow regaining control of the bucking Buick and screeches away in a trail of smoke. He makes another quick turn into a quiet residential street crisscrossed with hidden alleyways—good for giving someone the slip. "Damn, that was crazy, we almost died back there, Len! Sterling says with equal parts excitement and disbelief. "Are the po-po chasing us!?!" Sterling's query goes unanswered. "Lenny! Can you hear me!?! Are the po-po's chasing us!?!"

All Lenny can do is rock back and forth, corralling his head in incapacitating pain.

"Damn it, Lenny, what's wrong with you? Snap out of it!" Sterling says, trying to shake an answer out of him, "Come on, boy, are you alright? Can you hear me!?!

Lenny remains completely stuck in agony.

"Damn it, Len, I'll look back, then!" With the rearview mirror gone and both side views busted, Sterling has to twist his body back to peer out through the rear window. He looks out into the darkness for a good five seconds.

"I don't see any po-po back there!" No sooner than a sigh of relief escapes from his breath, that an object of considerable weight and size smashes into the windshield, tumbles over the roof of the car, and rolls awkwardly onto the middle of the street.

"What the hell was that!" Sterling shouts, slamming his foot down on the brake pedal. The stolen lowrider zigzags to a screeching halt.

The sweet aroma of night-blooming Jasmine—so common in a clear San Diego night—is marred by the bitter odor of charred rubber. The sudden stop in motion whips Sterling's head against the steering wheel and Lenny's cheek against the dash.

"Ahhh! What the hell, Sterl!" Pain sent Lenny into a daze, and pain snaps him back.

"Damn! What was that, Len? Man, I cracked my dome!" Sterling says, tapping on a small gash beginning to leak from his forehead.

Then, as if induced into a mechanical seizure, the stolen Buick convulses erratically, and then flatlines. Quickly, Sterling tries to turn the ignition over, but the car remains dead. Anxiety swoops in like a sand storm in the Sahara as the teenager's stare at each other speechless, but still communicating with their eyes, *What the hell is happening?*

They exit the car cautiously. White steam begins seeping out from the hood, followed by a snake-like hiss. It immediately grabs Sterling attention.

"Damn, the car's smoking! What the hell did we hit? It must've been a big-ass dog or something! It straight-up messed up our g-ride!" Sterling glares at the indentation on the hood as he slams the door shut.

"I...I...I think it was," Lenny tries to speak, "It was a," but his words skip, his eyes fixated on the blood and skull fragments encased in a web of broken glass on the windshield. *It wasn't a damn dog! It was a person! We straight-up hit a person!* His thoughts yell out loud and clear, but he can't seem to verbalize it.

"What is it, Lenny? What are you tripping off of?" Sterling notices the look of shock on Lenny's face and tracks his gaze. When his eyes hit the skull fragments attached to human hair, the fear knocks the air from his lungs, like an uppercut straight to the gut. "What the hell is that?" he says, losing his breath.

It takes two seconds for it to register—one for Sterling's eyes to meet Lenny's, and two for both of them to turn around and look past the rear of the car.

As they peer into the stillness of the night, the young boys become trapped, as if caught in Spider Man's web. Their mouths gape at a figure lying motionless in the middle of the street.

"Shit, Lenny, it wasn't a damn dog! It was a person! We straight hit a person! Let's get the hell outta' here!" Panic snaps Sterling into action, vanishing down a darkened alleyway like a phantom out of the corner of your eye.

A single lament entombs his thoughts as Lenny remains motionless. *Perdóname, ma, I broke my promise.* A hauntingly familiar scream pierces Lenny's eardrum, like an omen of bad things still to come. He covers his ears and drops to his knees—what else could he do. He peers around, expecting to find his mother beside him, horrified that she's about to lose her only son to the whims of the justice system. He realizes quickly enough that the shriek didn't come from her, or from anyone at all, but from deep within his soul.

Lenny was about to surrender to the grief when self-preservation shoves him into action."Sterl, where are you!?!" He stands and looks around." Sterling!?! Where are you!?!" He calls out again, now realizing he's a lone combatant in a cell of regret. His heart speeds as the fight or flight response kicks into overdrive. Fighting to keep his already tarnished soul clean, Lenny darts towards the figure lying motionless on the asphalt. The only thing he's sure of is that a terrible sensation stabs deep into his chest. A sensation that feels more like guilt than fear.

Lenny reaches the figure lying face down in a flash only to take a step back, shocked by a puddle of blood the size of a small fist leaking from the skull. He's never seen blood that looked like that before, like an oil puddle—thick and reflective under the glow of the moonlight. "Oh shit! It's a woman!" Lenny's guilt intensifies as he kneels and struggles to roll her body over. The cowboy's words from earlier replays in his mind, ju' be careful, ey', *la luna está llena. Muy peligroso*. Bery' dangerous." Lenny looks up at the moon, and then drops his head. His eyes gloss over as he tries to wipe away the coagulated blood from the woman's forehead with his long sleeve shirt.

Suddenly, an electric jolt rushes down the length of his spine when her eyes open and meet his—the desperation reflecting back sears into his subconscious. She groans as she tries to speak, but the only thing audible enough to hear is the gurgling of blood in her throat. With all the life she has left, the woman lifts her hand and points—her finger trembles towards the darkness. "*Mi hijo*."

Just as Lenny is trying to comprehend what she's saying, death strikes with his scythe. Lenny turns towards where she was pointing and notices a baby stroller standing near the side of the curb. He looks back down at the woman, confused, but she stares back with the eyes of doll—haunting and lifeless.

Lenny shakes the woman's shoulders, "Lady, lady, please don't die!" Her head limps over. "*Señora! Por favor, señora!* He shouts with desperation, fear, and sadness combined. Lenny shakes her again, "Wake up! Please, wake up!" He stops and looks into her eyes—they're open but soulless. He slides his hand over and closes them gently, and just as guilt is about to consume him entirely, a thought flashes. *"Oh, shit! The stroller!"* He lays the woman's head down and jumps to his feet, rushing towards the stroller as fast as he can. "Please be ok. Please be ok." Lenny pleads with all the faith he has in his heart. Inside the stroller, he finds a baby sleeping with his tiny head tilted to one side. He places two fingers near the baby's nostrils to make sure. He can feel the infant's gentle breath against the coolness of the night.

"Thank you, God!" Lenny exhales, relieved not to have another tragedy thrust onto his conscience. As carefully as he can, he pushes the stroller onto the sidewalk and secures it on a patch of grass. Then, he hurries back to the woman. "I can't leave her like this." Lenny grabs the woman by her wrists and pulls. He finds dragging a dead body a much more cumbersome task than he thought. His legs strain as he pulls her out from the middle of the street. "I can do this! I'm not leaving her like this!"

Lenny takes heavy breaths, and with adrenaline and determination pumping through his veins, the smaller than average-sized fourteen-year-old manages to lay her body next to the stroller.

A man taking a late-night stroll with his dog notices the odd-looking scene. "Hey, what the hell are you doing, kid!" he yells out.

"Call an ambulance now! There's been an accident!" Lenny shouts back and then sprints towards the Buick. He jumps in and cranks the ignition. "Come on! Come on!" He tries turning the ignition over to no avail. "Please start! Please start!" Again, he turns the key, and this time, the Regal rumbles to life. Lenny yanks down on the shifter and stomps on the gas pedal, skidding the Regal down the street. He can barely see through the broken windshield as he tries to keep the steering wheel from swaying side to side.

"I'm sorry, *ma'*." His's eyes water from the wind seeping through the cracks in the windshield. He bangs his fist hard against the steering wheel. "Why, why, why! Why did she have to die!?!" Lenny makes an unsteady left turn and slams right into an oncoming patrol car. The head-on collision sends the Regal spinning back. Within seconds, four other patrol cars screech to the scene—their sirens suffocating the silence of the night. Officers jump out of their cars, wielding their nine-millimeters pistols.

"Let me see your fuckin' hands, now!" they yell, "Or we will open fire. Show us your hands now!" The barrels of their pistols aim straight for the driver side window.

"That's the car!" an agitated voice says, "It was just involved in a hit and run."

As if in some surreal nightmare, flashes of blue and red hues cloud Lenny's perception. Muffled voices echo in the distance, and everything starts to spin out of control. An officer rushes towards the vehicle and shatters the driver side window with the butt of his pistol. He forces open the door and drags the dazed teenager out onto the pavement.

Lenny grunts, as an officer digs his knee into the center of his spine while another twists his arms back and handcuffs his wrists. A voice in the background recites the Miranda Rights while a single thought replays over and over in Lenny's mind, *I'm sorry, Mami, I broke my promise. I'm sorry.*

Time skips as Lenny is strapped onto a gurney and rolled into an ambulance. Like a person of great importance, he receives a police escort to the hospital, the same one his mother happens to be working.

Lenny's nervous system malfunctions as he drifts in and out of consciousness. Obscure images flash before his eyes—images right out of a Salvador Dalí painting (surreal and obscure). A nurse rushes towards the stretcher. Lenny doesn't recognize the hazy-looking figure dressed in all white. He thinks she may be an angel come to take him away.

"Ma'am! Ma'am, don't get too close! He's a suspect in a homicide hit and run." Officers restrain her. Again, Lenny drifts out of consciousness, but not before a familiar and haunting shriek invades his ear canal.

"*Por Favor,*" the nurse pleads, "*Es mi hijo,* he's my son! She says, looking up at the officer with desperation in her eyes. "Please, tell me what happened to my son!" Dolores struggles out of the officer's hold.

"Leonardo," she rushes to his side and grips his hand. *"Por Favor, hijo, contesta me!* Leonardo, answer me!" She yells out. *"Hijo!"* The intensity of the moment is too much to bear, and she falls unconscious into the arms of a police officer.

Present

"Oh, my God!" Lisa dabs the corners of her eyes with a tissue, the emotion too overwhelming. In that moment, she's whisked back to being that little girl who couldn't cry at her father's funeral, eventhough she wanted too. It wasn't until she was all alone in the garage sitting in her father's lowrider when her emotion finally broke free. She cried and screamed, calling out for her papa until she fell asleep exhausted, curled up under the steering wheel.

Diego twitches as El DaVinci finishes shading in the eyes.

"Relax, homeboy, I'm just about done, ey'." El DaVinci's dips the point of the needle into white-colored ink and maneuvers his hand in swift, circular motions bringing her eyes to life.

"That was," Lisa pauses for a breath, "Incredibly tragic." She blows the sentiment from her nose. "I'm speechless. Your whole life has been one tragedy after another."

"Simón, it seems like it, ey', *pero sabes qué?"* El DaVinci says, "Everything that happened to me was supposed to happen as it did. All my experiences, all the tragedies I've been through has lead me to this moment, right here, right now with you. I'm El DaVinci, the prison tattoo artist, and because of you, I get to share my story with the world."

"Oh, I believe it! I believe it was by divine intervention how I found out about you, and how your story ended up being the kind I've always wanted to do my entire career. I've always wanted an Oprah moment, and you gave it to me. I think both our paths have led up to this moment."

"That's a trip, ey'." El DaVinci dips the tip of the needle in the white ink and makes the final swirls. "Done, Big D." El DaVinci says, wiping his brow. He sprays Diego's back several times with the antiseptic and carefully wipes away the excess ink. Diego rubs his hand over his face as if his pain reached its climax.

So what about regrets?" Lisa asks.

"Don't get me wrong. I do have regrets, ey'."

Lisa leans in, "May I see how it came out?

"*Simón*, check her out." El Davinci's heart skips a beat with that familiar nervousness as he scoots back.

Immediately, Lisa is taken back by the beauty of the tattoo. Diego's skin is swollen and bright red, but the tattoo is wonderfully detailed and extraordinarily vibrant. "I have to say, that's the most beautiful portrait I've ever seen." Lisa cues Scott with a head nod. He's already in full zoom, sharing the intricacy of the tattoo through the camera lens.

"Her eyes are amazing. They look like they're telling a sad story," Lisa says.

El DaVinci sprays Diego's back once more, wiping away the tiny beads of blood that formed in the eyes.

"So, you were saying. You do have regrets?" Lisa asks.

"Yeah, I got regrets. One of my biggest is not finding that little *vato*. You know who I'm talking about, right? The baby in the stroller, he's a man by now, ey'. I wish I could explain things to him like Pastor Cris did with me.

"And if he were watching right now, what would you say to him?" Lisa nods towards the camera.

"*Chalé*," EL DaVinci peers into the lens, "I've been rehearsing this for years, ey'. Now that I have the chance, I'm kind of at a loss for words." He turns and wipes down Diego's back with a towel discolored with blood and tattoo ink.

"It truly is a beautiful tattoo!" Lisa attempts to divert the emotion.

"*Gracias*." El DaVinci rolls his chair back and analyzes it from afar. He rolls forward and focuses on her eyes, motivated by Lisa's comment. His speech slows, "*Simón*. You know what, you're right! She does look like she's telling a sad story, but she's still my masterpiece, my Mona Li…." He cuts off his own words as thought strikes like the Little Boy bomb over Hiroshima. "Wait a second! Those eyes," he pauses. "I know those eyes!" It hits him as hard as a spinning roundhouse to the side of the head from Bruce Lee. El Davinci quickly glances up at the old photograph on the easel.

"Those eyes. I know those eyes!" he says, once again finding himself frozen. Those eyes of desperation seared so painfully into his heart come reeling back as crisp and vivid as the night he shut them. His body reacts instantly as the hairs on the nape of his neck stand straight up.

"Oh, my Lord and Savior. This is why I'm here. I knew you were speaking to me, Lord!" Hit with the revelation, Pastor Cris bolts for the door.

"What is it?" asks the Warden.

"Please let me in there. I'm needed now!"

Diego stands and inhales deeply. He turns and faces El DaVinci with a murderous glare. He clenches his fists so tight his knuckles turn white. "Do you even know her name!?!" he asks as adrenaline pulsates through his body. "It was you! It's always been you!?!" His voice groans like an injured Grizzly. "All this time, and you were right here in front of my face. The *pinche vato* who killed my *jefita* and made me an orphan!"

"Oh, my God!" Lisa covers her mouth. Scott salivates as he catches it all on video.

"Holy Mary, mother of God!" says the director. "It's him! He's the kid!"

"What's going on? What kid?" asks the young, sound technician's assistant. The director points towards Diego. "The kid in the stroller. He's been here, listening the whole time. The whole damn time!"

Deputy Jones and Deputy Smith glance at each other with shock, their hands slowly slip down towards their OC canisters.

Time moves in slow motion as the intensity thickens. Scott stands there, capturing it all for the viewers. He zooms in on the inmates, hoping what he's filming is worthy of the Pulitzer.

El DaVinci suddenly breaks the silence. "Look, homes," he says, standing and raising his hands. "I've been waiting for you for over thirty years, real talk, homes. For thirty years." He slips off his latex gloves so he can show his hands. "I need to tell you. I'm sorry for what happened to your *jefita*, and for what I did to you. I never meant for it to happen."

Diego looks around, tears preparing to burst. His chest heaves, and his teeth grind.

Deputies Jones and Smith stand frozen, their hands glued to their utility belts

"I know this is gonna' be hard to hear, homes," El Davinci continues, "But what happened to your *jefita* made me who I am."

Diego's gaze fixates on the needles soaking in the jar of alcohol as Pastor Cris suddenly bursts into the room. "Listen to him, brother Diego. I know exactly what he's going through, and believe me, he knows exactly what you're going through, too. Just like your mother was taken away from you, his father was taken away from him. I know this is hard to understand right now, but it's all part of God's plan. We're not meant to understand it or even like it. We're only meant to accept it and grow from it."

El Davinci's eyes water as the pastor's words ring with excruciating truth. "Look, Big D, you do whatever you feel you have to, homes, but before you do, I want you to know, he's right. I do know what you're feeling, and I'm sorry for what I did to you. I need you know that." El

DaVinci lowers his hands and locks them behind his back, accepting whatever fate is about to befall on him on live television.

"If you let me, homes, I offer myself as your brother. I took your family. It's only right I become your family." El DaVinci's voice cracks with emotion.

"Listen to him, brother Diego. Your mother is with God. She would want you to take the path of forgiveness," Pastor Cris says, his heart filled with the holy spirit. "Why do you think we're all here together, right now? There are no coincidences, brother. No coincidences at all."

Right when Diego is about to lunge for the needles and jab them into the side of El DaVinci's neck, an image catches the corner of his eye. He twists his head back towards the security glass and eyes a portion of his tattoo.

El DaVinci quickly reaches for the shaving mirror. He holds it out, "Take a look, it's my best work. I was meant to do this tattoo, homes. I was meant to do it for you!" Diego turns and faces El DaVinci. He stares at him dead in his eyes and then snatches the mirror from his hands. "Yeah, well, a tattoo won't bring her back! Or take away all the shit I've been through." He holds up the shaving mirror and peers through it. Tears instantly form as he becomes spellbound by the image staring back at him.

"Are you going to do anything, Warden?" asks the lead executive.

"Huh? What?" Also stuck in a state of shock, the Warden suddenly jumps into action. He reaches for his hand-held radio and hails the captain of the guard. "Captain Briggs, what the hell are you waiting for!?! Get a hold of the situation, now!"

"Already on it!" The captain's voice echoes back through the walkie. The situation reaches full Defcon level as a small battalion of deputies storm into the room in full tactical gear. The captain orders the inmates to lie face down with their hands behind their heads.

El DaVinci lies down while Diego remains transfixed on the tattoo. "Hey Big D, get down before they let loose on you, homes." El DaVinci's voice snaps Diego out of his trance.

He looks down at El DaVinci, and then at the deputies with their protective suits, electrified shields, and tasers pointed directly at him.

"Get down on your stomach, Inmate Martinez, now!" Aggression accompanies Officer Jones' voice. Diego kneels and lies on his stomach. Deputies pounce on the inmates quickly, securing them with metal restraints from head-to-toe.

"We're clear. Inmates are secure." A pair of deputies hoist Diego up.

"Hey, homes!" Diego calls out. He stiffens his legs, stopping the deputies in their tracks.

El DaVinci looks up.

"It's a *firme* tattoo," Diego says, nodding his head—his rage subdued by the beauty of the tattoo.

Scott continues filming as the Deputies escort Diego out through the steel door.

"Lisa, doll!" The director shouts through his earpiece, "Snap out of it! Let's wrap it up! Time for an epic finish!"

Lisa looks around, confused. She stares into the camera, still caught in a daze. Deputies lift El DaVinci to his feet and begin hauling him away.

"Come on, Leese, snap out of it." Scott mouths the words. The crew jump in, waving their hands, urging Lisa into action.

She's finally pulled back and jumps right in. "Ladies and gentlemen, what just occurred right now," she says, shaking her head, "Was completely unexpected. I assure you, it was not an act, and I have to say, it took me completely by surprise." Lisa stands and places her clipboard on her chair. She turns and faces the camera.

"El DaVinci's story just came full circle right in front of our eyes. If ever there was a tale of redemption, we just witnessed it right here on live television. It was fate that brought us all here together to witness this extraordinary event, this extraordinary show, and I can't help but to feel humbled by it. I know, without any doubt in my heart, I'm now a better person for it. Though the circumstances may be different, his story, El DaVinci's story, is all of our stories. We all need to redeem ourselves from time to time, for the mistakes we've committed in the past, for the mistakes that hurt the people we love. God knows I do, too. And Leonardo Santiago, also known as El DaVinci, the tattoo prodigy, showed us first hand, that it's never too late to make amends, it's never too late for redemption, even if it's through a tattoo. Once again, I'd like to thank Warden Wiesel, his team of sheriff deputies, our sponsors, and you, our beloved viewers, for making this special broadcast possible. On behalf of Entertainment Weekly, this is Lisa Deveroe signing off. We hope to see you next week for another edition of Entertainment Weekly, the show that informs while keeping you entertained. I wish you, goodnight." The sound technician keys a switch, and the show's theme music activates.

The director jumps to his feet with his hands in the air, as if he just won the lottery, "Ladies and gentlemen, that's a wrap!" He turns towards the security glass and bows. "One hell of a show, folks! The ratings are gonna' go through tha' roof, through the roof I tell ya'!"

Lisa rushes out of the room, "Wait! Wait!" she yells down the hallway.

Captain Briggs and the escorting deputies stop as she rushes towards them. "I want to say, that was the most amazing thing I've ever experienced in all my years as an entertainment host, in all my life, to be honest. I can't imagine how difficult this was for you. Thank you for sharing it with us." Lisa stares at El Davinci, "Thank you for sharing it with me." She glances at Captain Briggs, "May I, Captain?"

He looks around and sighs, "Fine! But make it quick." Lisa places her hands on El DaVinci's shoulders and kisses him gently on the cheek.

Officer Briggs ushers her back. "Ok, that's enough."

El DaVinci bows, "No, *mija*, thank you. You made all this possible for me because you believed in me. And because of you, Ms. Lisa Deveroe, I found Diego and told him what I needed to tell him after all these years. I'm just sorry I don't have any more stories to tell." The shackles jingle as El DaVinci reaches to wipe a tear from her eye.

Captain Briggs quickly blocks his hand. "I'll take care of that for you inmate Santiago." He pulls out a handkerchief from his back pocket and hands it to Lisa. "Sorry, Ma'am, but rules are rules."

"I gotta' get back to my cage," El Davinci says, and with a nod of his head, he's taken away. Lisa stares at the men as they walk down the hall. "You know what? You truly are a rose that grew from concrete, just like Tupac wrote in his poem."

Back on the streets of LA, Lil' Playboy watches the conclusion of the show in awe. "What the hell! He killed Diego's mother?" he says, switching off his flat screen. "I can't believe Diego didn't do anything. I would've stuck that fool in his neck if he killed my mom, I don't care how good the tattoo came out. Man, that was crazy, for real!" Lil' Playboy reaches under his bed and grabs his pistol, concealing it behind his waistband. "I gotta' find the homies, tell them about what I just saw. They're gonna' trip out." He heads for the door but immediately stops. He stands there for a moment, contemplating. He reaches back in his waist and pulls out his gun. "I ain't gonna' need this right now," he says, and stuffs it back under his mattress and then heads out the door.

XIV. Lisa

Three-months later. **4:40 p.m.** "Let's get a move on..." bewildered yet again from not hearing the sound of his voice, the wily, old show director quickly raises the volume to the max on his megaphone. "Ok, boys and girls, twenty-minutes til' showtime!" With a sliver of enthusiasm hiding in his voice, the director scans the studio. "Hey, where the hell's my star hostess?!"

4:41 p.m. Just outside the studio, Juan (a.k.a. Smiley) and Carlos (a.k.a. Big Trips) childhood homies and employees of the network's janitorial crew, and who also happen to be a pair of old-school *cholos,* stroll through the studio parking lot.

"It's Friday, Smiley. You better be ready to get your party on tonight, homeboy!" Carlos says with the anticipation the weekend can bring.

"Fool, you say that every Friday, and end up passing out by eleven. You may be big, Big Trips, but you can't party like you used to. Let's face it, you're getting old, homes," Juan says with a smile across his face.

"*Chalé*! Not tonight, Smiley. Tonight we're partying til' the break of dawn!"

4:42 p.m. The two *vatos* approach a Chevy Impala pancaked several centimeters off the pavement.

"Check out that *firme* lowrider, homes." Juan says, motioning towards the car, "It's a six-four like yours, *qué no*, Big Trips? Only done up way more *firme*!"

"*Simón, limón*! That's a straight-up show car, Smiley! Damn, that burgundy flake is *firme*," Carlos says, awed by the paint job. "Those ghost graphics run all over the *ranfla*! That must've cost some serious *feria*."

"I know, huh. Check out those gold wire rims, homes, and it's in an executive spot, too, ey'!" Juan points towards the specially designated parking sign. "I wonder who it belongs to?"

"*Chale*, Smiley! It better not belong to some big shot executive faking the funk, ey', trying to pretend like he's from the hood!" Carlos says, shaking his head. "I'll come up on it, if it is, homes, *serio*!" his tone expresses a mix of anger and jealousy.

4:43 p.m. Juan lifts his pitch-black sunglasses and notices a woman sitting in the driver's seat. Quickly, he pulls them back down. "Hey, Big Trips? Don't be all obvious, ey', but you're not gonna believe this," his teeth become exposed through his smile.

"What is it, homes?"

"Check out who's sitting in the driver's seat. Isn't that, that *firme heina* from the show?" Juan motions with a nod of his head.

4:44 p.m. Carlos peers into the car. "Damn, Smiley! You're right, that is her, ey'! I can't believe that's her *ranfla*," he whispers back as if it's a well-kept secret.

"I know, huh. I thought she rolled a Benz," Juan says, returning the whisper, "Not a *firme* lowrider like that." He wiggles his hand in a gesture of disbelief.

"*Serio*, homes." Carlos pauses suddenly. "You know what," he says, snapping his fingers. "That's the lowrider she talked about with that tattoo artist from Donovan, ey'. It was her *jefe's*."

"*Orale*!. You're right, homes. I forgot about that."

"Damn, Smiley, I think I'm in love." He shoves Juan, playfully. "Don't go telling my ol' lady, *cabrón*!"

"I won't, fool," Juan returns the push, "Because she'll cut your *huevos* off!" He maneuvers his fingers in a scissor-like motion.

4:45 p.m. Carlos chuckles while nodding his head. "*Serio*, homes! She will, too, ey'. That's what I get for marrying your crazy ass sister."

"That's your fault, homes," Juan says, "I told you back in the day, she's one crazy *heina*, but your stubborn-ass wouldn't listen."

"Shut up, Smiley. It's all your *jefa's* fault!" he says.

"What!?! Why is it my *jefa's* fault?" Juan cocks his head in confusion.

"Because your sister bewitched me with that booty, that same big ol' booty she got from your *jefa*!" Carlos says, and takes off in a sprint.

"What, *cabrón*! Don't ever talk about my *jefa* like that!" Juan gives chase.

4:46 p.m. Lisa peers into her rearview, outlining her lips with designer lipstick while conversing on her cell phone.

"I know it, girl," she says. "I can't believe it's been so long. Have you heard from any of our homegirls from back in the day?" Lisa maneuvers her lipstick, staying perfectly in line with the shape of her lips. "No, I haven't heard from any of them either, but don't trip girl, I gotta a homegirl down here at the network. She's like our own private investigator, and girl, let me tell you, she's talented at what she does. She'll find out where they are. She found you. I'm so glad you can make it down next week," Lisa pauses, rubbing her lips together to spread the lipstick evenly. "Don't worry about that, Sasha, you can stay at my place, you'll love it. You can see the Hollywood sign from my balcony."

4:47 p.m. Lisa ends her call and caps her lipstick. She peers into the rearview, swaying her head from one side to the other, admiring how her lips shimmer. "There, Daddy. Now I match with the color of our low-low." Reconnecting with her best friend from high school has brought back an old feeling, a feeling she hasn't felt since like forever, like the future holds limitless possibility. Though it's taken some time—a stretch over twenty years—but she's finally liberated that part of her that's been locked away for far too long.

4:48 p.m. Lisa peers down at her diamond-studded watch. Although her experience at the prison helped her to find the courage she needed—the courage to be true herself—she hasn't lost the taste for the more finer things in life. "Twelve minutes! I better hurry!" Her eyes glimpse the tiny skeleton key bracelet hanging from her wrist. She stares at it for a moment. "Thank you for bringing me luck, and for unlocking my past, one I wouldn't change for anything."

4:49 p.m. Lisa taps on a switch, and the top end of the impala rises. She taps on another, and with a *zzzt-zzzt* from the hydraulics echoing through the parking lot, the back end lifts leveling out the car perfectly. She steps out of her low-low—the custom license plate reads, *DADSGRL*.

Lisa heads towards the studio, rocking a beige firm-fitting Armani suit, and white blouse opened teasingly at the neck to show off her striking diamond necklace. Her matching colored Christian Louboutin high heels tap on the asphalt, sending word that a classy lady is roaming about. Lisa glances up to the sky, "I know you're watching from up there. I love you both!"

4:50 p.m. Smiley and Big Trips wait by the side employee entrance sharing a cigarette.

"Here she comes, homes, I'll get the door!" Carlos says.

"*Chalé*, I got it, homes!" Juan quickly reaches for his employee badge.

"*Nel, pastel*! I said I got it!" Carlos also reaches for his badge. The two hard-looking *vatos* bump into each other, trying to get the door open like Larry and Curly in an episode of the three stooges. Somehow, they manage to get it open.

"*Muchas gracias, Caballeros.*" Lisa winks as she enters.

"*De nada, señorita.*" The vatos respond like a pair love-stricken parrots.

"Did you hear that, Smiley? She called me a *caballero.*"

"Shut up, Big Trips! I'm telling my sister!"

4:51 p.m. Lisa enters the back room adjacent to the set. Similar to most talk shows on cable tv, the studio is arranged so that an enormous jumbo screen serves as the backdrop. Several tan leather couches are positioned so Lisa and her guests can sit and conversate while remaining visible for the audience. There are also several gold-trimmed coffee tables with silver trays containing coffee cups with the networks logo imprinted on them.

"Geez, it still amazes me how different everything looks on this set," Lisa peers through a large curtain, scanning the audience. She spots her special guest and smiles. She still can't shake the feeling like she took a life-altering trip and came back a completely different person.

Donovan Penitentiary is infested with the worst society has to offer, at least, that's what she thought. That was one of the many things that captivated her about El Davinci's story—how the worst society has to offer reached the highly coveted of society. Even though the interview with him and not someone of significance, celebrity wise that is, it was the most significant for her personally, even eclipsing the one she had the opportunity of doing with her childhood idol, Janet Jackson. It was he who changed her perspective on many things. It was he who encouraged her to embrace the past and to let go of any shame because of it. But perhaps the most important thing she took away from the interview with El DaVinci, is that we all possess something special— our own little hidden gem—and we shouldn't ever shy away whenever we get the opportunity to let it shine, even if it is from behind the walls of a maximum-security penitentiary.

4:52 p.m. Like clockwork, the crafty, old show director ambles about several minutes before broadcast, checking for anything that may be a miss. He waves at the audience and cuts across the stage to get behind the jumbo screen to check the cable connections.

4:53 p.m. The director walks passed the sound amplifiers when a thought strikes him. *I have to make sure there's no static interference coming through the mics.*

4:54 p.m. The director's seeks out the sound technician's assistant to bark orders at him, a thing he's been getting joy out of doing. "Come on, son, stop your damn lollygagging and make sure there's no static comin' from the mics!"

4:55 p.m. The director settles back in his custom-made chair, the one his crew got for him as a show of appreciation—the one with, *Best Director Ever* embroidered in elegant gold lettering across the backrest. He peers into the monitors. "Well done, Scottie boy. The cameras are in optimal position."

"Of course they are, chief," Scott responds through his nearly invisible microphone. "I know what I'm doing after all these years under your most excellent guidance."

"Yeah, yeah, mister smarty pants. You should take your handkerchief outta' yer' back pocket, my friend, because yer' nose turning brown," the director responds back.

4:56 p.m. "Here's today's script and an espresso Ms. Deveroe," says an attractive, long-legged young woman as she hands Lisa the items. "And I just want to say, I can't thank you enough for making me your assistant. I hated working for the higher-ups. They never took me seriously."

"For goodness sake, Carla, call me, Lisa. And no, thank you! You're a great assistant, and it was time for me to start grooming a worthy protégé," she says, taking a sip from the tiny cup. "I don't want you to worry, Carla. I know you have ambition for the spotlight. It'll happen sooner than you think," Lisa places her hand on Carla's shoulder, "You'll be in front of the camera soon enough, I promise."

4:57 p.m. Lisa glances to her right, where an overweight security guard with In-n-out's secret sauce stains on his light blue company shirt stands watch. His hands rests on his protruding belly as he maintains a vigilant stance by the side entrance.

Lisa shakes her head, "My personal guard dog." She turns in the opposite direction and peers at her reflection coming from a large, backstage mirror. She turns to the side and lifts her shirt, "Hey, papa."

4:58 p.m. "Two minutes, everyone," the director announces through his trusty megaphone. Again, he gestures angrily at the young sound tech, "Son, please, please, please, tell me you checked Lisa's mics?"

"Yeah, boss! I double and triple checked them!"

The director knifes the young man with a sharp stare.

"Fine," says the young sound tech with a frustrated breath. "I'll check them again, ok!" He hustles over to Lisa and unclips the microphone concealed in her collar. "Sorry about this, Miss Deveroe, but you know how he gets." He brings the microphone close to his mouth, "Mic check one, mic check two."

"Don't worry about it, Chucky. And call me Lisa. Ms. Deveroe makes me feel old, and I consider myself anything but." She leans in close. "By the way, I know it doesn't seem like it, but the old man really does like you," Lisa says with a wink.

"Mics sound good," yells out the lead sound technician, "No static."

"See, boss, I told you, everything's good to go." Chucky clasps the tiny microphone back onto Lisa's collar and rushes back to his place next to the lead sound technician before he's assigned another dubious task.

4:59 p.m. The director raises his thumbs. "Alright, folks, we're ready in sixty seconds!"

Lisa inhales deeply and then exhales slowly. She still hasn't been able to conquer those pesky pre-show jitters. Even after all her years in the spotlight, her stomach still goes for a rollercoaster ride before every countdown. "I'm pretty sure Oprah gets nervous before every show, too," she tries to convince herself. "OK, Lilyboo, let's give the fans another great performance."

"Positions everybody, we're on in 5-4-3-2," the director's index finger goes up, and the show begins.

5:00 p.m. Lisa struts onto the stage with the swagger of a pop star, ready to entertain with her newly signed multi-million-dollar contract. "Good evening, everyone, I'm your hostess, Lisa Deveroe, and welcome to another edition of Entertainment Weekly," she says with a smile. A cue card goes up, and the sound of live applause reverberates through television sets around the nation.

"Before we begin with some juicy gossip floating around in the world of entertainment news, I'd like to say, hey *nanay*, I love you," Lisa blows a kiss into the audience. "My mother happens to be sitting in the audience. *Nanay*, I know you don't like to be embarrassed, but can you please stand?" Scott punches in a few buttons on a switchboard, and camera two zooms in on Lisa's mother. "That's my mother, ladies and gentlemen. I love you, *nanay*!" Lisa says as applause and cheers spread throughout the studio.

"Thank you all for that. We have another great edition for you today. We're going to try to confirm or refute some juicy gossip floating around in the world of entertainment." A pair of high-profile celebrities caught in a loving embrace flashes onto the jumbo screen.

At Scripps-Mercy hospital in Los Angeles, a nurse who recently transferred in from San Diego and is already beloved by her patients begins her evening shift. She enters a room in the intensive care unit, checking in on a fourteen-year-old boy recovering from a savage assault at the hands of rival gang members.

"*Hola*, Juan," she says. "Oh, I'm sorry, I mean, Lil' Playboy, right?" She gives him a warm smile. "How are you feeling today?"

"Why do you always check up on me? Don't you have other patients?" he asks, grunting as he tries to sit upright.

"Because I promised your *mamá*," she says. "I know what she's going through. I know what it's like to lose a son, I mean, to almost lose a son."

"Did your son die?" he asks, surprised.

"Kind of." She answers and then quickly turns away. "So, you're an artist?" The nurse picks up his sketch pad from a rolling table and flips through the pages. "Wow! These are really good. My son was an artist, too. A good one like you." She digs into her pockets and pulls out several freshly sharpened number two pencils, and rolls the table next to him.

"Here," she says, placing the pencils on the table and opening the sketch pad to the half-finished drawing. "It looks like this one needs finishing. It's going to be beautiful, I can already tell. Those were my son's favorite, by the way," she says, pointing at the pencils. "I always keep a few on me so they remind me of him."

Lil' Playboy sits back and the stares at the drawing. After several painful breaths, he picks up a pencil.

"There we go." The nurse reaches for the television remote. "How about a little TV?" She activates the remote and cycles through several channels. "Tell me where you want me to leave it." Lisa suddenly flashes on screen. "Leave it there! I like that show. She interviewed a bad-ass tattoo artist in prison who ran over a lady when he was a teenager," he says.

"What!" The nurse drops the cup of water she was serving him and quickly looks up at the TV.

Back at the show, Lisa turns towards the audience. "We also have for you an intimate conversation with a certain A-lister and academy award winner, I won't reveal who just yet," she winks into the camera, "You'll just have to stay tuned. And finally, we're going to end with a follow up with none other than El DaVinci, the tattoo prodigy from Donovan Penitentiary. By the way, we'll be re-airing the entire interview with El DaVinci by popular demand on Monday at 6 p.m.

pacific time." An image of El DaVinci tattooing Diego flashes onto the screen.

"See, I told you," Lil' Playboy says as he begins shading in his drawing. Dolores stands frozen in her nurse's scrubs with her mouth wide open. Quickly, she reaches for a pencil and rips out a page from Lil Playboy's sketch pad.

"Hey, what are doing, nurse Dolores?" he asks, bewildered.

She scribbles down the date and time, "I'm sorry, but that's my son!"

From a small television secured on a rolling cart, inmates at Donovan's maximum-security wing watch the show with anticipation. Cheers erupt in the day room as Lisa mentions the tattoo artist by his prison name.

After the interview, El DaVinci was removed from general pop and placed under protective custody. Even though he's held in high regard within the walls of the prison, Warden Wiesel couldn't risk giving a random inmate a chance at making a name for himself by taking a stab at their very own prison-house celebrity. He put it to El DaVinci rather eloquently. "Look, Santiago, I understand you don't like it, but you have to understand my position. There's a price for fame. I have to say you did something short of a miracle. There's a strange sense of unity radiating around the prison of which I've never felt in all my years working in these institutions. We haven't had a single incident of violence in these past few months, and that's unheard around here, wouldn't you agree, Captain Briggs?"

The Captain of the guard removes his sunglasses, exposing his full drill-sergeant like face, something he rarely does. "That's affirmative. What you've done in here, Mr. Santiago, is short of a miracle," he said with no emotion. "But I'm a realist, and prison will always be prison," he puts his mirrored sunglasses back on. "I assure you, it won't last. Look, Santiago, you're stay in isolation will be temporary, until we can guarantee your safety."

That was three months ago to this day.

Sporting tan, starch-creased khakis, a black collared shirt and matching tie, and a pair of freshly polished French-toed Stacy Adam dress shoes, El DaVinci stares at the barren walls of his temporary cell, fighting the urge to etch out another masterpiece.

The show did in fact go viral, and the ratings skyrocketed far beyond the network's expectation, once again elevating Entertainment Weekly back to the top spot in the Neilson ratings for entertainment news. Lisa also signed a new contract with a certain clause—insisted upon by the president of the board himself—stating that after the current year is up, Lisa will transition into the role as a new member of the executive board. They're already remodeling her new office overlooking downtown L.A.

After airing, a mass show of public support for El DaVinci inundated the network via letters, emails, Youtube videos, blogs, Twitter feeds, etc. Many want to know about his fate, while others want to offer prayers and words of encouragement. It so happened that an email was sent directly to Warden Wiesel from a prominent government official, stating that he was so moved by the show he feels that the inmate known as El DaVinci should be given special consideration, especially after such a public display of redemption.

The Captain of the guard and Deputy Smith escort El DaVinci to an undisclosed location, where three very professional and uptight looking individuals await his arrival.

"So, *Capitan* Briggs, is today my lucky day or what, ey'?" El DaVinci says, preening his hair back. "I'm all dressed up, but where's the party?" He tries to get a response from the man with no emotion. Captain Briggs shakes his head as he scans the cell block with his trademark intensity. Like a pair of secret service agents escorting the president, they scan every nook where an ambush can occur. They reach their destination without incident.

"Inmate Santiago," Capitan Briggs's voice carries its usual indifference, "Good luck." He cracks what seems to be a smile from the corner of his mouth. Not quite sure if his mind was playing tricks on him, El DaVinci does a double-take. Whatever expression crept out of the Captain's face is long gone as he turns and walks away.

"*Órale, Capitán* Briggs. You're not a robot, after all," El DaVinci says, shaking his head and smiling. "This just might be my lucky day, homes." He enters the room and heads for the chair placed in the center. Behind a long conference table, three members of the parole board discuss El DaVinci's case, dubious to his presence. After several minutes, one of the members turns and faces him.

"Good afternoon, Inmate Santiago, my name is Mr. Ryan," he motions to his left. "This is Mr. Whitey," he motions to his right. "And this is Mrs. Stern." He clears his throat. "Now that the introductions are out of the way, Mr. Santiago, I want to ask you a question before we begin. Do you know why you're here?"

"*Simón*. I'm here because I committed one count vehicular manslaughter, one count grand theft auto, and one count evading arrest."

Mr. Ryan shoots El DaVinci a perplexed look. "Well, yes, we've reviewed your file, we know what got you in here. However, what I'm asking is, do you know why you're here today, at this unscheduled hearing?"

EL DaVinci scans their faces. "*Simón*. The warden told me I was granted a special parole hearing, *qué no*?"

"Yes, that's exactly right, Mr. Santiago, this is, in fact, a very special hearing especially after being denied parole for the past ten years. I can tell you this is the first time I've ever sat in one, and I've been doing this for over fifteen years. Not many inmates are given this opportunity," Mr. Ryan says.

Mr. Whitey jumps into the conversation, "Apparently, Mr. Santiago, some big wig in government feels you deserve a chance at parole, even after being denied so many times for your close associations with various prison gangs. I'm sure you're aware that such associations merits automatic denial because of their far reaching influence outside of these walls. I mean that alone is why you haven't been released. Personally, I think this hearing is just a ploy, this being an election year and all."

"However, if I may," Mrs. Stern also jumps into the conversation. "We need you to understand that we take our jobs very seriously, Mr. Santiago. You've associated with practically every prison gang throughout our state's prison system. Your popularity makes you a powerful man, a dangerous man, to be frank." She leans in and crosses her hands. "Look, Mr. Santiago, it doesn't matter to us who you have advocating for you. We've dealt with some pretty high profile cases before, cases with mass public support. We want you to know, that your popularity does not influence our decision one bit. If this board feels that you will be a continued danger to society, even a slight one, we will not grant your parole. We have a responsibility to the public, and that's the bottom line. Do you understand, Mr. Santiago?" she says, staring straight into his eyes.

"*Simón*, I mean, yes, ma'am. *Y sabes qué*, I respect your candor."

"Alright then, now that we have come to an understanding," Mr. Ryan continues, "Let's begin. We've recently reviewed a letter from an inmate at Corcoran, Sterling Jackson is his name, who is also serving a life sentence."

"What!?! *Serio*? Why did he write you guys?" El Davinci asks, surprised by the revelation.

"We honestly don't know. But he reveals some rather incriminating information. Information that can add significant time to his already prolonged sentence."

"What are you talking about, ey'?" El DaVinci facial expression begs the question.

"He states he was the one behind the wheel, the one who committed vehicular manslaughter, and not you. You were just the passenger. Is that true, Mr. Santiago?"

EL DaVinci sighs with disbelieving eyes. "I don't know what you're talking about."

"Are you sure there isn't something you want to tell us, Mr. Santiago?" Mr. Ryan asks, "Because now would be the appropriate time."

El DaVinci shakes his head, "Nah', homes, I don't have anything to say about that."

"I'm going to ask you one more time. Are you sure there isn't something you want to tell us?"

"Yeah, homes. I'm sure," El DaVinci says.

"Well, alright. Let's hear from your character witness, then."

El DaVinci cocks his head to the side, again confused. "Character witness? What are you talking about, ey'?"

As if perfectly planned, the door cracks open. Inmate Diego Martinez enters in full-body restraints, followed closely behind by Deputy Smith. He approaches El DaVinci and reaches out his hand.

"*Q'vo, hermano*," Diego grasps El DaVinci hand. "Look, homes, after all the drama that went down, I didn't get a chance to say, *gracias*. My *jefita's* tattoo came out way more *firme* than I imagined." Diego bows his head.

"Thanks, homes," El DaVinci says, "Like I said, she's my Mona Lisa."

"I want you to know I figured out what she was trying to tell me, homes," Diego says and pulls El Davinci in close to whisper in his ear. "She forgives you. And so do I, homes!"

El DaVinci's eyes gloss over, like a freshly sprayed clear coat over a candy pearl paint job. He grinds his teeth, trying to keep his emotions in check.

"Hey!" shouts deputy Smith, "That's too close!"

Diego winks at El Davinci and approaches the parole board.

"Welcome back to Entertainment Weekly," Lisa announces back at the studio. "Before we close out today's show, I would like to share a few posts made on our website by some of El DaVinci's new-found fans. If you would like to post a comment about tonight's show, please join our newly revamped Facebook page at *#entertainmentweeklyrocks*." Lisa waits for the post to appear on the jumbo screen. "This first comment is from Carlos Villarreal, 19 years old. He wrote;

Hey El DaVinci,

I'm an artist just like you, man, though not nearly as good. I want to thank you for inspiring me to keep my dream alive. I gave up on becoming a muralist like Rivera and Siqueiros. But now, after listening to your story and how you kept at it even after everything you've been through, it motivated me to keep painting. I mean, if you can become a famous tattoo artist in prison, it has to be easier for me to become a muralist out here. Thanks for sharing your story, man. You're freakin' awesome. I hope we can collaborate on a mural one day.

Your homie, Carlos.

Amazing idea, Carlos, keep painting!" Lisa says. "I'll make sure your message finds him." Again, she turns towards the jumbo screen. "This next post is from Diamond Girl, 32 years old. She wrote;

Hey El DaVinci,

Damn, you're one fine-ass, vato. If you ever need a pen pal, you can hit me up anytime. I love your tattoos, they're amazing. I'd love for you to tattoo a portrait of my daughter on the upper part of my chi-chi when you get out. By the way, you can write to me at....

Con Amor, Diamond Girl.

I'm Sorry, Diamond Girl. We can't give out any personal information over the broadcast," expresses Lisa. "But I'll make sure he gets your message. This next post is from Jeremiah King, 18 years old. He wrote;

Yo El DaVinci,

Your tats are the straight shiznit'. I hope you get out soon and open up a shop. Man, I'll sweep your floors for free for a year if I can be your first customer. Stay strong, my brotha' from anotha' motha'. I'll be praying for you.

Your Lil Homie, J-King."

Lisa shakes her head. "My goodness, Jeremiah, free manual labor for a year. You must want a tattoo pretty bad. I can't say I blame you. He is the best. This last post I'm going to share with you is one I'm sure El DaVinci will be particularly interested in. It's from Miriam Kahlo, 43 years old. She wrote;

Dear Leonardo,

I saw the show and couldn't believe it. Back in middle school, I had a serious crush on you, too, but I didn't think you liked me because you never tried to talk to me. I remember my friend Maria told me you were going to ask me out when you won the art contest, but you never did. I even waited in front of the school for an hour, hoping you'd ask me. Anyways, I don't have a boyfriend anymore, but I have a 12-year-old daughter. If you're still interested, my address is...

Your Middle School Crush, Miriam Kahlo.

Sorry folks, we had to blur out her personal information, but I'll make sure your message finds him, Miriam. It looks like El DaVinci has many fans out there. These were just a few from hundreds of posts and letters that found their way to our station. We'll make sure he gets them all. And now, a final update on El DaVinci, the tattoo prodigy from Donovan Penitentiary. We recently confirmed, from an anonymous source, that he's been granted a special parole hearing, and I want to say, on behalf of our entire crew, our network, and especially myself, we wish him the best of luck. Thank you all for tuning into another exciting edition of Entertainment Weekly, the show that informs while keeping you entertained. Tune in next week for some more juicy gossip floating around in the world of entertainment news. Also, be on the lookout for another Entertainment Weekly special, where I get the profound honor of interviewing the Pope, yes, that's right, folks, the venerable Pope Francis himself, and at the Vatican!

Talk about life-changing! Oh, and one last thing before we close out the show." Lisa turns to the side and lifts her blouse halfway up, revealing her side profile, and a freshly healed tattoo. Scotts zooms in, showcasing a striking portrait of Lisa's father smiling and waving goodbye. "Now, you can add my name to El DaVinci's list, and now I can boast that I got inked by the very best."

The day room at Donovan's Maximum security wing turns eerily silent as credits roll on the screen. A deputy walks over to the television set and switches off the power. An inmate stands and begins applauding. Like dominos of different colors—browns, blacks, whites, Asians, Pacific Islanders, middle easterners—all one-hundred and fifty inmates who were allowed to watch the show, stand to their feet, applauding and cheering. A tidal wave of positive energy—of which has only been felt once before—flows throughout the maximum-security wing as inmates who don't normally associate, shake hands and give each other high-fives.

The final cue card goes up, and cheers echo throughout the studio. The video monitors fade to black, and the director concludes the broadcast with his trademark saying, "And that folks, is a wrap!"

The crew high five each other.

"Come on, Chucky, I dare you," says the lead sound technician.

"No way! He'll fire me," responds his young assistant.

"No, he won't. Come on. Lunch will be on me for a month," says the sound technician, egging him on.

"Alright, but he better not fire me." Chucky approaches the director, "Um, Chet, I just want to say, it's been awesome being part of your crew."

"Wait a beat, young man, what did you just call me?" the director asks a bit perplexed.

"Chet, that's your name, right? Chet Smears?"

The director stares the young man down, long and hard, then reaches out his hand. "That's right, young man, that's what my dear mum and pop named me." They shake hands. "You know what, son? I have to say, you got a big pair on ya'." He suddenly pulls Chucky close. "But the next time you address me, you can call me boss, chief, director, hell you can even call me God." He tightens his grip, squeezing the blood from the young man's hand as he whispers, "But listen good now. If you ever call me by that name again, I'm gonna' kick yo' snotty little ass from here to kingdom come, you understand me, right, boy! I may be old, but I can still inflict serious pain in ways you can't possibly imagine! Catch my drift?"

With a scared-straight look etched all over his face, Chucky nods his head, "Yes sir! I'm sorry, sir! I mean, boss!"

The crew break into a stupor, watching it unfold exactly as they knew it would. And that, homes, is a wrap!

Glossary Of Caló Terms (Chicano Slang)

Carnal- brother; close friend

Chalé- expresses disagreement or surprise."

Chavala- an insult for someone who lacks courage

Chingón- bad-ass

Clecha- status; class

Dispensa- excuse me; sorry

El Mero-mero- boss; the boss

Firme- cool; hip

Heina- girl; girlfriend

Jefa- mother

Jefita- expression of endearment for mother

Jefe- father

Jefito- expression of endearment for father

Jura- police; the cops

Mija- my daughter; my dear

Mocoso- little boy; kid

Órale- right on; alright

Pinta- prison

Qué onda- expression for, "What's up?"

Ranfla- car; lowrider

Sabes qué- expression for, "You know what?"

Serio pedo- serious stuff

Simón- yes; that's right.

Tinto- Person of black skin

Torcida- jail or prison

Vato- dude; guy; man.

Veterano- person with experience

Acknowledgments

Wow! What can I say? I've been looking forward to writing this page for a long time. This is where I get to thank and pay my respects to those who have influenced me. Those I have mad respect for, those I love deeply and have had a hand in making this book possible in some way or another, even though they didn't know it. I will name them by nickname because that's what we Chicanos do. We go by our nicknames, our family monikers, and they'll know who they are.

I'll start with my *familia*. I'd like to first thank my wife, Carina—my Diamond, my daughter Bri, my boys Nick and Z, *mi jefe, Güicho y mi madresita*, Sonia, my brother's Adrian, Cuban B, James, Playboy, and Johnny (rest in peace), *Mis Abuelita's* (who are the gold standard for strong women) Sonia *y* Lilia, *mis Gran Tios*, Pancho (rest in peace) *y* Angelita, *mi gran Tio* Beto (may you rest in peace), *mis tios*, Marc and Letty, Pat and Mark, Sergio and Luz, *mi tia loca*, Laura (may you stay forever young), Uncle Captain San Felipe (a.k.a Bub) and Ana, *Tio* Humberto (may you rest in peace) and Gigi, my *Tia* Nilia and Uncle Fern, Uncle Jorge, Uncle Frank, *Tia* Rosa and Bibi, *y mi tia* Linda (may you rest in peace, you had an impact on my life, even though it was for a short time), my cousins, which I have many, Big E and his sister B, Beto, Rich, Yvette and Daniel, Cindy and buff-ass Marquitos, Big Savage and Danny, Pila and Tati, my amazing Tia Claudia, and even though we're always clashing, this is for you too, Serg. I know, I haven't mentioned all my family, know I do carry you in my heart as well. Thank you all, and I love you.

Man! And now for my peeps, my boys, my homies, who are more like family than friends, I want to thank you too, on the real. Thank you, Toro (rest in peace), Chino, Assassin, Sterl, Forrest, Khalil, Hanif,

Sharif (rest in peace), Khalil, Mr. Frosted Flakes-Jose, The Legend-JP, and Orangutan Toes-Juan.

To those who have helped me professionally in this endeavor, I want to express my most sincere, *gracias*. To the Megaphone-Cris and Billeci, thank you for your advice, encouragement, and suggestions for this novel, while keeping it on the down-low. To my colleagues and probation staff in that facility—you know of which I speak of—Thank you! Thank you, Big Mike, Galindo, Legge, The bad-ass-Chino, Mira, *Chocolate*, The shit-talking—but I have mad respect for—Supervisor Greene, Mr. Hold All Traffic-Osorio, Vega, Iniguez, Valdez, and everyone else putting it down at EM, and trying their best to motivate the young, crazy-ass generation behind cell doors.

And to you, who this book was written for, you young-ass knuckleheads, those thousands of youths who have crossed my path. I want to tell you, again, you all have mad potential, you just need to find the right avenue to apply it. I told you, anything is possible with a little determination and lowrider full of perseverance.

I know there are still many I haven't mentioned who I also need to thank. My apologies, and I want to say, thank you, too.

And finally, thank you all for reading my novel, I mean, your novel, because it now belongs to you, to anyone and everyone willing to read it and possibly learn from it. Keep your feet moving forward, especially through the hard times!

-With lots of love, *y con todo mi respeto*!

EL Incognito

About The Author

I bet you're wondering why El Incognito? It's simple, really. It's a pseudonym for an author who wishes to remain anonymous, while also trying to create an aura of mystery. El Incognito holds a B.A. from SDSU and is currently working in the field of education with at-risk youth. He also occasionally writes for a small, non-profit publication called, The Beat Within (www.thebeatwithin.org).

EL Incognito's literary works of fiction focus on inspirational content, primarily for young adults and teens. His themes include urban and Chicano culture, friendships and social circles, and urban street lore. He is currently editing a short novel he recently completed titled, Eagle Warrior. It's meant to be a middle-grade reader, but can be enjoyed by all. El Incognito has two more books in the very beginning phases, with the hope of completing them by the end of 2020.

His motto is-

Without failure, there can be no success. Without perseverance, a dream will only be a dream.

Visit his Facebook page at *Soy Unsecreto* for updates, more about this mysterious author, and just for some general cool-ass content

www.ingramcontent.com/pod-product-compliance
Lightning Source LLC
Chambersburg PA
CBHW050019180626
46810CB00002B/485